SCORNED

LEGENDS OF THE CAROLYNGIAN AGE

Joseph S. Samaniego

Within this book, I've taken some steps forward in detailing, and with storytelling, the culture of the world of Caelus. While the majority of this came from the Lotcalan culture, derived from the Gota culture, others were explored.

Notably, independent Quarmi civilization was presented in more detail. This along with introducing more beastfolk will help to give readers a better picture of this particular fantasy world.

Also, the addition of languages has been introduced. While there are hundreds if not thousands of languages within Caelus, there are some that are common. Akin to our use of English, Mandurian Chinese, or Latin and Greek in the middle ages. Many languages also derive from other root languages, such as English having its root in Germanic or Spanish from Latin.

Just some thoughts to keep in mind as you read, and hopefully, enjoy this novel.

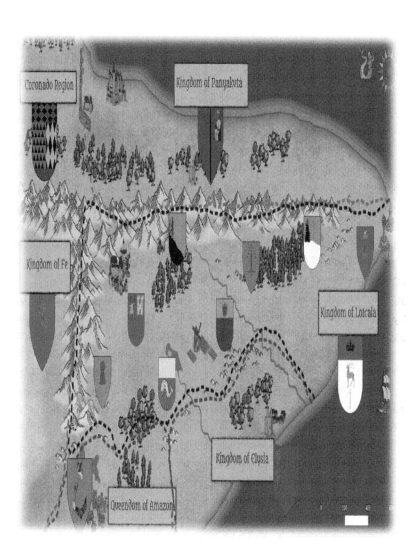

KINGDOM OF KIIROI HANA

KODAI KINGDOM

ROTASU

WINTER KINGDOMS

Table of Contents

Memories

istorians, or at least those that profess to have some sort of authority on the subject, can tell any student that life on the Falcon Coast wasn't always peaceful. Later scholars look to certain kings, and later on queens, as being gentle or fair. Monikers added to someone's name stated as much. The Fair, the Bold, the Conqueror, or the Fat. Yet, this wasn't usual for those under such a lofty station. Commoners did not get fancy nicknames or fancy titles. In fact, life for most non-landowning folks was brutal. So brutal was the average life of a commoner that most felt living to forty was old age.

Wars were near constant. When barons ruled large swathes of land, governing everything except the mage's guilds (though they tried to wield influence) and the churches, life was hard. Was it bad? Not always. The king ruled all the land in Lotcala, another king ruled Elysia, a king for Panyakuta, and a queen ruled Amazon. Each had trials, each had glories, and most were through war.

The king in Lotcala had little power to control the barons on most local matters. Further down the line of nobility, things got even murkier for the monarch. So hard was it to keep track that the king ignored many of the local squabbles. The manor lords fought each other for land and castles, and the gentry fought amongst themselves, as well. Fighting among nobles was almost seasonal and the power changes were frequent. Forty men would fight, another forty and thirty-two would die. All for five acres of land. This was life in Lotcala just two centuries after the conquest.

But the lands that historians and other scholars knew as Panyakuta were much different. That matters in this story and the background of what the legends say about the dwarven princess. Of course, the Lotalans called her something else...

The bastard princess.

Lotcala was human. Elysia was human. Amazon was human. Panyakuta was dwarven. That meant, in the eyes of humans, they were beneath the human nations. The humans would trade goods, but would they associate beyond that?

No.

The humans would kill each other over little strips of land, but should a dwarf kill a human in self-defense, and the entire tribe would pay. That was the life on the falcon coast before King Charles I.

* * * * *

In the days before Charles I, the borders were wild and dangerous. The south contained an unfriendly kingdom, and the west housed elemental terrors. That was the nature of borders. The dividing lines of kingdoms will be perilous. None more dangerous than the border to the north, along the Blue Mountains. This was the border to the dwarven lands, Panyakuta.

The lands of the northern dwarven people were mostly lawless and ruled by powerful warlords that would encroach on trade routes or pilgrims. These were the final dwarven lands to reach a peaceful accord with each other. Dwarves around the world had already found a measure of cooperation, using it to great influence. That was a hard thing to come by in the north.

King Charles, through no action on his part, had seen a dwarven tribal alliance create a kingdom out of warring states. It was a momentous occasion, and one welcomed by their neighbors. Yet, not all was well or safe.

Previous to the reign of Charles, relations with the dwarven tribes were frigid. The marauding bands created high tensions, and the march-lords were there to protect the border. Yet, when the dwarves would not provide any help, most of the lords only did what they felt was enough to protect their lands. It was a slow and effectively losing effort fighting back against the different tribes. That was where Guntram came in.

King Guntram was a dwarven warlord who had the foresight to unite the tribes under his banner. Those that submitted to his will were rewarded. Those that resisted were conquered. It was ruthless, efficient, and shift. In the end, it was necessary. Another tactic was to build alliances. Who better than the closest neighbor, and a trade partner already established among some of the former warlords?

All of this was great for the world's stage, but for the march-lords, little changed. The lords that guarded the border were still battling the roaming bandits that Guntram had failed, or ignored, to reign in. That was an issue, and one that was fraught with controversy.

What King Guntram had planned was to keep his border wild. It allowed the dwarven warriors a proving ground, while the bandits drove the prices of trade goods up. It was a terribly kept secret, and one that kept the tensions high.

That is the world that Rowena, the aforementioned princess born to King Charles and a dwarven tavern worker, was born into. There was still a hatred for dwarves, and Rowena felt the sting of that prejudice daily.

This is the beginning of her story. Told by someone who knew her best, and can describe the events in the fairest details of her and others. Was she a villain or was she the hero? She was the...

Daughter of the King

"I don't want to stay with Leif!" Rowena said as she walked along the western corridor of the palace in Jovag.

"It's Baron Leif or Baron Hardstone." Queen Sirie replied sternly.

Rowena huffed. "He lets me call him Leif or Uncle Leif."

"Therefore, you must go to stay with him. It'll teach you manners and respect for the court hierarchy." Sirie shot back. "When you are not in the War Academy or here for an important event, you will be in his home, attending to whatever he assigns to you. As a princess, I'm sure you will be an attendant to the baroness or their children."

"He loves Lostwood."

Sirie sighed. "Baron Lostwood." She corrected. "Baron Lostwood and Baron Hardstone were not married and therefore, each took a bride to have heirs. What they do in their private time and amongst themselves is their business, and theirs alone."

The queen's tone gave a note of disapproval that Rowena noticed.

"I still don't want to go." Rowena frowned. "I didn't want to go to the academy either."

"You don't want to be a warrior like your father and I?"

Rowena thought back to four years earlier when she killed a man protecting her father. It still gave her nightmares. She thought of the time she had spent in the academy, simply called the War Academy, and the strict life her stepmother forced upon her more so than the other students.

"Sara Ramsey will act as your attendant." The queen said, continuing the conversation. "She is thirteen like you, and a respectable young lady. Besides, your friend Elva will be there." Sirie sneered.

Rowena understood Sirie wasn't a fan of the younger Hardstone cousin, but she knew the girl's skill was impressive and Elva had taken a liking to Rowena during their time at the academy.

Sirie's feelings on her stepdaughter were mixed in the best of times. She didn't love her by any stretch of the imagination, but she tried to help her grow strong. King Charles, however, loved his firstborn and his only daughter. She was his favorite, and he wasn't above showing that to the world. That bothered Sirie. In the queen's mind Rowena, the half dwarf and half human daughter of a drunken affair, had no place above her children in the line of succession or in the king's eyes.

That line of succession was just the tip of a very rigid iceberg. All those born in the Kingdom of Lotcala were expected to fall in line with the courtly hierarchy. Gentry lords answered to manor lords, who answered to barons, and they all answered to the king. Beneath all the lords were the landowning taxpayers, such as yeomen or freeholders, and the land-tenants, such as husbandmen.

All these positions paid homage and taxes to their lords above them, and that fueled the kingdom. The men, and some women, of the kingdom were expected to fighting in their lord's wars. Soldiers fought in return for safety and land. Land they had to pay taxes on and safety that they had to fight for.

Charles had tried to outlaw fighting amongst the lords, but that was not a simple task. Still, he did his best to keep peace in his kingdom. One such way was the King's Army that was being built with recruits expected to come from the War Academy and from each of the barons. Often, the castaways from their personal armies filled the ranks, while nobles became the officers.

The War Academy was where Rowena came in. She was to be part of that first class, and any extra education from the Hardstone Barony would only strengthen her prowess.

Sirie's plan to help solidify her husband's fragile peace coincided with her plan to ensure her eldest son's rise to the throne. Both depended on Rowena being the protector of the throne, but not the one sitting on the throne. The queen knew that the Lotcalan hierarchy of lords would accept her son over an illegitimate daughter. All except Hardstone. However, one baron didn't worry her.

"Now get your things and have them loaded in the wagon. We will leave at first light." Sirie said, leaving little room for any further argument.

Rowena kicked the wall after the queen turned. She hated the idea of leaving her father, but the queen commanded it and Charles was nothing if not a devoted husband. If under pressure, it was the queen he'd stand beside. Rowena knew that and understood. She did as instructed, because her father would want her to.

The next morning, King Charles escorted Rowena along the route to the Barony of Hardstone.

Their carriage, ornate with gold trim, was not uncomfortable, but the thought of taking one's own daughter to live in another lord's house was. However, Charles was a king about keeping peace, and that meant his own house as well. He tried to comfort Rowena and cheer her up, but the ride through the countryside was not a pleasant one, no matter what he tried.

"You know, this is an important thing you are doing." Charles chuckled. He was trying to help his daughter feel at ease. "Leif is one of the march-lords and it's his duty to guard our borders."

Rowena furrowed her brow. "I thought Panyakuta were our friends?" She said, looking at her father. Rowena, though a half dwarf, felt no allegiance to the dwarven kingdom. Her own physical stature, dwarven in appearance, and height, gave people enough information to view her as less than human. Not all came to such conclusions, however. Many, once they spoke to Rowena, found her to be much more than a half dwarf. Yet, Rowena couldn't help but feel the scorn of being mixed race.

Rowena looked at her father. "I just think that with Panyakuta being allies, that Leif won't be so busy guarding the border. And besides, my mother was…"

"Yes." Charles interrupted her. "Yes, she was a dwarf. And, yes, Panyakuta are our allies. It is still the duty of a march lord to guard the borders."

"You never let me talk about her." Rowena said, returning the subject to her mother.

Charles sighed. "There isn't much to tell."

Charles was right, at least in his memory. He was drunk for much of the war with the Sile Empire that saw him march to the Dwarven Wall, and with his allies in Panyakuta, defeat the Sile emperor. The victory celebrations were well deserved and full of inebriation. Rowena's mother was a dwarven tavern worker that had been serving the king. He took her into his bed and a year later, the tavern owner delivered Rowena to the unsuspecting king. Rowena's mother had died. Charles recognized his own flesh and blood the moment he saw her. Therefore, he took her without hesitation. He was ashamed that it wasn't until they brought Rowena to him that he hadn't known the mother's name, Mildri.

Charles smiled at his daughter. "You favor me more than her, except for your physical stature and hair. You have my eyes and nose. Regal features." Charles chuckled. "At least, my mother used to say they were." The king sighed. "Rowena, you need to remember that sometimes, the cause of something isn't what's important. Only the outcome."

It was an answer that stuck with Rowena. The outcome. That was her life. Her existence came from Charles' drunk decision, but did she believe that's all it was? Did her father? She tried to find more meaning in her life, but being so young, that wasn't a simple task.

Rowena leaned her head back on the headrest of her seat and stared out the window. She saw the trees, in their summer fullness, pass her by as she drifted off to sleep.

The ride was uneventful. Riding in the carriage most of the day, except to stop for relief and to eat. Then camp in the evenings. A few inns along the way, but mostly a boring ride in the carriage.

Thirteen days later, Charles and Rowena, along with their royal entourage, led by Gentry Lord Torin Ramsey, arrived at the formidable Red Lass Castle. The fortress, built from stone from the Blue Mountains, was named for Lady Maeve Hardstone. Maeve was a fierce warrior and confidant of King Theodorif I, who sailed with the first raiders during the War of Conquest.

The castle was like everything in the Hardstone Barony; large and imposing. It was a border fort built on the southern end of the Hardstone lands. Two centuries old, constructed during the days of the First Barons' War, a war that saw an uprising against the weak Haakon I. Maeve, the acting baroness, had ordered the fortress built to protect the king. The fort stood as a symbol of Hardstone loyalty to the crown. Now, it would serve as the meeting place for Leif Hardstone and King Charles.

As they exited the carriage, Leif walked out of the castle gate and greeted Charles and Rowena with an enormous smile. Leif was a giant of a man, nearly seven feet tall and as broad as a small house. His beard, light brown with flecks of red, hung down to his massive chest. He was a sight to behold and one that was hard to miss.

"Beloved ones!" Leif called out in his Harsh Hardstone accent and dialect.

Leif wrapped Charles in a bear hug that engulfed the king. He let the king go when the guards approached and turned his attention to Rowena. "Darling little one!" Leif grinned. "Not so little now, yer gonnae be a warrior like me soon enough." He said, picking Rowena up in a hug.

He put Rowena down just as his family came out to join him. His wife, Lady Agnes, was the Lady of the Moorwood gentry estate, vassal to Baron Lostwood. She joined Leif at his side, holding their newborn son Torin, while his five-year-old daughter, Torvi, ran up to the group.

"Thank you for having us, Leif." Charles said with a smile. "And to you, my lady Agnes." The king gently kissed Agnes' hand.

Agnes curtsied lightly. "It is our pleasure, your majesty." She turned to Rowena. "And to you Princess Rowena."

Rowena curtsied in reply, but she felt a coldness from Lady Agnes. She just couldn't tell if Lady Agnes directed the coldness at her or if that was her nature with everyone.

"Come, let's head in. The rains are a coming soon." Leif said, guiding the king towards the castle.

"Two things we can always count on in Hardstone; loyalty and rain." Charles laughed.

The group went inside, the nobles to a large banquet hall and the guards to their barracks. A couple of hours later, after washing off the dirt from the road, the king and Rowena joined their hosts in the great hall for a feast.

The hall was festive, with the tables laid out according to the proper etiquette of the kingdom. The king sat next to Hardstone at the head table, along with their family. Rowena sat next to Lady Agnes. As was customary in the Kingdom of Lotcala, the hosts served pork as the main course, however, the Hardstone specialty of quail was also served.

As the minstrels came out to begin their performance, Lady Agnes leaned over towards Rowena.

"Your stepmother and I are not too particularly close. She's not fond of the arraignment that my husband and I share. I'll play the dutiful wife when I can, and Leif is a good man. Normally, we're left to our own life here. However, Sir Ramsey is a Canton gentry lord and therefore he is reporting back to his overlord,

Sirie. So, please forgive my earlier brevity around him."
Agnes whispered. "Hardstone is a safe place for you
once he leaves back to his own hold. Assurances from
Baron Lostwood that you will have a home there as
well, should you need one."

Agnes straightened up and smiled. She glanced
at Ramsey, who had been watching the princess. She
smirked at the man when he caught her eye.

"Hardstone isn't a welcoming place for spies."
She whispered to Rowena. "He should be mindful that
he and his daughter won't find a warm welcome here
after the king leaves."

The princess breathed a sigh a relief at the
lady's words and did her best to enjoy her meal. It was
the last meal she would have for some time with her
father. The next morning, after a bittersweet and tearful
parting, the king left Hardstone to return to the capital.
At Leif's urging, the king took all the soldiers, including
Ramsey, who rode with him. Sir Ramsey and his
daughter leaving with the king was something that Sirie
had recommended that the king not do. However, King
Charles trusted his friend Leif and was naïve to his
wife's intrigues.

The next day, Rowena walked the corridors and
found Leif and Agnes looking out over the courtyard,
where Torvi played with an attendant.

Rowena curtsied when she approached. Leif
smiled in reply.

"No need to do that here." He said to the
princess.

"She should still mind her manners, even here."
Agnes corrected.

Leif snorted. "Bah!" He retorted. "I donnae make
the others do such nonsense."

"The 'others' are not princesses, and they aren't being watched by the queen." Agnes said.

"There are no spies in me hold. Ye sent that scurvy Ramsey away. Without him and his daughter, there ain't none to spy on Rowena." Leif replied.

Agnes rolled her eyes. "That you know of." She whispered. "That woman has eyes and ears in every hold, I'm sure. If nothing else, hold to the courtly manners, Rowena." She curtsied to the princess. "Yet, your stepmother had suggested I take you on as a lady-in-waiting or as an attendant for Torvi. Both roles would be beneath your station as a princess. The firstborn at that. Were you a gentry or manor lord's daughter, then fine, but as a princess, I should wait on you." Agnes said. "Besides, I think that you and our cousin Elva would be better suited training for your next year at that brutal academy that Sirie created."

Leif turned back to the ladies and burst with excitement. "An excellent idea! The kingdom will need many warriors with the likes of them orcs in the northwest." Leif grinned.

Rowena smiled. "Yes, my lord, my lady."

Leif clasped Rowena's shoulder. "I'll be takin' you and Elva hunting in a few days. We'll be goin' with me sister, Lady Catherine of Hollerton."

Rowena smiled. Her heart grew with excitement. The entire kingdom knew of Lady Catherine, the lady that oversaw the Hollerton gentry hold. Hollerton was the second biggest mining community after Silverstone, and Lady Catherine was the sole ruler of the land.

One reason Rowena loved the Barony of Hardstone was their belief that women could rule alongside men. If any place in Lotcala gave all people equal footing, it was Hardstone. As long as you contributed to the society, then you had a place in the barony. Rowena intended to make her mark as a friend within the barony and prove her worth. Showing her hunting prowess to Lady Catherine would help.

Rowena was eager for the three days she spent waiting for Lady Catherine and Elva. Her friend, Elva, was the daughter of Sir Alain Hardstone of Briwathun, a cousin to Leif and Catherine. He was the lord of the ancient border fort that stood over the Blue River along the Lostwood Border.

Briwathun was the ancient Gota translation of *River Fort* and that was the original intention of the structure. Slowly a town grew up around it, and over time a trade route, mostly to supply the soldiers. Yet, the town's chief claim to fame was its role in the First Baron's War. It was the prison for the kidnapped Gentry Lord's daughter. A young lady, kidnapped by King Haakon I, kicking off a year's long war that ended with Haakon's victory over the barons. Now rumors flew about the fort being haunted with her spirit, but that didn't bother many of the Hardstones. Finding something that scared them when their bedtime stories were of the dead creatures from the War of Conquest was a tough task.

The morning of Lady Catherine and Elva's arrival came, and Rowena had spent the night before awake, dreaming of the fun she'd have. She ran to the front gate and watched the two women dismount from their horses. She had only seen Lady Catherine once, and Rowena was a young girl then. Now she saw her in a better light, and Rowena stood amazed.

She watched Lady Catherine approach. Catherine stood over six feet tall, was broad shouldered and chested. Her armor hid her frame, but Rowena knew from the stories that Lady Catherine did not look like the ladies of most courts, and instead was robust and larger in frame. Mostly because of her heritage, but also her love of physical activities and delicious foods. She cut her dark auburn hair short with exception of three braids coming off the top. She was smiling and looking at her brother, Leif, nearly eye to eye. The beautiful woman before her, a champion of the Hardstone family, mesmerized Rowena.

At Lady Catherine's hip was her famed bastard-sword, *Svikarar Bölva*. It meant *Traitor's Bane* in the old Eire language that the Hardstone family often spoke a broken form of. The Hardstones were not only descendants of the warriors coming from Gotistan during the Conquest, but also of the people from the mysterious isle of Eire.

Laying just north of Gotistan, Eire had been home to tribal Eirens, or *Sky People*. The Eirens were dark-haired and thinner in build, but much more rugged than they looked. While the Gota had developed settlements, the Eirens remained nomadic and moved between seasons, following the caribou or fish migrations. While some openly traded with the Gota, many stayed away from them. Only small bands ever mixed with the Gota. One such band was the family that became the Hardstones, with Maeve Hardstone being half Gota and half Eiren.

Leif and Catherine turned and walked to the castle.

"We'll be staying here during the hunt. The forests to the south along the border give the best chance for deer. Agnes will take the wee ones back home to Hardstone." Leif said. "The city." He clarified.

Catherine chuckled. "Our people were never that creative. Our name is Hardstone, as is our capital." Catherine laughed. "Our heads too!"

"It was all Maeve found. Hard stones!" Leif laughed.

"Ye would ne'er catch a Hardstone poet." Catherine said with a hearty laugh. "He'd run out o' words."

The family named the Barony of Hardstone for the town that Maeve founded when she was given control over the land after the conquest. That it was the smallest parcel given out wasn't lost on many, especially not Maeve. However, any resentment felt quickly dissipated when the riches from the mountains were discovered. Gold and silver, along with building stones, made the barony one of the richest in the kingdom. That was more than enough to appease Theodorif's general and earn the undying loyalty of the family.

The barony considered whatever Maeve said law, even over two centuries after her death. The name stuck, and no one questioned it.

Elva ran up to Rowena, passing Leif and Catherine. Anywhere else that would have been seen as an insult to the kingdom's hierarchy, but here it was greeted with a grin by the baron and the lady. Elva grabbed Rowena in a hug and lifted the young girl up.

"Good to see you too, Elva." Rowena said with a gasping breath.

Elva laughed, lowering Rowena. She was tall like the rest of her family, pure Hardstone. Her dirty blond hair was long and unkempt. She was lankier than most of the women in her family, but she was just as headstrong.

"I've missed ye, lassie!" Elva said. She looked around and lowered her voice. "Did ye bring it?" She said.

Rowena smirked and nodded, pulling a small glass bottle from her pouch. "I said I would."

"Aye, ye did. I shoulda known that whatever Princess Rowena says she'll do, she does." Elva smiled. "King's own mead. I heard it was the best."

"We'll find out tonight." Rowena smiled.

Just then, Lady Catherine appeared. "The sun hits emerald glass just right lass, might be best to keep it hidden in yer pouch."

Rowena and Elva looked up at the woman and then nodded in shame.

Catherine grinned. "I guess the queen ain't been teaching ye girls to sneak. How else can ye win our wars?"

"She has been teaching us to fight in the open fields. Pitch battles." Rowena answered. "My lady." She finished properly.

"All well and good when yer in a pitch battle, but I prefer to meet me foes when they can't see me or me army." Catherine replied. "Yer highness." She added with a wink. "Come on, let's get in and get some food in us. I'm famished, and I know Elva can eat with the best of us."

Elva smiled at the remark.

Later on that night, another banquet was held, but unlike the dinner with the king from some nights prior, this banquet felt more festive. Ale was served directly from barrels, Catherine reserving her own and sharing amongst her entourage. Trays of roasted lamb, pig, and quail were brought out to the middle of the hall and everyone pulled off pieces of the meat as they went by. It wasn't long before singing and dancing erupted with the hall, followed by the usual tests of strength and a good natured wrestling match that spilled out into the courtyard.

This was a Hardstone party and Rowena was in awe of the festivities. She grew up in the strict and stifled environment of the king's palace, a place ruled by Queen Sirie.

Not that Sirie didn't enjoy a good banquet. No, in fact, she had thrown a few in her days. It was more about her growing rigidness to courtly life and duty. In the days since the Knights of the Silver Seal rebellion three years prior, Sirie had not felt up to parties. The only time they used the great hall as a banquet hall was for diplomatic affairs.

Rowena sat back in her chair next to Elva and enjoyed the rowdy scene around her. A band of minstrels played a raucous tune while men and women swayed to the rhythm. Across the hall Rowena spotted Lady Catherine as she was downing a tankard of ale, her feet propped up on a table. One of the lady's men at arms was sitting with her and drinking from his own tankard. Rowena smiled at the freedom that the people of Hardstone seemed to enjoy. Something she long for herself.

Elva tapped the distracted Rowena on her arm and motioned with her head to follow her down an adjacent corridor.

"Let's open the mead." Elva said in a low voice.

Rowena pulled the glass bottle from the folds of her dress. Another reason to like Hardstone; most of the women's fashion had folds within the dresses to hold insignificant items. Ladies from the other courts didn't get to know such luxury when it came to pockets in their dresses. She popped the cork and took a swing before passing it over to Elva.

The mead was aromatic and strong. Rowena grimaced at the sharp alcoholic taste of the fermented honey. Elva's reaction was the same. Both of the girls drank wine, as was the standard fare, and Elva was not unfamiliar with mead like Rowena was, but this was stronger than the typical recipe. It was bitter sweet, with a powerful aroma of honey and juniper. More juniper than Rowena would have preferred. Elva passed the bottle back to Rowena, who took another sip before handing the bottle to Elva again. The girls repeated the process until the bottle was emptied.

Elva started walking back to the banquet hall, but stumbled from the mead's effects.

Rowena laughed, watching her friend trying to walk before she took a step and stumbled over next to Elva. Their combined laughter brought a curious Catherine to the corridor. She smirked at the two girls, slumping along the wall and laughing like fools.

"Ye two took a dip in that there bottle, did ye?" Catherine said. She bent down and lifted the two girls up. Catherine hoisted Rowena on her shoulder while holding Elva under her arm. "Yer a bit too old for such foolishness." She said. "Or too young, maybe." She corrected.

Catherine took the two girls and deposited them, as they were still laughing, in Rowena's chambers. An attendant sprang up and walked over to the lady.

"See that they sleep off tonight's festivities. We leave just before dawn and these wee ones need to be ready." Catherine said. She took a gold piece and flipped it to the attendant. "They'll be heavy in the head in the morn, make sure they feel it." She grinned before walking back to the banquet hall.

* * * * *

A few hours later, the sun was still below the horizon, but its first rays were peaking. The scullery maid came with a large pot and an iron ladle. She grinned at the two girls, passed out in their clothes from the previous evening and in a deep sleep. Each sprawled out on Rowena's bed and was in no shape to wake up on their own at this early hour.

"Wake up!" She shouted while banging the large pot with the ladle. "Wake up or the baron and Lady Catherine will leave ye both where ye lay!"

The girls, reeling from the night before, both clutched their heads in agony.

"Not so loud." Elva groaned.

"This would never be allowed in the palace." Rowena said.

"Well, ye ain't in the palace, princess. Besides, her ladyship and the baron gave me strict orders to make sure ye two were up and ready by the time they left for the hunt." The maid replied. "Now up ye both and put on some fresh clothes."

Rowena frowned. "I have to wash up."

"Wash up?" The maid replied. "Ye going out into the wilds. Ain't no reason to be cleaned and proper out in the wilds. Just put on some fresh tunics and breeches. Ye both smell of mead." The maid looked outside. "Rains a'comin so there's yer wash, princess." She smiled before leaving the room. "I had many a good washes in the rain. Best memories from me youth." The maid finished as she closed the door.

The girls dressed and rushed down to the stables, where two attendants patiently waited for them along with their provisions.

"Yer late." Rowena's attendant, Bowen, said when Rowena approached.

Bowen was the son of a Hardstone retainer but not from a gentry's family. His father, Owen Leckey, was a husbandman from the Briwathun Hold.

"Sorry, Bowen." Rowena replied, trying to produce a smile through her sleepy façade.

"Think it odd that Queen Sirie dinnae send you with an attendant?" Elva asked as the four mounted their horses.

"She tried, but Lady Agnes said that she sent them away." Rowena answered. "Sir Ramsey's daughter, Sara, was to be here as a lady-in-waiting."

"Sara Ramsey?" Bowen asked. "She's a proper one, I hear. Pretty too."

Rowena nodded. "That's probably why Sirie wanted her to stay here with me. She thinks you Hardstones are too rough around the edges."

Elva's attendant, Gilda Leckey, rode up on her horse. "Aye, we're bad influences on the princess." Gilda joked.

Rowena smiled. "It would have been nice to have a lady-in-waiting, though."

"Ye never had one?" Bowen asked. "I thought all princess get one."

"Not me." Rowena sighed. "There are chambermaids in the palace, but no one assigned to me directly. They are there to do the normal work, but if I wasn't there, they would do the same job."

"I guess that's so you donnae get soft like Ramsey." Gilda laughed.

The group joined her in laughter as they trotted up to Leif and Catherine's entourage.

Leif grinned as the younger riders approached.

"Alright, seeing as we're all here, let's be off. It's a full day's ride to southern forests." Leif said.

The baron kicked his horse and took off, his companions following behind. The group, numbering around fourteen, rode throughout the day, only stopping to water and rest the horses.

The lands on the southern end of the border weren't as barren as the lands near the mountains. Along the mountains, sandier soils dominated the landscape. This was in contrast to the southern end of the barony, where richer soils from the river's basin helped provide healthier crops and harvests. Tall deciduous trees also marked the landscape, giving the plentiful wildlife a fertile home.

The group of hunters rode forth to the tree line and ventured deeper before the sun was setting.

"This is the area we'll set up camp." Leif said once he found a suitable clearing in the trees. "Rowena, Elva and the Leckey kids, start setting up the tents and building a fire." He ordered.

The younger party members did as they were bid. That was all part of their training and, for the Leckey pair, it was part of their duties. With Leif, however, all four were more or less equal and needing to carry their own weight. Other parts of the kingdom might look at it differently, but not in the Hardstone

Barony and certainly not when Rowena and Elva were expected to lead others one day.

The two Leckeys were fast in their tasks of setting up a camp and starting a fire. Faster than Rowena and Elva, though the two knew how. Here it was more of a matter of experience creating speed.

Night soon fell over the woods and the campfire became a warm and welcoming beacon for the hunting party. Salted pork and hardtack bread was the meal for the evening. Most were tired from the day's ride and sleep found everyone quickly on the first night.

* * * * *

The morning sun was a welcome sight for Rowena, who slept little. The forest reminded her too much of the entrance exam for the War Academy, and she wanted to put that ordeal behind her. Still, the quietness of the forest was something to enjoy.

Later that day, the group split up and went hunting. In the southern end of the barony, deer were plentiful, as were the boar. However, it was a hunt for the winter stock. Two hunting parties could kill more deer or boar than one party. That way, they could fill their larders quicker.

The winters in the Barony of Hardstone were rough and harder than most other baronies. This meant that meat, from any source, was welcomed throughout the year. Dried and or salted, the summer and autumn hunts would keep during the colder days. Of course, the trappers would hunt for mountain goats and caribou during the winter and closer to the mountains. However, these animals were much more difficult to hunt. The baron had ordered his hunting party to bring out any animals they could. Of course, Rowena and the other younger members flushed out the game.

Rowena wasn't thrilled with such a task, but she did as ordered. Elva walked alongside her as the pair hit shrubs and tree trunks with sticks. The goal was to scare an animal toward the hunters.

"I wish we could do the hunting." Rowena said.

"Aye, but someone has to flush the beast out." Elva replied. "The baron donnae want to use his hounds."

Rowena scoffed. "What good are they for then, if not to hunt?"

"They're gifts from Baron Lostwood." Elva smiled. "Me uncle would never let them be used in a way that might get them hurt or worse."

"Your uncle is a sweet man." Rowena grinned.

"Donnae tell him that." Elva smirked.

The girls continued walking through the forest, hitting the brushes, trying to scare up game.

Coming to a clearing, the two young ladies came upon five soldiers in tattered armor sitting by a campfire. The soldiers were cooking a stew with a few squirrels. They looked different from Hardstone soldiers. They were darker in complexion and spoke an unfamiliar language. Definitely foreign mercenaries, yet they wore Goldwater sigils on their armor.

One soldier spotted the pair, motioning for his buddies to look up.

"What do we have here?" The soldier said, standing up. "Lost little girlies?"

"No, are ye?" Elva asked.

Rowena and Elva, neither wore a blade or anything other than the sticks used to swat the bushes, were defenseless if the men took offense.

The lead soldier grinned. "We ain't lost. We're hunting for a bit of fun."

The soldiers behind the leader laughed.

"What's this here?" The taller of the soldiers motioned to Rowena, "Your pet dwarf?"

"Ain't a concern for ye other than to get yer asses back to the south with yer golden fish banner." Elva spoke defiantly.

"Come now, we just came to the barony here to take care of a quick matter of business. That doesn't mean we can't have a good time with two peasant girls." The soldier grinned.

"We ain't peasants!" Elva replied. Both girls raised their sticks. "I'm Lady Elva, daughter of the gentry Lord Briwathun, and this is the fooking princess!"

The soldier raised his left eyebrow. "That's even better. Gold for a ransom."

"Aye, if ye get out of me realm alive." A voice boomed from the tree line.

Leif Hardstone, Lady Catherine, and their entourage walked out of the woods. Swords out.

Lady Catherine looked at the girls. "Best get behind us." She motioned.

Rowena and Elva quickly did as they were asked.

"Ye wearing Goldwater sigils. Hugo know yer this far to the north?" Leif asked.

"Hugo?" The soldier chucked. "Hugo's dead. We're retainers of Lord Edwin Langley, the new Baron of Goldwater."

Leif hid his shock. "I just saw Hugo, not more than a month ago at the king's assembly." Leif stuck his sword, a mighty two handed blade, into the ground. "Ye will be kind enough to send condolences to Lord Edwin. Ye can leave in peace, if ye leave now."

"Our lord, wanted us to take stock of debts owed to the barony. Loach owes a debt." The soldier replied. His comrades stood behind him. "We intend to collect from him or his liege."

Leif scoffed. "I'm that liege, and I say ye ain't going to be dealing with me vassal."

"It's a simple matter." The solider continued. "We take what's owed, and then we'll leave."

"Ye ain't Lotcalan, are ye?" Lady Catherine asked.

The soldier shook his head. "We're from Zaragoza."

Catherine spat on the ground. "I thought I smelled bilge rats."

The soldier's smile faded. "Don't forget, rats have claws."

Leif's eyes burned with rage. "Aye, and we have swords, and plenty of experience killing rodents."

The soldiers rushed Leif and Catherine. Both Hardstones leveled their weapons with expert strikes. Leif cleaved the lead soldier in half, slicing down from the left shoulder to the waist.

Catherine's blade found an unguarded neck. *Svikarar Bölva* did its job, separating a Zaragozan head from its body.

Two other Hardstone retainers killed more soldiers, but Leif stopped them from killing the final one.

"This one," Leif said pointing to the man lying on the muddy ground, "he'll go back to his new lord and tell him what happened here." Leif grunted. "That'll be the last time some southerner sends bill collectors into my realm."

The Hardstone men gathered up the bodies and roped the prisoner.

"Take him to the capital. There is a dungeon cell he'll hit nicely into." Leif said. "We'll be along soon."

The hunt would continue, but the mood shifted. If gathering meat was not of such vital importance, then Leif would have gone back to Hardstone himself. Winter survival was always the priority in his barony. Discovering the motives of the new lord would have to wait.

It wouldn't wait long, however. A new lord meant the king would call upon his nobles to share in the news. This sort of meeting was necessary indeed.

The King's Assembly

our weeks later, Rowena and Elva joined Baron Hardstone and the other lords of the barony on a journey to Jovag. It was a special occasion. A new lord was being brought to the court. Even the notoriously reclusive lords from Highwind came out for the event. Hedge knights, yeomen, and husbandmen made up the rest of those being called upon to witness the new lord. A Baron, no less.

While conferring the title of baron was not usually a major occurrence, passing down from scion to an appointed heir carried more ceremony. Often, this was from father to son. This time was one of the rarer occasions when the heir was not appointed prior to the death of the former baron. Instead, Edwin Langley, the son of Hugo Goldwater's niece. Edwin, a young man raised in Elysia and Aran, was now expected to take the title of Baron of Antei and pay proper homage to the crown. While he was already acting as baron, he had yet to receive the king's blessing.

The capital was abuzz with commotion and energy. Without counting the commoners, or the hedge knights with Leif's band, his entourage numbered fourteen lords, and fifty men at arms. While most had to find accommodations among the crowded inns and hostels, Hardstone and the lords kept apartments near or within the palace.

Leif stayed in the palace, along with his family and four manor lords. Rowena and Elva also stayed in the palace. The homecoming gave the girls a chance to wander around the halls.

Their second day within the palace, the pair walked in on Rowena's younger brother Liam during his studies. An elderly tutor, the royal sage Damon Claremont, an uncle to Lord Gerald Claremont, was going over the finer points of the lesson on noble families.

"And coat of arms of the Moray family?" Damon asked. He pulled the baggy sleeves of his cloak up to his forearms.

"A red crab over a blue field." Liam answered.

"Azure, not blue." Rowena said, correcting her brother, as she entered the room. Elva followed behind. Both sat at Liam's table.

"Azure." Liam said.

The old tutor smiled. "Good." He said, with a nod to Rowena. "Their seat?"

Liam thought for a moment. "Crabber's Keep."

"Which is in what town?" The tutor prodded.

Liam scoffed. "I don't know. Why should I?"

"Because one day you will have to visit the lords as an official envoy of the royal court." The tutor replied. "Your sister, too." He looked at Rowena. "Care to answer for the young prince here?"

Rowena smiled. "The Moray family seat is Crabber's Keep in the town of Widow's Cape."

The tutor nodded. "Excellent."

Liam slumped in his chair. "Well, of course she knows. She gets to leave the palace and see places. She's the lucky one. I'm stuck reading books."

"You will venture out, too. You'll travel plenty in the years to come, but first you must be prepared." The tutor replied. "Now, let's continue. The coat of arms of the Seamist family?"

Rowena and Elva walked out of the room, leaving Liam and Damon to their studies.

"How do ye know that about the coat of arms and castles?" Elva asked.

Rowena shrugged. "Sage Damon used to teach me. It's important for lords and ladies to know the seats of the places we have to visit." Rowena looked up at her friend. "We're the ones that our fathers will send to make the diplomatic deals and niceties."

Elva scoffed. "I rather they send me to fight." She said, pounding her fist into her hand.

"There hasn't been a baronial war for years." Rowena smiled. "You'll be stuck in banquets for the rest of your life. You better get to reading the great poets like Maritus and Sylvania. It'll be a good idea to brush up on your history prose, too." Rowena put her hand to her chin as if in deep thought. "How about Calisoro's *Philosophies of the Red Moon Age* or *Mairism* by Jovan Rutter? Both splendid books for a lady wanting to find a husband and spending her life in a stuffy court."

"Donnae say that!" Elva yelled, pushing Rowena in fun.

The two girls laughed as they continued down the hall.

They walked down the hall, passing servants, guests, and a few squires. The area was bustling with the thought of a new baron coming. No one knew a lot about the man. The gossip was that he had been a soldier in Aran for the Sile emperor, but was exiled for his brutality in some previous war. Lotcala forged an uneasy alliance with the Sile Empire in the eleven years since the war, leaving the idea of Langley's baronial title as a continuous thing.

His soldier's treatment of Rowena and Elva, threats to the young ladies, was also a point the king meant to rectify. Leif had sent the prisoner to Antei after Langley gave a suitable apology. In short, it pledged that his men would respect the baronial boundaries. Time would tell if that promise would hold.

In another stately room, the sounds of laughter and song. Venturing into the room, they saw a host of knights and gentry in merriment. Among the group was Sir Varis Breakspear, the son of Lord Harrel Breakspear, Sir Morgan Jest, Sir Oleg Longshanks, and Lord Donovan Cullenhun. The men had a few tankards of wine, and were sharing their stories of past fights or tournaments.

In the corner was Grainne Cullenhun, her nose in an enormous book, and her shoulder length light brown hair hung around her face. The girls slipped into the room and walked over to Grainne, sitting under a stag's head.

"What ye reading, Grainne?" Elva asked, pulling a chair next to her friend.

"A book." She replied, without lifting her head.

"We can see that." Rowena chuckled. "What's it about?"

"It's about the Far-Off Kingdom and subsequent explorations trying to find it." Grainne answered, now looking at her friends.

"Yer wanting to go off and find it?" Elva joked.

Grainne nodded. "Beats hanging around here waiting for some stupid lord my father wants me to marry." She said. Grainne turned to look at her father, laughing with his friends. "They get to have the fun while we sit as pawns or envoys for their achievements. Our spring and summer years spent in toll and scrolls, eyes dimmed in waning candle light, yet to dream and fly away as the birds in song. To see the world and marvel at the heavens. Breathe the thoughts and memories of yore lost for our sex and cursed with duties not fitting our hearts." She sighed and returned to her book.

Rowena and Elva looked at their friend. In silence at first.

"I donnae know what ye said, but it sure sounded pretty." Elva remarked with a laugh.

"We're here for a celebration and you're stuck reading. Elva and I are heading to grab some smoked meat. You should join us." Rowena said.

Grainne smiled.

Lord Donovan walked over to the group. He was tall, and nearing his mid-forties. His dark hair was greying, but his beard was still as dark as the evening skies. He wore the coat of arms of his family, the hound, upon his grey tunic.

"My daughter has told me of your two. Hard to mistake either of you." Donovan said. He looked to Elva. "As tall as me with the look of Lady Catherine. You're Elva Hardstone, I'm sure."

"Aye, mi lord." Elva smiled, and curtsied, though clumsily.

Donovan looked at Rowena. "The dwarven princess." He smiled. "You look like your father... not counting your height, of course." He motioned with his hand, showing Rowena's shorter stature, only coming up to his waist.

"Father!" Grainne exclaimed, her head shooting up from her book.

"I meant no disrespect, your highness. Simply stating the fact." He said, holding his hands up.

Rowena grinned. "It is alright my lord. I know my father isn't the most handsome man in the kingdom, but I don't mind when people say I resemble him."

Donovan smiled at the joke. "You are his daughter, that's certain." He chuckled.

Rowena curtsied. "Are you here for the ceremony, my lord?" Rowena asked, making polite conversation.

"I am, as is my entourage here. Sirs Jest and Longshanks are two of my vassals, and Sir Breakspear was a squire of mine." Donovan motioned. "They've come as my guards for the occasion. Your father is naming me his chamberlain."

Rowena smiled at him. "A great honor. I remember him talking about your valor in the war with the Knights of the Silver Seal a few years ago."

"I just did my duty." Donovan shook his head. "It was a terrible war. I'd be happy to know a war like that can't happen again. An old fool's hope, I fear."

Grainne closed her book and looked up at her father. "You're no fool, father. It's a good hope, but it'll take all of us to make something like that realistic."

"Sure enough." Donovan replied. "My daughter is wise beyond her years. That's why I brought her." He beamed. "She'll do well to help the house in diplomatic matters one day."

Lord Donovan bowed to the princess and then went back to his fellow knights to further celebrate.

Grainne stood and put the book on a nearby table. "We should go. My father will tell his stories about winning the Great Tournament two years ago."

The girls left the knights in the room.

"I remember that tournament." Rowena said. "That's when he unhorsed Sir Tyros to be the champion."

Grainne nodded. "He hasn't stopped talking about it."

"I thought he would tell stories of the war with Elysia." Elva commented.

Grainne shook her head. "He doesn't. He only ever told me that story once. He was uncharacteristically drunk when he did it. He doesn't realize he is doing it, but I know he only tells the story of the tournament because of what happened during the war."

Grainne stopped, the others two did as well. "My older brother wants to take part in some tournament Harbor is having. Says he will unhorse a great knight. He isn't knighted yet, and my dad is thinking of asking the king about knighting him. He wants me to be his squire."

"That's great!" Elva exclaimed.

Grainne shrugged. "Maybe for you and Rowena. I want to enroll in the Mages Guild."

"I didn't know you could do magic?" Rowena asked.

"I can't, but I can learn the arts of being a sage. They don't know magic, but they help the guild, and they travel around the world learning many interesting things. History, alchemy, medicine, and more." Grainne smiled.

The girls continued walking down the corridor, where they came upon a few other lords in a chapel. A priest of the Creator was saying a sermon on teachings from one of the prophets, while the lords and ladies present sat and listened.

Rowena and Grainne stood by the door way, but after a moment Elva walked off, scoffing. Her friends followed behind a few moments later.

"What's wrong with her?" Grainne asked, as she and Rowena tried to catch back up with Elva.

"She's a Hardstone. They don't follow the Creator, they believe in the Old Gods. Most of Hardstone and some of Coldwood do, actually. Even Baron Harbor has a shrine to Helisn, but he claims to believe in the Creator." Rowena explained.

"Helisn?" Grainne asked.

"I thought you were the smart one." Rowena chuckled. "He is the god of the seas and oceans."

"I have read little about the religions of the world. My father doesn't put much stock in it, not even in the Creator."

Rowena nodded. "Mine doesn't either. My step-mother does though. She is zealous for the Creator. I think that's one of her dislikes about my heritage. Dwarves have their one pantheon and the Creator isn't on it." Rowena sighed. "She doesn't think my belief in him is sincere."

Most scholars knew the Lotcalans' views on spirituality well enough, but for many of the families, organized religion was an afterthought. Half a world away, however, a former associate of the king was dealing with machinations from fanatical faiths and believers.

"Let's catch up with Elva." Rowena said, jogging with Grainne.

* * * * *

As the sun set, the lords and ladies of the kingdom adjourned to the great hall of the king's palace. It was crowded, standing room only. Many of the attendants were bunched together, arm to arm, in a sweltering humidity. The king, sitting on his throne, looked down at the new lord. Around him were his family's vassals.

Though they had all publically sworn loyalty to the new baron, few knew him really. It would be a tough fealty to enforce. The Goldwater name was respected and loved. This was a distant relation. Time would tell if he could live up to his stately predecessor.

It was the baron's turn to swear his fealty to the king. Langley dropped to one knee, putting his hand over his chest. He swore obedience in all earthly matters. His oath also bonded him to answer the call to join in the king's wars, should any ever arise again.

The banquet for the new baron was as lavish as any banquet had ever been in the kingdom. Barrels of smoked pork, chopped and stewed vegetables, and they served more than fifty fattened geese to the attendees. So many nobles and their families came to witness the event that seating was provided throughout several of the halls and in the courtyards. After the meal, which included nearly three hundred barrels of ale, mead, and wine, dancers came to provide entertainment. A few jugglers and jesters made their way through the crowd as well.

Mostly, life was happy and everyone celebrated with a renewed sense of optimism. Though, no real consequence came of Langley's men at arms, nor of Hardstone's defense of his lands. This left a void. The king did not call for action. Even in his daughter's stead, Charles let it pass without as much as a stern word.

Baron Hardstone felt slighted, but he was stoic. He held his tongue, as he was the king's friend, and he cared little about himself. However, the insult to the two ladies, Rowena and Elva, he felt shouldn't go unpunished. If others could have seen the foreshadowing, then perhaps some of what was to come to pass might have been avoided.

* * * * *

While life returned to normal, the seasons changed, and the days shortened. The harvest was collected, and the stored meats, salted or smoked, were brought into the larders for winter's meals. It was now the months of the chilled air. A time for gathering within the homes, near fires, eating stews, and telling tales of days gone by.

In Hardstone, the days were chilly, and the nights were colder. Snow blanketed the ground. Deep, soft layers of frozen joy for the children at play.

Leif knew, as did his vassals, that the encroaching Langley had eyes on the riches of the mountains. Ore, and precious metals. Leif Hardstone may have been thought of as simpleminded outside of his barony, and his people were looked at with scorned for their traditionalist ways, but they were hardy folk. Hardy, and knowledgeable of the world's nature.

The baron of the cold, mountainous region set to work at bolstering his defenses along the borders. New forts were raised on the frozen ground. Stone and timber made the walls of his barony. Soldiers were trained to man the new forts and walls. Langley's trespass would not happen again.

However, for the Rowena, she was away at the War Academy. She and her friends, who would make up the next generation of the king's soldiers, still had years left before they could take command.

The Academy

knew we'd find you here!" Rowena exclaimed to a lone young lady sitting at a wooden table with several opened books in front of her.

"And where else would you think to find me, Ro?" The girl replied, without looking up. Her dark hair was down, and it covered her face as she was over a table reading.

"Studying again, Grainne?" Rowena asked. Elva stood next to her.

"It is a library, is it not?" Grainne said coolly, looking up at her two friends. "Besides, staying in here allows me a break from everyone calling me a crone or woods witch."

Rowena nodded at her friend. "Corin still giving you trouble?"

"It's no bother. I just try to ignore it."

"I'll see him at fencing later. I'll make sure he knows not to mess with you." Rowena said.

Grainne shook her head. "And then they'll just increase their attacks on you. I'm sorry, but those sound worse than being called a crone."

Rowena sneered.

"Besides, I like it in here. It's peaceful." Grainne added. "And with you two joining me, it feels more like home." She finished.

In their four years at the castle, Rowena and her classmates had seen the structure rebuilt and made livable. At one point, the library was opened with a meager selection of books and scrolls. Now, however, the students were finding more reading material when they entered. Grainne was the student that entered the library the most. An unofficial librarian.

"You know that it's not proper for a lady in this kingdom to keep her nose in so many books? What's the research today, gnomes, centaurs, or alchemy?" Rowena, now feeling happier, teased as she sat across from Grainne. She pulled a book towards her. "*The Study of Wyverns, Wyrms, and Drakes.* I was close. Dragon research is definitely not fitting for a young lady." Rowena slid the book back to Grainne with a wink.

"Yes, and a group of young ladies fighting with young men, hoping to be officers in some army that the barons and manor lords don't want within the kingdom is?" Grainne shot back. "Besides, dragonkin are interesting. Lots of beasts are, and it's good to know about them."

"Ain't you gonna be marrying some lordy boy? Why do you need to know about beasts?" Elva asked after taking her seat.

"I doubt that will be much of an issue, not that it matters. My father is already searching for a potential husband for me, but most *lordy boys* don't want a studious wife. Nor one that can kick their ass." Grainne replied. "You've seen the looks we keep getting. Think about the ones I'm getting for reading so much."

"Then stop." Elva said.

"No!" Snapped Grainne. "This is what I love. Just because the Hardstones only care about books when they need paper to wipe their asses doesn't mean the rest of us don't enjoy them for their words. Besides, I don't plan on staying in Lotcala after my time in the King's Army is up. I'll move on to another country and study there. I'll work my way up to be a sage."

Rowena grinned. "There aren't many women sages."

Grainne scrunched her brow. "So?"

"Yea, so?" Elva added, seeing Grainne's point.

"Just saying that maybe things will not be so easy without the King's Army." Rowena sighed. "If the queen is being honest about it all."

"Yea, I guess so." Grainne conceded. "I'm still not planning on sticking around. I can't inherit, unless my three elder brothers die, and I don't know of many men that would take a wife with such a passion to learn and travel. Best to stay a spinster. I'll help raise the next generation of Cullenhuns."

"This isn't always going to be a kingdom run by men for men." Rowena said.

"And are you, miss dwarven princess, going to change that? Look around you in this school." Grainne countered her friend's notion. "There are fifty-three students and eight are female."

"Don't forget Paul Somerled. He says we should count him among us ladies. Given Paul's preference for his own gender, I figure it makes sense." Elva pointed out with a wink.

"Fine. Nine." Grainne corrected. "That's just less than twenty percent of the total number. Next year's recruits are expected to bring us fourteen more classmates with three females. That would keep our numbers at just under twenty percent. No change, and that's only if they pass their exam."

"Did you figure all that out in your head just now?" Rowena asked, amazed by her friend's mathematical skills.

"Yea, and?"

Elva was just as impressed. "That's damn special, that is!"

"It's math. Simple math, really."

"Not for most of us here in the academy." Rowena said. "It's a gift."

Grainne cracked a smile, but then frowned. "Too bad math isn't too useful for a noble woman in Lotcala. Neither is horticulture, alchemy, or astronomy. Not in the way I want it." She leaned back in her chair and crossed her arms. "We're halfway out of this school and in the King's Army. I don't know what I'm going to do without the army unless I can be of use to someone." Grainne said, realizing Rowena's earlier point.

"Why not be of use to yerself?" Elva asked. "Wasn't Sirie some sort of mercenary captain?"

"She was." Rowena answered, nodding. "Maybe we could be too. We can all fight, and with Grainne, we'd have more intelligence than most armies."

"Being a mercenary?" Grainne raised an eyebrow at the idea.

"You'd get to see the world." Rowena said.

Grainne nodded her head thoughtfully. "Okay, I think I can get on board with that. Better than sitting around waiting for a husband to come home from war."

"Fighting, world travel and more fighting? You donnae have to ask me twice!" Elva responded, slamming her fist on the table.

* * * * *

In Antei, the new lord was building up a great host of mercenaries. His eyes had been engulfed by the gold coming in and filling his coffers. It was immediately spent on arms, armor, and something grander. He built a new keep. A large keep, away from the protective motte and bailey that had served the Goldwaters well for centuries.

Like much of the Goldwater family, the previous lord, Hugo, was not a man to live above his means. He was almost miserly with his gold, saving instead of spending it. Yet, the new baron was the opposite.

Langley was ready to let the gold leak from his hands like the water that nourished his new lands. Soldiers were expensive. Good soldiers were even more expensive. The age old secret with mercenaries; you get what you pay for. You don't get to demand a lot of gold for your service unless you can prove you're worth it. Langley, a former mercenary himself, knew such nuances of hiring men. Boastful men rarely became old soldiers, and old soldiers rarely bragged.

The baron looked out over his lands. He stayed in the ancient manor that had housed generations of his predecessors. It wasn't enough. A new keep was rising just to the east. One that would tower over Antei without the need of a motte. Langley smiled as troops camped out and drilled nearby. One day, his time would come.

* * * * *

What the War Academy lacked for in an open atmosphere, it made up for in dedicated training. Rowena and her two friends, fellow outcasts, excelled in the physical activities. Hand to hand combat and swordsmanship were Rowena's favorite skills. Grainne took a liking to archery instead, while Elva was top of the class with the spear. These learned skills helped earn the girls' spots at the top of the class.

Queen Sirie kept her eyes on Rowena and her two friends. She had a hand in her training since the princess could walk, and now Sirie was more focused than ever. Her goal was to install Rowena as a protector to the kingdom, the throne, and the crown prince.

The prince in question, Alfred, would need a protector. The barons were too hard to control from a central throne, and the manor lords and gentry were even more fickle. Sirie knew the minds of the nobles. Any excuse would do for the nobles to take advantage of a king. A new king could be impressionable. Charles had been, Sirie knew that well enough from her own manipulation of him. Alfred was like his father. Too much like him. They would then need Rowena to enforce his reign.

That was the trap Sirie set. The nobles weren't always too friendly with the queen, but they practically hated the princess. In Queen Sirie's mind, that would hopefully shield Alfred from any scorn that he could pass off on his sister. Let Rowena be the scapegoat if she was too heavy handed.

Sirie sat in her office with her lady-in-waiting, Lady Ginesa Mortimer. Lady Ginesa was a former mercenary from Sirie's old company that married into the Lotcalan nobility. One of Sirie's many political power moves. Ginesa was as shrewd as any of Sirie's former soldiers. Deadlier than most.

"Do you think it's wise to keep the dwarven bastard around?" Ginesa asked while sitting with Sirie. "A simple slip from one of my vials, and she won't pose a threat any longer."

Sirie grinned. "While that would solve future complications, I can't risk it."

"It'll be untraceable to most skilled healers. Even the best apothecaries won't catch on. My mother-in-law's healer couldn't detect it." Ginesa smiled. Her face contorted like a cat after catching a fat rat.

"So that's how your husband was so fortunate to inherit while so young?" Sirie responded with a smile. She had disliked the former Lady Mortimer, a mistress of her husband's father. "No, that won't do here. The king would be much too despondent over her death. Besides, with my firm guiding hand, she'll be Alfred's greatest protector."

"She's being influenced by the Hardstones. My husband has mentioned their ways in recent months. Do you think their past actions could influence her?"

Sirie waved off her friend's notion. "What the Hardstones did two hundred years ago, while despicable, is long gone and in the past. But if she enforces our ways too heavy handed, then Alfred need only say the word, and she's charged with treason, leaving Alfred as the savior of the people."

Lady Ginesa smiled wider. "A perfect plan." She quipped, taking a piece of sweet bread from a nearby plate. She ate the bread and licked the honey on her fingers. "Let's hope the upcoming tournament casts young Alfred well. These students will be his court one day."

Sirie nodded. "He is good on a horse, and his jousting technique is nearly flawless."

"A feat for one so young."

"Aye, it is." Sirie replied. "Many teachers have schooled him. He will be hard to beat."

"What of Rowena?" Ginesa pondered aloud. "I've heard she is far more skilled in combat than any other student."

"She is, yet she is a dwarf. They don't ride as well as humans." Sirie grinned.

While that fact was true enough for nationalistic or racist stereotypes, many dwarven warriors excelled at horsemanship. In fact, they could rival the Lotcalans in such activities, though most Lotcalans wouldn't admit that.

"My lady Sirie, you've seen to so much with her upbringing. Why not send her to some foreign land and be rid of her, though not in death? A tool for an alliance or married off to a foreign noble?"

"My husband might ask too many questions." Sirie said, her smile fading. "The most dangerous thing I can allow to happen is for the king to see what is truly within his power to do."

"You mean to make the dwarf legitimate?"

"Exactly. I must keep my hold over Charles, or my life's work has been for naught. From the moment I influenced my father to place me in the king's court until my conquering Charles' bedchamber, every moment has been a part of my plan for power. That dwarven bastard is the key to unraveling everything." Sirie turned to her friend. "I'd see this kingdom soaked in blood before I'd let her win over the king!"

* * * * *

The seasons changed as they are meant to, and before long, a cool wind blew across the land. Harvests were brought in after the arduous labor of collecting the grains and fruits. Soon the days would end early as the sun's light would fall earlier in the day. The coming of Yule would bring smiles to children and warm spiced wine for the adults. It was a time for families, friends and cheer.

Rowena and her friends roamed the halls of the dreary old castle that housed their school. Their thoughts on the future. All in secret, of course. Still, they knew that one day they would form a mercenary band, venture off into the wider world. A world without such rigid duties as that of the courtly life.

Grainne stopped and looked out of a window. Down in the courtyard, a group of students were hauling in pine burrows.

"Dammit. It's nearly time for the Yule Festival. That means the Yule Banquet." Grainne lamented.

"If I dinnae have to go to another banquet, I'd die happy." Elva smirked.

The trio walked off, back to their rooms for the night. The banquet and festival was still a month away, but it was so important that the festivities had to begin earlier each year. Rowena would be expected to help set up the tournament grounds, other students would help in other areas of the academy. Everyone was excited, especially Rowena, who loved the frosting mornings. Yule was her favorite time of the year, and while she never took part in the tournament, she loved the spectacle it brought.

That was why she volunteered to lead the set up for the tournament grounds. Not that there was any competition for the job. Rowena was a natural leader, and such a simple set up showed several classmates that away from the royal court, she was someone special.

Gathering Allies

nother lavish banquet held within the palace in Jovag was Sirie's favorite event these days. A harvest season feast called for braised chicken stuffed with pork. Sweet sugar glazed breads were laid out on platters and thick fruit sauces were drizzled on anything edible like a gravy. Red wines flowed, adding a warmth to the body and a lighthearted spirit to the room. It wasn't so strange that a banquet was being held in Jovag. Rather, it was the reason. Queen Sirie, in her scheming reasoning, had deemed it necessary and critical to think of suitors for the young princess, Rowena.

"My husband, the loving father he is, would rather we wait to discuss this, but Rowena is at the age most Lotcalan women think of marriage. The barons will mostly shut me out and most don't have eligible sons. Certainly the young lady would do well as a manor lord's wife." Sirie said to one of the ladies at the table.

It was Sirie's plan, sitting at a table among ladies from the noble families and several of their husbands, to wed Rowena well. Keep her close in the kingdom to keep an eye on her but also to use, in case the need arises.

Her nearly eighteen-year-old stepdaughter was at the right age for betrothal, but that did not ensure that she'd wed. Several factors went into such a decision. The king's approval was only the final matter. The two parties and their families had to agree on the terms governing households, land, and any trade opportunities with the land. Soldiers often played into the discussions and even gentry houses, should a baronial family think it prudent or helpful. Then the financial implications that went into that agreement had to be met. Once those details were worked out, the ruling overlord would give their consent. Often that occurred first as a courtesy, to avoid any work that would only be in vain. It was fair to say that any wedding among nobles was first and foremost a political and business matter before it could be called a matter of the heart. If one's heart even came into the picture.

After all that, the king had to give his consent. Not usually a fearful matter since most kings trusted their overlords with such trivial tasks. However, a baronial daughter and or son might warrant more attention than lesser houses.

A princess was an entirely different story. That meant the king had to be at the forefront for the duration of the talks.

King Charles was not one for such talk. He knew, as any father knows, that one day his beautiful little girl would no longer be so little and would fall in love. She'll want to marry. Like all fathers, he dreaded such a time. However, one reassuring notion he tried to tell himself was, since he never legitimized Rowena, she might be able to marry for love. Whether that was some half-assed attempt to justify his inaction on the subject few could say (in reality, it was to not anger his wife, who had been pregnant at the time of Rowena's arrival). He was left unaware of his wife's plans for his daughter.

One saving grace might have been the bigotry of the kingdom itself. The truth was that Sirie needed to do a lot of convincing for a marriage, the marriage she wanted, to happen.

"Maybe within Coldwood?" Sirie said, before sipping a goblet of red wine. "You have a son, don't you, Lady Blacktower?" She said.

Lady Blacktower's smile, which had been rather wide, faded some. "You expect my family to mix with dwarves?" She said, obviously taken aback. "Maybe the Torson Family or Breakspears would accept such a bride." She scoffed. "They might if the dowry is high enough."

Sirie grinned at the remark. High dowries were often reserved for less than desirable daughters.

Lady Gwain, already feeling drunk from the spiced blackberry wine, added to the conversation. "Of course, you are aware, your majesty, that most families aren't needing a warrior for a wife. Certainly not a dwarven one."

"We've allied with them to fight wars and trade goods. Not to breed with. That is how we'll dilute our own strength from Gota." Lord Curr, a sickly man with a thin chinstrap beard and greasy hair, from the Greenfield Barony said to the group.

Lady Gwain nodded. "You are a bit harsh, but honest, my lord Curr. The barons might not want to saddle such a burden on their vassal houses."

"Dwarves are good for fighting and mining ore. She's where she'll do best. With those backwards, rock-humpers, the Hardstones." Lady Blacktower said, mockingly.

Lady Gwain sneered. "To think that Baron Leif's own sister, that Catherine brute, tried to ask for my son's hand." She huffed. "A Hardstone is only slightly better than a dwarf. Your Majesty, I think that you'll have better luck sending the bastard back to her own kind. Let them deal with the ugly children she's sure to sire."

Sirie turned to Lady Gwain. "I think it's quite obvious that I can't turn to a baronial family, but I think a manor house would do well with such a lady. I've been able to train most of the dwarf out of her, and she has good genes." Sirie said with a smile. "At least half of her genes, that is." She finished with a chuckle.

The group erupted in laughter.

Charles, with his chamberlain, Sir Donovan Cullenhun, caught the last of the conversation from the hall. They missed the worst of it, but even an imbecile could get the gist of what they were implying. With a red face, his anger boiling over, he stormed into the hall and slammed his fist on the table.

"Enough!" The king roared.

Everyone in the hall turned to their king with shocked eyes. Instinctively, everyone in the hall stood with the king. They knew that when a king was standing, so too did the audience.

"That is my daughter you are speaking of, and laughing about, like she was a jester for your entertainment. One more word out of anyone's mouth in her regard, and you'll forfeit your life to the chopping block." The king's expression let each person present in the hall know he was not to be tested.

"My love…" Sirie began.

"No!" Charles cut her off. "Rowena is my daughter. My first born and one day, when I deem the time right, I and I alone will decide who she marries." He said.

"Charles…"

"Woman, I have spoken!" Charles yelled. "She is not legitimized, so what the hell does it matter to you? She won't be able to claim the throne, though I'd wager she'd do a damn fine job as queen. She might clean up the kingdom." Charles finished before walking out of the hall.

Lord Cullenhun, who had walked in with the king, looked to the group. "My daughter is a classmate of the princess. They're good friends, she tells me. I'd be honored if she were to join my family. The Cullenhun family doesn't hold any animosity to the dwarves."

Several of the lords and ladies murmured to themselves.

"You're from one of the oldest families. Surely, you know of the wars in the early years." Sir Horne said, stroking his bushy grey beard.

"Aye, and my family did their duty, fighting alongside Kings Haakon the Weak and Kjetill Stonebreaker. They fought, bled, and died with many of your ancestors. We lost many brothers during those days and that's why our house fell in numbers more than any other." Sir Cullenhun stopped and nodded, thinking of the old tales. "We Cullenhuns have plenty of reasons to distrust the dwarves. Our house was almost wiped out except for two sons and a daughter. We've rebuilt over the last two centuries, but perhaps our glories are behind us. It wasn't the dwarves' fault, though. Grainne and her friendship with Rowena have helped me see that. I believe my daughter and her words about Rowena, and should the princess need a husband in a few years, I'd gladly offer my one of my own sons."

Sirie feigned a smile. "Well spoken, Sir. If only it was your decision."

"Yes, your majesty, if only. However, I trust the king's decision, and as he said. It is his, and his alone." Cullenhun said with a nod before excusing himself from the hall to rejoin the king.

Sirie sneered as the man walked off. The others at the table felt an uneasiness, but they stayed, fearing to move. The queen relaxed and turned back to the table.

"Of course, whomever she marries, I'm sure we will have the most wondrous games and tournaments to mark the occasion." Sirie said, smiling uneasily along with her guests.

* * * * *

Grainne rushed through the corridors of the academy. She passed several sons of high ranking lords, brushing by all of them. Several stopped and called out to her to apologize, but Grainne wouldn't turn around. She might not have even heard them. She burst through Rowena's door, startling the princess.

"You need to read this!" Grainne demanded. "It's from my father." She said, handing a letter to Rowena.

Elva, hearing the commotion, ran into the room.

"What in the hell are ye going on about?" Elva asked, looking at Grainne. "I'm hearing the likes of some baron's son shouting that ye knocked him over in the hall."

Grainne looked over at her friend. "If he was in my way, then he probably deserved it. Now shut up. This is important." Grainne handed the letter to Rowena.

The princess read the letter in silence. Tears welled up in her eyes.

"How could she?" Rowena said, as she read. "The queen wishes me to marry. Some gentry lord in Pern."

"Ironhand." Elva said. "The queen loves them almost as much as those Canton bastards." She grunted.

Rowena continued reading. "There's more. These things she and the other ladies have said about me at a recent banquet." Rowena dropped her hand with the letter. "I'm just a monster to them."

Elva and Grainne saw the pain in their friend's eyes. The hurt was palpable.

"Yer not a monster." Elva said, walking to her friend and draping her arm around her. "Yer a fookin' princess."

"Not only that, but you're top of your class here at the academy." Grainne added. "That's pretty special."

Rowena tried to smile. "Sometimes I wish they had left me in Panyakuta. My mother didn't have anyone, I guess, so they sent me here, but maybe it would have been easier. Everyone treats me so different."

"And what's wrong with that, lass? Ye are different. So am I. So is Grainne." Elva said.

"How?" Rowena asked.

"Grainne can read better than the sages and priests. She knows more than anyone, and can speak better than yer patriarch. As for me, well, I'm a Hardstone, so everyone already thinks we're strange. They think we can't read or write and only want to fight and drink."

"What's wrong with that?" Grainne asked, her arms folded.

"Not a damn thing, if yer a Hardstone." Elva chuckled. "We enjoy going out getting drunk, fighting a bunch of highborns and then humping each other afterward." She laughed with a hearty breath. "I figured being here would help us get to know folks, but it ain't working." Elva grinned softly.

"It's working. I'm just realizing I don't like most of these assholes here." Grainne responded. "Bunch of pompous pricks." She finished looking toward the hallway, where nosey students were walking by. "I'll close the door." She said, turning and sneering to the others students as she slammed the door in their faces.

Elva smiled. "So, which of ol' Ironhand's gentry sirs is going to be blessed with a princess for a wife?"

Rowena looked at the letter. "Sir Rodrik Longpine's son, Ioan."

"I've heard of them, the Longpines." Grainne frowned. "They've harbored a longstanding hatred for dwarves and Hardstones."

"Aye." Elva said. "They tried to pick a fight with us a few years back. Killed a few of me relatives, but we killed a few of theirs too." She smiled at that last remark.

"Yeah, Ioan has a habit of tossing stones at me when I walk through the courtyard, and calling me a smoke colored bitch when he sees me." Rowena said. "Same with a few of his friends. They all hark on my height or sink color."

"This sort of marriage can't be some coincidence." Grainne said.

Rowena shook her head. "It isn't. It's her plan to get rid of me and away from my father. I honestly think that she'll keep pushing these sorts of things until I'm dead. I can't stay here while she's alive." Rowena tapped the letter in her hand. "I know what we have to do. We finish this year. Once we finish, we leave."

"Leave?" Grainne asked. "Leave to where? Doing what?"

"Mercenaries. We'll start our mercenary company, of course. We've been saying it for months now." Rowena said, standing from the bed.

"Just the three of us?" Elva raised an eyebrow.

A knock at the door caught their attention.

"What?" Elva yelled out.

"May I enter?" A voice answered.

"Paul." Grainne said.

Rowena nodded to Grainne, who opened the door.

"What do you want, Paul?" Grainne asked. "Why is there yellow paint on your tunic?"

The peach fuzzed young man walked into the room. "A jest from some of the other boys. Nothing more."

"Somehow, I think there is more." Rowena said.

"Two other guys caught me writing a poem to a page from back home. Oliver. He wrote to me saying he is going to squire for my elder brother so I wanted to give him something as a token. A poem and a lock of my hair." Paul said. "Corin and his lot thought that less than manly, so they painted me yellow and tossed me down a bit."

Rowena scoffed. "He wouldn't know what it takes to be a man if a man punched him in the face." Rowena smiled at Paul.

Grainne, still stone faced, tapped Paul on the shoulder. "You came for a reason other than to tell us about Corin, I assume?"

Paul straightened up. "Oh yes, I wanted to speak with Rowena. About the final test next week. The sparring match during the tournament."

"You want to be my partner?" Rowena guessed.

Paul smiled and nodded.

Rowena returned the smile. "Okay, Paul. If you do something for me."

"Sure." He answered.

Rowena smiled. "Join our mercenary band."

Paul was taken aback. "What? You were serious about being a mercenary?"

"Yes!" Rowena answered. "We're starting a mercenary band when we get out of here and we need members. We want you." Rowena explained.

"Are you sure? No one wants me." Paul asked, obviously confused. "At least not to fight with."

"Well, there aren't many to choose from." Elva said.

Rowena shook her head. "Paul, you're one of us, and we need to stick together."

"One of you?" Paul looked confused.

"An outcast. Grainne is too studious for a woman, Elva is too rough for a woman, and I'm too much of a dwarf." Rowena answered.

"What am I?" Paul asked.

"You're a man that loves who you love and you don't deserve judgment for it. Where does that put you with the other lords running around bedding any woman that looks at them?" Rowena said.

"Okay, I see your point about that, but what about the King's Army?" Paul asked.

"Do ye think they'd use any of us? A Hardstone that the queen hates, a weird girl that reads too much, and the bastard daughter of the king." Elva said. "We're rejects in every way but name."

"Four is a pretty small company." Paul responded.

"Yeah, it is." Rowena conceded. "However, we're not the only outcasts here. We can get at least six more. We are different, but we are valuable and we can do great things without the judgement and restraint of others. But we have to stick together."

Paul nodded. "I think I can help with that. Let me go speak with the other ladies and we can be on our way. Ten is better than four."

Paul was out the door in a flash. Elva and Rowena smiled.

"I always liked Paul." Rowena said.

"Yeah, well, let's hope the other ladies do, too." Grainne replied.

* * * * *

"Why would he send away the tenants from his lands? Hiring mercenaries when he has sworn vassals?" King Charles said to several of his advisors. "This Langley is not making friends of his bannermen."

The king was in his study, surrounded by his council of trusted advisors. Nearby, a fire was smoldering out. Candles lit the room in its place, their wax melting around the bases. Natural light entered the room, but the wood and stone walls still kept the study in a dim light.

In his hand, Charles held a letter from Antei. Like many nobles in the area, the author of this letter wasn't happy about recent events.

"Your majesty, we can't simply assume that Lord Redmayne is correct in his complainants. We shouldn't be too concerned just yet. Not without more evidence." Baron Coldwood, the Lord Chancellor, responded.

Other lords standing around the room seemed to agree with the baron.

Chamberlain Cullenhun shook his head. "I know Lord Redmayne. He is a serious man, with a very stern outlook on his lands. He is also slow to make assumptions. He wouldn't make such accusations without justification." Cullenhun was a gentry-lord of Antei like Lord Redmayne, but he had been away from the barony for some time. "Your majesty, perhaps I should ride home and see the matter for myself."

King Charles thought for a moment before turning towards the window behind him.

"Stay here for now, Cullenhun. We might have to send you later on, but for now, I think it is safe to do nothing." Charles replied. He held his hands behind his back while looking out to the eastern horizon. "We have more letters to go through. Hopefully no more on Langley."

* * * * *

Throughout the world, training for war was often brutal. It had to be difficult so that those being trained would be ready for whatever they might face. Would they ever be truly ready?

Most teenagers, as these young nobles would be once they left the academy, and the mighty Amazons were when they left the Herd, would see the true horrors. Lives broken, bent, or lost. Those that survived fared much worse than those that died. Swords and spear points leave terrible wounds that may never heal. Blades and points that spread the blood of others, the dirt from the muck, and leaving it in new victims to fester. Camps and healers' tents were full of disease and infection. Men shitting themselves to death from drinking the stagnant water. Nothing but stagnant water to drink. Unless you count the water that flows by the camp, where the army cleans off the blood from blades, armor or themselves. Water that the soldiers used to piss or shit in. Flowing water full of dirt, grim, and the waste of human life. That water would be certain death for those that dared to drink it. In a camp where soldiers were dying of thirst and that water looked like an oasis.

That would be the life of those who served in the wars. Songs of glory may reach their homes, but those songs would be song so loud to drown out any of the cries of anguish from those that lived through the haunting memories. Ever notice that the only ones singing the songs are the ones that never picked up a sword in their life?

Queen Sirie, when she was at the academy, and her staff trained the students hard as they could. Sirie, a former mercenary captain, was no stranger to a scene of battle. She had fought in more than a few, many spoke of her deeds in whispers. Though she had grown much more settled in her life as a queen, few would dare to challenge her. Her second in command of the academy was Sir Brandon Riverman, the son of the elderly Lord Roger Riverman.

Brandon was as tough as anyone. A veteran of many skirmishes with the Elysian Kingdom, and the war against the Silver Seal, Brandon was an expert on war. His expertise would be handy in the days when Sirie was away with her youngest Liam. Alfred, her oldest and the Crown Prince, was already in his second year of the academy.

That wasn't so odd, given that Princess Rowena was already a student. However, while Rowena was often taunted or chastised, Alfred was popular. He didn't excel in his studies, as his sister did, but he held sway with the other nobles' children.

There wasn't a rivalry between the two. Neither spoke to one another often. Rowena tried to reach out, but Alfred would ignore her or join in with the other students' torment of her. His actions were worse, being her brother. Alfred would toss stones at her, throw paint on her tunics, and steal her writing materials. Once he and a few others, pulled mud over her, telling her that dwarves like the dirt and she looked better covered in mud.

Throughout their years in the academy together, most did not imagine them as siblings. Rather, a prince and his unfortunate familial inconvenience. A family that would come together at the Yule Festival and Tournament.

The tournament, an annual affair with joisting, feats of strength, and a melee, was held to celebrate the time of the winter solstice. In the older Gota traditions, the old gods Ymir and Varis would lead a hunt with Atino and Guerra during the fortnight of Yule. While the citizens of Lotcala (a kingdom named for an old goddess) were followers of the Creator's faith, the old Gota traditions permeated through the society.

The joust was the favorite event, by far. This was also the sporting event Alfred excelled at. He was the champion in the joust. Was it because he was that skilled or the other students were afraid to risk hurting the son of the king? That was up for debate, but that debate didn't happen within earshot of the young prince.

"You should enter the joust!" Paul told Rowena one day as the pair walked into the courtyard. "The other sisters think you'd win it. Even against the prince. If you unhorse him, then you'll gain the respect of the others. Even Sir Brandon." Paul remarked.

While Rowena couldn't prove it, she always felt that Sir Brandon wasn't someone she could count on being an ally.

"I'm not looking for his or anyone else's respect if they can't give it to me for who I am now." Rowena countered. "Besides, he thinks that all the crap the other students give me is good to toughen me up."

"You're already pretty tough. Also, it would also look good for a mercenary to have experience in battles and tournaments." Paul added.

"I suppose I can see that. But winning a stupid jousting match isn't enough to erase years of ridicule."

"Perhaps, but it's enough to make them fear you." Paul replied.

"Fear?" Rowena stopped walking and raised an eyebrow at Paul. "I'm already a bastard to them, and from the wrong race. Fear isn't what I want to add to their hearts that are already hardened against me." She sighed. "No, I'll take my lot in life as it comes, and the respect of those closest to me is more than enough."

"How do you know those closest to you will fight beside you? How do you know they won't betray you?" Paul asked.

The question caught Rowena off guard.

"Your father isn't doing you any favors by not giving you a true place in the succession. He betrayed you the moment he learned of your existence." Paul continued.

As Rowena looked at her friend, she could see the sadness in his eyes. Still, his words rang true, and he didn't back down from them. The sting of the cruel words that echoed true was always bitter and deeper than any blade could ever pierce. Rowena felt the tears form in her eyes. She shook her head and left her friend standing there in the courtyard.

The truth was the confidence that her new friends, dubbed the sisters, felt for her flattered Rowena. Paul had done what he had said he would do. His friendliness with the other students, particularly the female students, had been enough to win them to Rowena's side. Now she had friends apart from Elva and Grainne. The pair of her original friends gained new allies, too.

One, Ingrid Hafmen, had come to Rowena for insights during an assignment on battlefield tactics. Rowena was gifted in that role. However, most took notice of her prowess on the field. Ingrid, known for her temper, athleticism and height, had sparred with Rowena, and was always bested by the much shorter princess. Now, as her ally, the pair practiced daily in friendly matches. Yet, their sparring never developed into a rivalry. Paul was adamant about the two royal children meeting head to head. For better or worse, he wanted to use them.

Ingrid had been within earshot of the conversation, and she made her way to Rowena's hiding spot along the academy's outer wall.

"Seeking solace in the loneliness, Rowena?" Ingrid said, approaching Rowena.

"Yes, alone please." Rowena said, wiping away a tear.

"I'll leave you be in a moment, but please hear me out."

Rowena nodded.

"Paul is not good for us. He seeks his own form of legitimacy. Maybe in the short term we can work toward a mutual benefit, but his goal is to be within the winning circle. If that's us, then fine, but if it's Alfred, so be it." Ingrid said. "I know of his dealings with the others, like Alfred. He leaves your room and goes to your brother. He sneaks off at night to whisper in the dark halls. One day, he'll have to make a choice between the Sisters or Lotcala, and I'm not sure we can count on his vote."

"Paul will make that choice, but for now I have to trust those around me." Rowena paused. "Do you really think it has to be me against my brother like Paul does?" Rowena asked, unsure of her new friend's logic.

"It's been that way since the day that merchant brought you to the king. It's the inevitable road. The only thing we don't know is how deep the rift will be when you prove to be the better of the two." Ingrid replied. "As much as I don't like, nor do the other sisters, Paul's forcing the issue, but we wonder if that is a bad thing in reality. Get it out of the way here and in a place that is fair."

"Fair?"

Ingrid nodded and then sat next to Rowena along the wall. Even sitting Ingrid was at least a head above the princess.

"The Yule Tournament is open to all challengers and if he is beaten, Alfred won't be able to cry foul or spout about some law against harming a prince." Ingrid continued. "He's taking the same risks as the rest of us. Each noble son is, and you can use that to show them your skill."

"You counsel me to watch out for Paul and his advice but then you offer me similar guidance."

Ingrid smirked. "I don't like the boy. He shows two faces. However, I can't deny that his direct approach might be the best. It could also draw Paul's true self out."

Rowena thought for a moment. "Fair enough. I sign up for the tournament, possibly beat Alfred, and then live with their fear?"

"Fear or respect. Either way, no one will ever like you the way you deserve." Ingrid snapped her fingers, producing a small flame before snuffing it out in a fist. "At least not around Lotcala. Too many backwards nobles. Commoners too."

Rowena liked the flames that Ingrid could produce. "Will you use your magic in the tournament?"

"Now that will get me arrested. I'd have to join the guild and learn to be a battlemage." Ingrid smiled at Rowena.

"Do you want to be a battlemage?"

Ingrid smirked. "Nah." She chuckled. "I rather like looking at my opponents up close as I knock them on the ground."

"Too bad you'll never see me on the ground."
Rowena joked, nudging Ingrid, shoulder to shoulder.

"Maybe one day, but I'm sure it won't be easy."

Rowena and Ingrid laughed. The friends stayed
by the wall until later in the day, watching the sun set
before heading in.

Later on that day, Rowena put her name down
to compete in the joust. It would be a decision that
would resonate for years to come.

The Yule Tournament

The air was chilly and the wind bit like a frost hound starving for its next meal. That was winter in Lotcala, a northern kingdom on the Falcon Coast. Known for its falcon beaked shape, the famous coast was a beacon for travelers and merchants during the winter months. Its main harbor, Ter Nog, was usually bustling before and during the Yule season.

Lords would host feasts in all the holds for such a great time. In the War Academy, the tradition was no different. Feasts and parties were common during the Yule Season. The biggest event, however, was the Yule Tournament. Nobles came out to cheer on their youth. Seeing some of their own vassals, or future vassals, was a treat. It was also a way to strengthen your position for the coming years.

It was certain that the king would show. Two of his children were attending the academy. He had to be there to support them. A spectacle was expected and the wards of the academy made sure that everything was going to be perfect for his majesty. That had to be done. Sirie would not allow for anything less than the best for her husband, nor would she ever show the academy in any state unfit for noble born children.

A momentous occasion that had to be perfect. The Yule Tournament was planned perfectly, right down to the type of cloth used for the upholstery in the chairs.

Within the combatants' tents, each participant was readying themselves for the day's events. Rowena fidgeted under her chainmail armor. Elva was finishing tying the coif around her neck.

"Stop yer moving about las. This coif is hard enough to tie without ye moving this way and that." Elva said.

Rowena grunted what sounded like an apology.

"It's the nerves, girl." Elva continued. "Yer about to joust that pompous puss, Ioan Longpine." Elva stopped and smirked at her friend. "Ain't he to be yer husband soon?" She chided.

"Fuck you." Rowena said, lightly pushing Elva back. Both friends burst into laughter.

Just as they subsided, Grainne entered the tent. "Rowena, they're calling for you at the list."

Grainne picked up Rowena's nasal helm. Hung beneath was an added guard of thick chainmail. That simple addition would help protect her face during the joust. She helped Rowena put the helm on. It wasn't always a simple thing for a warrior to prepare for battle.

The three walked out to the list, the area where the joust was to take place. Arriving, they saw the other ladies from the academy, and Paul standing near her horse. Ingrid held the stallion's mane.

"He's ready for you, your highness." Ingrid said once Rowena reached the group.

Elva and Dona Redwater helped Rowena onto the steed, while Paul handed Rowena her kite shield, and Ælfthryth Elbe handed her the blunted lance.

"Ride well, lass." Elva said, just before Rowena pulled the reins and guided the horse toward her mark.

The herald was announcing the participants as they trotted up. Some gasps were heard when Rowena's name was called.

Rowena Carlsdotter.

She heard the herald yell. She looked to the stands and saw her family, her father, in the middle. He looked confused, and she wondered if her stepmother was confused or angered. Sirie's face was as much a stone as it ever was.

Rowena saluted the king, who nodded, and then she turned toward her opponent.

Ioan was a tall and lanky young man of seventeen. Already, he had seen some skirmishes in his home county against the Mortimer family. Nothing too drastic like against the Hardstones in years past, but enough to give him more combat experience on a horse.

Truth be told, several of the students had already been in battle. Mostly in skirmishes against other families. A painful reality that the king allowed, or at least couldn't control. The gentry families would fight for small parcels of land, and while that wasn't exactly legal, it was overlooked, as long as it didn't spill over into larger conflicts. Most battles turned into duels between champions, so the casualties were minimal.

Rowena had some experience, and she was the only student to have killed a man to protect her father from an assassination attempt a few years prior. That gave everyone at least some thoughts about her skills. Ioan, not too happy with his arraigned marriage to the dwarven princess, wanted let loose some of his frustrations. Now he had his target.

The pair saluted each other, as was custom. The flag bearer waved the academy's standard, and the combatants kicked their steeds hard. Both shot off at a hard gallop. Rowena wasn't quite as steady on her horse, but she maintained herself and lowered her lance. Ioan did the same on his end. Their horses huffed and blew steam from their nostrils. The mud from the ground flung as the hooves stomped at a treacherous pace. Within seconds, the pair were mere feet apart.

Rowena pulled her lance back slightly, and at the last second heaved it straight into Ioan's guarded shoulder. The shield on his left arm took the brunt of the hit, but the young rider flew off of his horse by Rowena's perfect hit.

The horses slowed their pace. Rowena pulled the reins of her steed and turned him to see the field. Throughout the crowd, the spectators were gasping and in shock at the scene they had witnessed. Ioan was slow to get up, but he finally rose, with the help of his second. Pushing them away, Ioan tore away his helm and flung it to the ground.

"I demand her disqualification!" Ioan shouted. "She cheated!"

The crowd grew silent. It was a heavy accusation that was rarely heard at such tournaments.

"Liar!" Elva shouted. The surrounding ladies yelled affirmations of agreement. "Yer just mad ye were beaten by a girl!"

The ladies around Elva burst into laughter, as did many in the crowd.

Ioan scowled. He would not stand for such humiliation.

"No, she is a dwarf and her unnatural strength is grounds for cheating!" Ioan replied. "Dwarves are nothing but brutish barbarians, no different from cave trolls. She's just smaller since she's a bastard bitch!"

Sounds of shocked nobles echoed through the tournament grounds. Ioan had spoken ill of a noble, a royal, the princess, no less.

"How dare ye!" Elva roared.

She drew her sword and rushed onto the field. Ioan's seconds stood with him, but the ladies that stood by Elva were right behind their friend.

The king rose, intending to speak, but before he could say anything, he heard a metal clang.

Everyone stopped in their tracks and looked at the sound. There they saw Rowena, her helm removed. She slammed her helm on her shield.

"Longpine! You've cast an insult my way and that will not stand. Before the king here I challenge you to a duel for vindication!" Rowena roared.

She dismounted and called for her sword. Ingrid brought it over.

"What say you, Longpine?" Rowena asked.

Ioan looked around. He smirked and shook his head. "Not worth my time."

A voice rang out through the crowd.

"Coward!"

Ioan turned to the crowd and scowled. "You call me that, but I've beaten many in battle. What say all of you?"

Most stayed silent, but one spoke.

"You do not know the horrors we've seen, boy." King Charles said. He was still standing, watching the events unfold. "You say she's cheated you and then you insult her. Accept the duel and prove your accusation or refuse and face my dungeon."

"Husband, mere words should glance off your daughter." Sirie said.

Charles ignored her. "Do you accept or...?"

Ioan lowered his head. "I accept, but my champion will fight for me. I'm the first born of the Longpine family and so I'm needed in such capacity."

A large framed man walked onto the field and stood with Ioan. The man was at least twice the height of Rowena, taller than Ioan even, and nearly six hands across the chest. Upon his face was a large scar, healed poorly from a war long ago.

"This is Sir Gerald Olbe. He'll act as my champion today." Ioan said with a wicked smile.

King Charles shook his head. He was about to call it off when Sirie stopped him.

"This is what she demanded, and you encouraged. Ioan is within his legal rights by the customs according to duels." The queen said.

Charles looked at his wife and nodded solemnly. "Aye."

Rowena noted the scene and nodded. "Fine." She grinned and put her helm back on.

The princess gripped her sword in her right hand and her shield on her left. The sword, a present from Hardstone, was single handed and simple in design. The blade was steel, and the hilt was ebony wood, with a steel pommel.

Sir Gerald put on his helm. He already had on chainmail. Not sure why, but maybe he wore it often. No matter, he was ready once he pulled his sword from its scabbard. The two inched closer to one another until they were close enough that Gerald took a swing at the princess.

Rowena was fast enough to move out of the way. She crept low and saw an opening in the larger man's defense. His sword was larger. Hand and a half hilt and most of the weight was in the blade. That meant he had heavy swings and more recovery time. Rowena also saw that the chainmail didn't cover his legs. Simple trousers, perhaps two layers, but not nearly enough to protect from her blade.

She dodged a second strike, trying to line up her own swing. A third came and Rowena brought her shield up to deflect the blow. The princess turned and spun behind the larger man and kicked at the back of his knee. Gerald dropped low onto his knee.

Rowena took that moment to bash her shield into the back of his head. Gerald fell face first onto the ground. The princess wasted little time, rolling him over, removing his helm, and slamming her shield onto his face three times. Rowena pulled back as Ioan's seconds came over to Gerald to check on him. There was breath left in him, but it was shallow. Doubtful that he would make it through the night.

Ioan writhed with rage. "Cheat!"

Rowena leveled her sword at the young man. "Call me that again and this sword will find its way into your stomach."

The young man gulped back his air before talking, keeping his voice to a whisper. "My father accepted the queen's proposal. You're going to be my wife, and I'll be sure your life is hell every night. You'll feel no pleasure at what I have planned for you, bitch." Ioan grinned wickedly.

Rowena seethed with an internal passionate fire. "Not sure you'll get much pleasure, either. Touch me once and I'll slice your throat as you sleep."

Ioan backed off, scoffing, and taking his seconds with him off of the field. Rowena turned to the crowd. She removed her helm and looked at the king. He was seated, his face looked unnerved at the scene. Sirie grinned.

"I withdraw." She said before walking off, back to her tent.

Within her tent and surrounded by her sisters, Rowena wiped away the tears that she had held back on the field. She knew her fate was sealed if the marriage took place.

Ælfthryth looked at the sister on her right, Bega. "That Ioan needs to be killed before their wedding."

"Let them marry, but then we kill him before the bedding ceremony." Bega Galdur replied.

"No, if he dies before consummation, then she can't inherit his claim. They have to have the bedding and conceive." Another sister, Pega Fairhair, remarked.

"What the fuck are you three going on about?!" Grainne yelled in anger. "He threatened our sister, and you want her to have his demon spawn?"

"And then kill him." Pega answered.

Grainne shook her head. "That fucker isn't getting within ten feet of Rowena. Ever! Or I'll gut him myself."

The princess sniffed back her tears and stood up. "That's enough." She said, stopping the argument. "I understand what everyone is trying to do, but there is only one course of action." Rowena looked at the others. "Tonight, we leave. We all leave. This is what we've been planning, and tonight it has to happen."

* * * * *

Rowena and her sisters scurried through the halls of the academy. They had to be quick and quiet, or they risked capture. What they were attempting was actually breaking their oaths as King's Army soldiers. Still, the die had been cast, and they made the choice. Leave and take their chances in the world, or stay to be fodder for other people's schemes.

The sisters had gathered all the belongings that they could carry. For several, this meant leaving many changes of clothes or other personal items from home. Rowena instructed them to take only the items that they would absolutely need. Grainne left a good number of books, taking only two, a book of medicinal herbs and plants, and a book on southern languages. Others took stores of food, skins of wine and water, or cloth for garments. Each had their weapons and armor already on their person. Still, the group had to travel light so that they might travel fast. Rounding corners and avoiding light, the ladies were close to the gates.

Paul was waiting by the exit. He would help them escape and then join them on a journey to the south.

Rowena smiled at Paul as she approached with the sisters in tow.

"Good on you, Paul, for getting rid of the guard." Rowena said. "I have your gear." She finished, handing him his satchel.

"He won't be needing it." A familiar voice spoke from the shadows.

Rowena's smile faded. It was the same voice that echoed in her head each night as she slept. It was the voice she heard in every mistake. Sirie.

"You're taking a trip?" Sirie asked, coming out of the shadows with several guards around her. "I would have missed it had Paul not been such a good boy and told me your plans." Sirie looked at the scared young man and winked.

Paul hung his head low. His former friends sneered at him and his betrayal.

"A mercenary, really? Do you honestly think you have what it takes to do something so dangerous?" Sirie chuckled. "Of course not. However, that doesn't matter, anyway. I'm afraid you're needed elsewhere, Rowena. These Longpine soldiers will escort you to their liege's estate." Sirie looked around at the rest of the sisters. "The rest of you may go back into the castle and we'll forget any of this ever happened."

The Longpine guards scowled at Rowena. Nothing but hatred within their hearts and minds for the young dwarf.

Sirie motioned for the guards to move in. They grabbed Rowena by her arms. One held out a length of chain and shackles.

"This can be easy for you, Rowena. Just do as I say and you'll make it easier on yourself." Sirie chided.

Rowena kicked and a guard and another clubbed her with the pommel of his sword, knocking her to the ground. Blood oozed from her forehead.

The ladies were frozen in place for a moment. A couple backed away until Elva stopped them.

"No." She said in defiance. "We're all leaving. Rowena too. Ye can't stop us, even if you are the queen." She knelt down to help Rowena stand up.

Two guards tried to pull Elva away before Grainne rushed in to help. Followed by the other sisters. They pulled Rowena from the guards reaching in for the princess.

Sirie feigned a smile. "My step daughter's best friend always trying to protect the little bastard." The queen's smile faded. "Another thorn in my side. I'm the queen, and that means you don't get to tell me what you're doing. No one does."

"That's not entirely accurate." Another voice, a man's voice, spoke from behind the girls.

Everyone turned to see King Charles, followed by Sir Cullenhun.

"Thankfully, the queen isn't the only one with spies within these walls." Charles said. He walked over to Rowena. "You're wanting to leave?" His voice was softer than normal, almost breaking.

Tears, blood from her forehead mixing in, ran down her cheeks. "I can't stay and be married to a man that would rather hurt me than to know me." She sniffed. "I would stay for you, father, and be at your side, help you in any way, but I need to control my own life. I know that as long as I'm here, I'll never have the life that I need within your court."

Charles nodded in agreement. "You are a wonderful daughter and deserving a better father. I'd never let you marry such a coward as Longpine. You're eighteen and though you are a subject to the crown, I can't stop you as a father. As a father, I must see you grow."

Charles looked at the guards near his wife. He waved them off, but they stood for a moment. Sir Cullenhun stepped up from behind the king.

"The king ordered you away." Cullenhun said, placing his hand on his sword hilt. Several king's guards appeared nearby. "We're not alone so I'd be gone if you're wanting to make it back to Dustcairn in one piece."

The guards begrudgingly walked away, leaving the queen alone.

Charles looked back at Rowena. "You may leave. Your friends too. I only ask that you return to us should I ever call for you."

Rowena sobbed. "I will, father. I always will."

The pair hugged. Charles held her close for as long as he could and Rowena held on tight.

Around them, the ladies walked through the gate. Elva and Ingrid looked for Paul for retribution, but the coward had run off at the first sign of a fight.

Queen Sirie, having lost her pawn, cursed and spat on the ground before walking away.

Rowena released her hug from her father and waved goodbye to him and Sir Cullenhun. She caught back up to her sisters.

King Charles watched his daughter fade from him. He felt a tear run down his cheek, not knowing if or when he'd ever see his little girl again.

Journeys through the World

n the days of the Carolyngian Age, a great host of beasts roamed the world. Not as many as in centuries past, but plenty to put fear into the mortal races. Be it minotaur, centaur, troll, or any number of creatures, mercenaries would be called upon to protect pilgrim roads. Even drakes, dragons, and their terrible kin would haunt the roads taken by caravans. Yet, wars still raged, and often enough soldiers could find work in the armies of lords fighting for lands.

A year passed since Rowena and her Sisters left Lotcala, and life was not as easy and carefree as they might have dreamed. Sure, they all knew that hiring themselves to lords or other companies would not be simple, given their youth and the fact that they were women, but jobs were scarce. In the year since they struck out on their own, the group took seven actual jobs. Four were hunting destructive animals, two were security for trade caravans, and the last was stopping a bandit attack. That final one turned out to be nothing more than a bunch of teenage boys stealing local crops from grain stores.

Of the seven jobs, only the trade caravans paid any real gold. The others paid in food, welcomed, but not exactly what was offered. The last job decided not to pay, so Rowena let the boys go. After that last job, Rowena marched her band, now numbering fifteen, towards a small fishing village, Puck's Landing, along the Bay of Souls. She had heard of a few pirate raids, nothing too large, but the Zaragozan pirates didn't need numbers when their reputation usually did all the work for them. Villagers feared the black sails of Zaragoza, even though most ships only had a small crew of pirates.

Rowena stopped the group on the low ridge overlooking the village nestled below. A steady rain fell on their shoulders. All were covered in cloaks, but the sea winds whipped up the surrounding chill. No matter, the sight before them, with its prospects of coin, warmed them enough. For now.

The Bay of Souls was a deep water refuge for trade ships. Most were larger, and slower, cog ships that were well equipped to carry cargo but not as great in a fight, apart from tall sides, deterring boarding. The galleys, provided by local lords, would protect the ships in times of peace, but they were often away at war. For many years, those wars occurred with the seasons, and that meant that there were known times when the cogs were left to their own protection.

The sisters knew enough of the rumors of a renewed war coming and heading their way to Puck's Landing to possibly make a decent share of coin. They made their way down to the village, passing the locals, all either retreating into their houses from fear of the strangers or coming out with curiosity. Mud flung from their horses' hooves. Another truth of life in a fishing village. Add that to the gloom of a dreary day with overcast and raining skies, and it would be miserable.

Ingrid looked around and scoffed at the miserable village scene. "Not a damn thing worth protecting. What are we here for?"

Rowena pointed to the docks. "That." She said with a grin. The docks were broken but still functional. However, the men that huddled around the area looked even more broken that the docks themselves.

"Puck's Landing is the only deep water port in the area. This place used to have more people, but pirates ran most off. However, the deep hulled ships can't dock anywhere else, so they risk it. Most have armies, so the pirates leave them alone." Rowena continued.

"It's the villagers and the smaller cogs that are in danger from the pirates." Grainne replied. "Those armies leave with the ships, leaving the village defenseless once again."

Rowena nodded.

The group stopped in front of a tavern. It was a dingy looking place, much like the rest of the town. It was old with several broken or missing windows. The place was rundown, probably well over fifty years old, but the tavern had seen its better days.

"We need shelter for the night. If nothing else but to get out of this rain." Rowena looked to the building. "As small as this place looks to be, I doubt they'll have enough room for us."

"A barn nearby, maybe?" Elva said, looking around.

"I'm guessing there is a village leader. An elder, maybe?" Matilda Greenfield remarked. "He'd be able to point us to friendly nobles. If there are any."

Elva smirked. "Send in Severa. She's a snake charmer. She'd make anyone feel friendly."

The group laughed at the remark.

"Come on." Rowena said after catching her breath. "Let's head in and see about the job and quarters." She finished, dismounting from her horse.

The group went into the small building. Within, the scene was no better. Men, a couple passed out from whiskey, were in a drunken or somber stupor. Several left the tavern, leaving only three sleeping off the booze.

"No wonder they can't defeat any pirates. They're too drunk." Ingrid said, pulling out a chair and sitting down.

A tavern girl noticed the group, but made no attempt to serve them. Instead, she sat behind the bar and knitted. One of Rowena's newest members, Hadiza, a southern kingdoms woman from the Free Cities, called out to the girl.

"We're looking for drink and shelter." Hadiza said, loud enough to wake the men, they quickly scurried out of the tavern at the sight of armed women.

The tavern girl looked over at her, then went back to her knitting.

"You'll find neither here." The girl said. "Best to leave before you meet the raiders and the others around town."

Rowena looked over at the tavern worker. "That's exactly why we're here. We heard this village and the trade ships needed protection."

"You're here to offer that? A bunch of girls?" The tavern worker replied with a scoff.

"We prefer women." Rowena answered.

The worker rolled her eyes. "Too bad these men around here do, too. Ain't nothing here for you lot. If you're smart, you'd leave."

The Sisters sat around four tables, whispering their next plan. Most were inclined to leave, but Rowena, Grainne, and Elva all knew that they had to earn some gold or get food. Their stores were getting low and coin was becoming lower.

Rowena looked over at the woman and noticed she was pregnant. "Your belly is swollen, I see. A baby coming soon?"

The girl nodded.

"What's your name?" Rowena asked, standing up and walking over to the bar.

The wood floors creaked as she moved, and a few looked to be close to rotten.

"Juniper." The girl said.

"I'm guessing this place isn't too hospitable to strangers." Rowena said.

Juniper shook her head. "Most strangers aren't the friendly type. Respectable travelers avoid coming to this village. If you're respectable, you should do the same. Leave while you can."

Rowena nodded. "I forget that sometimes there are places like this in the world. Not like back home."

"Yep, not everyone can live in a fantasy land where everyone's nice." Juniper quipped.

"How old are ye? Ye look and sound like ye rather be somewhere else." Elva asked, walking up to the bar.

"I'm eighteen."

"A young one like us." Elva replied.

"Old enough to be the owner of this place." Juniper shot back.

"You own this tavern?" Rowena asked.

"Yeah, ever since my father went to the waves last year."

"My condolences." Rowena said. Elva made a noise, sounded sorrowful.

"No matter. This place is his legacy to me and my baby."

"What of the babe's father?" Elva inquired.

"What of him? Just a villager, take a pick." Juniper replied. "A regular customer, I'm guessing."

"One of the men that was in here is the father?" Rowena asked.

"One of them or possible another from the village. Every man in the village has taken a turn. Well, a couple hadn't, but I'm expecting it soon enough." Juniper grimaced. "Most preferred not to risk a baby, but several have tried to plant their seed within. One lucky son of a whore succeeded." Juniper replied, throwing her knitting down. "I just hope it's a boy so I can teach him better than this lot."

Rowena shook her head. "They don't have wives?"

"Aye, what of other women around here?" Elva continued. "I know in our homeland brothels exist. Houses for men to get their rocks off, women too if they're inclined. Where are they?"

Juniper sighed. "There are only a few wives left, ugly hags. The pirates took most wives. These cowards didn't fight for them. The men that did fight, died or were recruited to fight in the lord's wars. They don't always come home. And some just never return from the sea." She stopped. "Ain't had many whores come through here during the off season. When the armies dock, women from the main land come and pry their trade."

"Then the armies leave, pirates move in, the women leave." Rowena reasoned.

"Aye, and leave me and a couple of other lasses to be ravaged by these assholes." Juniper finished.

"How many other women are in town?" Elva asked.

Juniper thought for a moment. "Eight or so. A couple of little ones, too."

Elva softened her tone. "Do ye have any options besides this town? Can ye leave?"

"And go where?" Juniper shot back. "We have no money, or any support, away from this place. Anyone that did left long ago."

"Fucking shit hole. This ain't the place for us, lass." Elva cursed before walking away.

Rowena wasn't ready to leave just yet. "How many men are left in the village?"

Juniper shrugged. "Twenty five, I think. Some don't venture out of the house too often. Just to collect from the crab traps. Some come out in the evening for a drink and to harass me. Best to leave as soon as you can."

Rowena looked up at the woman and nodded. "We'll see what we can do."

"Do?" Juniper asked.

"Just wait a moment." Rowena answered before walking to her group.

Elva was already in the midst of telling the tale.

"I think it's better we leave, captain." Dona said once Elva finished.

"We are." Rowena answered. "With the women and as much gold as we can carry."

The group looked confused.

"I'm not leaving them here in this shit. Grainne, you, Ingrid, and Pega find the man that put out the contract and get whatever info you can. We need to be watchful of pirates, but these men might be the biggest threat."

"Captain?" Elva interrupted. "Where do you expect us to take the women?"

Rowena pulled out her map and laid it out over the table. She traced the route they had come. "The town of Brekkenfield is three days' ride south. However, I think East La~Porte is the better option. Fortified, larger, and further up the coast. The pirates stay away since the lord of the region maintains a standing army and navy."

"What of the men?" Severa inquired. "They won't be happy and word will spread."

Rowena shook her head. "No, it won't."

Everyone looked more confused until they realized her meaning.

"That's a good way to never get hired again." Grainne said. "We need the gold."

"We'll get it." Rowena answered.

"Why?" Elva asked.

Rowena grew angry that her sisters couldn't see it the way she did. "These bastards are hurting their own people. They can't or won't fight to defend them, so they just take them as they see fit, and leave them to suffer in squalor!"

The others lowered their heads. They knew it to be a terrible situation, but they didn't want to make it personal.

Elva was the first to speak up. "Ye know we cannae be going about making these jobs personal, Rowena. We have to make coin and continue to make coin if we a gonnae survive. We cannae kill an entire village!"

"It's not the entire village." Rowena replied.

"Ro." Elva said. "Ye know what I'm meaning."

"Look, we have to get these women away and that's that." Rowena responded to Elva.

Rowena sat down and motioned for Elva to do the same.

The group sat silently. Juniper walked over with platter holding two pitchers of ale and some goblets. The goblets were as clean as a busy bar maid, fighting off men all day, could manage.

"Since you lot are more stubborn than smart, I figured you could use a drink before leaving. Besides, you seem to be good folk. Something this village has been missing. I'll fetch a couple more pitchers of ale for the rest of you." She said, walking back to the bar.

The sisters poured the alcohol when several men entered the tavern.

"Juni, pour us some mead, and park that sweet ass over here!" One called out as he took a seat at a table along the back wall.

"I'll get you the mead, but you'll have to wait while I serve these ladies." Juniper replied.

The man looked over at Rowena and gave a wink. "Fancy a roll, dwarfy?"

Rowena smirked. "I'd be willing to bet my dick is bigger than yours."

The man shot up from his chair and stomped over to Rowena's table, while his friends and Rowena's had a hearty laugh. Elva and Ingrid both stood up. Each matching his height.

"Sit down, boyo." Elva said, her hand on the hilt of her blade.

"I won't be made fun of by some dwarf bitch!"

"She ain't making fun of you, Tormin. I've seen what you got, and it is a wee bit of a thing." Juniper said.

Tormin looked at her and scowled. "So these ladies waltz into the place and you grow a pair of balls under that skirt? Funny, I never noticed them before."

Rowena quickly stood up and kicked the back of Tormin's knee, bringing him down to the floor.

"We heard about pirate raids and that we could make some gold protecting the village. Anyone we should speak to about that?" Rowena said.

"Yea, me." A voice said from behind the group.

Everyone turned to see an old woman standing at the door.

"Some men said we have well-armed visitors. I had put the word out for mercenaries. I had expected men. Hoped for men." The old woman said.

"Why men?" Grainne asked.

"Because we don't have any gold and the men could have helped themselves to the women instead." The old lady replied. "Unless you women prefer ladies, then it might be best for you to move on."

Pega grinned. "I like women just fine, but if you're any sign of the type of women I'd get around here, then I'll pass."

"Shall we vote?" Rowena asked her friends.

"No need. Your plan works fine." Elva said. The others nodded.

The old woman raised an eyebrow, but Rowena ignored her look. Her mind was made up.

Rowena looked at the old lady. "How long before the pirates arrive?"

"Most times with the first full moon of autumn. Should be tonight."

"That's convenient." Rowena grinned. "We'll stay and see what happens tonight. Anyway, we're tired from the road and need some shelter from the rain and cold. If they don't attack, then we'll leave in the morning. If they do attack, then maybe we won't be any trouble for you any longer."

The old woman nodded. "Fine, but I want you gone by midday, no later." She finished before walking out of the tavern, followed by Tormin and his crew.

Rowena looked to Juniper. "Sorry for scaring your customers away."

"They wouldn't have paid, anyway." Juniper said.

"Who's the old hag?" Grainne asked.

"Ettaine Wilte. Everyone just calls her Grandma Etty." Juniper scoffed. "Bitch, that lets the men treat all the women as commodities. She owns the village. She's the reason this village is so bad off with the pox and poverty."

"Fuck me." Rowena responded.

"Stick around and they will."

Rowena shook her head. "Okay, so we have a plan. Forget the pirates, we're taking all we can and whichever women that you think will want to leave and getting you all out of here."

"What?" Juniper said.

"You're not safe, nor is your unborn baby. We'll get you to East La~Porte. Just a week away." Rowena said.

Juniper looked shocked. "You can't be serious. I can't just leave my father's tavern."

"You want to stay here and live in this hell?" Grainne asked.

"Well, no... I've just never known another place." Juniper replied. "I wouldn't know how to begin."

"We have allies in the northern towns, doctors and clerics, that can help heal whatever you've caught, and they can help with the baby. I know people there that can help you set up a better life. It won't be easy, but you have a better chance there than here."

Juniper began to tear up. "Okay, yes."

"Great, we can get you to safety. You and whoever else you think deserves it." Grainne said.

"None of them." Juniper replied.

Rowena looked confused, as did her Sisters. "I don't understand." Rowena said.

Juniper looked out the grimy window. "These people sent my dear father to negotiate with the pirates. He was the town elder, so he and two others went to make a deal, but his companions betrayed him and made a deal with the pirates for Grandma Etty. The pirates chained my father up and threw him off the ship. Sent back the other two men. Then Etty took over the town. They get to have their way, as long as the men leave them alone." Juniper wiped away her tears. "Fuck them and let the pirates murder the lot." Juniper looked back at Rowena. "I'll go with you."

Rowena stood with her group. "Is there any gold in the village?"

"Etty's place." Juniper said. "I don't know how much, but any gold that comes through here, any trade, all of it goes through her."

Rowena nodded. "Elva, take five Sisters and get all you can carry." Rowena said. "Make sure that Etty doesn't live."

Elva sighed. "This town needs to be wiped off the map. Pega, Bega, Dona, and Hadiza come with me. You too, Severa. Let's get the coin." Elva and the others walked out of the tavern.

Rowena looked to Ingrid. "Torch it all."

Ingrid nodded before walking out of the town.

Grainne and Matilda rushed Juniper to gather whatever she could take and quickly got the horses ready. The sun was setting as the first fire rose into the sky.

Rowena took the other seven sisters to wait for the commotion of the town's men. They didn't have to wait long as more fires sprung up and people took to the road that ran through the middle of the town.

Night fell as more people fled from the flames. Rowena watched them, men and women. Some approached her and her Sisters. The wrong idea.

Two men brandishing axes ran towards the Sisters. Maita, another woman from the Free Cities, and

Gunhild, a northern woman, were quicker than the men. Each cut the men down with ease.

Emma Ota, a master with a spear, thrusted her weapon at another attacker. Groups of men rushed Rowena and her band, but the highly trained warriors were quick to cut down any others that came too close. While the original nine had been trained in Lotcala under strict rules, the newest members had their own training and learned further skills with Rowena. The village's folk were out matched. Still, that did not deter any from trying.

Rowena, her sword in her right hand and a war ax in the left, swung with ferocity as a woman attacked her with a meat clever. The woman's body fell prone as Rowena left her where she lay.

Two wagons trotted out from behind some ramshackle buildings. Elva pulled one, guiding a mule. The other sisters were following along, weapons drawn. They were all bloodied, but it was hard to say whose blood it was. The other wagon was Grainne, with Matilda and Juniper riding inside. Grainne had loaded clothes, ale, mead, and some food as well.

Ingrid came running from the side of another building. "There's a shitload of whale blubber in that last building. We need to take some to sell. We can blow the rest." She said to Rowena.

Rowena gave the order. Several sisters rushed off with Elva and Ingrid to load up some of the blubber. The expensive resource would fetch plenty of gold in another town.

"Grainne, take your wagon and you two get Juniper out of here. We'll provide you cover. Get up to the high ridge and wait for us there." Rowena ordered.

Her friend did as instructed while two other sisters fired arrows into attacking villagers. Rowena turned back to helping defend the second wagon, while Elva and a couple of others loaded it with trade goods.

"We have to go!" Ingrid yelled, before casting one last flame spell to a haystack drenched in whale blubber.

The band rushed out of the town, hauling the last wagon, full of pilfered goods. Within an hour, the village was engulfed in flames, and every villager was dead. Rowena and her band were making their way up to the ridge when she looked back at the scene. In the distance, she thought she could make out sails. The pirates, she figured. However, in the bright glow of the fire, she wasn't sure if she could see anything well enough.

It didn't matter. The job was done, and they had made it out with plenty of goods to sell, and most importantly, Juniper was safe.

Later on, by a warm campfire. Juniper was sleeping on one of the wagons, while two sisters kept guard. They set some tents up, but with the rain stopping, most sat near a fire or on the wagons. Rowena sat looking into the fire when Grainne walked up behind and sat next to her.

"I did what was right. What was necessary." Rowena commented without looking at her friend.

Grainne spoke up. "No one doubts that, but what we did wasn't the best plan. Do you know what —"

"If you say her name..." Rowena cut in, looking at Grainne.

"I wasn't." Grainne replied, holding her hand up. "You know I'd never say her name, but I was going to ask if you know what your father would do. You still respect him, right?"

Rowena's eyes narrowed. "You know I do."

"Well, he'd never kill all the men in the village just to spare a one woman's heartache and misfortune." Grainne said.

Rowena sighed.

"He'd kill the entire village." Grainne finished.

Everyone gasped, but Grainne sat stone-faced.

"In southern Lotcala, near the border with Elysia, there was a small little farming village in Greenfield, just like the one we just left. Hopemire or something like that. My father and yours rode an army into it and slaughtered everyone." Grainne said.

"What? I never heard of that." Rowena replied. Others echoed the comments.

Grainne shook her head. "My father wasn't a big talker about the wars, as you know. However, he told me about that one battle, by mistake. He cried at the memory of putting innocents to the knife, but bandits had been using the town for resupplying their winter stores. The villagers couldn't stop it so they aided the bandits. It grew to be a yearly occurrence. To stop the bandits, our fathers had to stop the supplies. The king also wanted to send a message. So he did."

Rowena looked at her group. "Matilda, did you know?"

Matilda Greenfield, daughter of the Baron of Greenfield, shook her head. "I remember the name Hopemire but it was so far south, I never realized it was one of our villages. I thought it was Elysian."

"Your father committed murder to end a war for a country. We committed murder to save a girl and her baby." Grainne said.

The group was silent for a while before Rowena spoke up. "All that is done with. We know my family has issues and dark secrets, but this is our time. Juniper wasn't safe, and there was nothing redeeming about that village."

Rowena stood up and walked to her tent. "Get some sleep, everyone. We leave at first light. Grainne, you're on guard duty next."

Grainne nodded. "Aye." She said, throwing a small twig into the fire.

Several days later, the band entered the gates of East La~Porte. The town was just as Rowena had described it. It was much larger than Puck's Landing could ever have been. Market stalls dotted the streets and alleys. People were hustling about the area, most with the daily chores but others in a more jovial nature. The homes and buildings were all taller than any of the buildings in that crumbling old village.

There was a bit of a sanitation problem. In the larger towns and cities, horse manure and human refuge would be left on the street. Cleaners would shovel it up in wagons, but that was an understaffed labor field. Still, that didn't dampen the glow that Juniper had while looking around. She rode on the wagon with Grainne and Matilda. The entire town was a sight for the young lady. One that she was happy to have.

Rowena sent Ingrid and Elva to sell some of the trade goods, while the rest were to go to a friend's house.

The pair left the group with a wagon full of supplies, hoping to cash in. They left some of the food and alcohol with Rowena and the others. That would get them through the next week.

Rowena rode up to a stately manor. Her sisters stayed behind the front gate while she walked up to the front door to knock. After waiting a moment, a woman answered.

"Rowena! War wounds to heal? Or a social call?" The woman said with a smile.

"Not for us, Adela. We have a friend who's with child and was in a bad way before we got to her. She needs your medical expertise." Rowena said.

Rowena motioned for the group to join her.

"Bring her in." Adela replied.

After a while, the sisters exited the building, Adele following behind Rowena.

"She'll be safe here. This sort of pox is a common disease and one that will clear up with clean water and some salve. The baby will be fine when it comes. She's carrying low, my guess is a boy but you can never be sure.

"She's hoping for a boy." Rowena smiled.

Adela smiled. "Creator's will be done, no matter our wants."

Elva appeared from the street. She handed a bag to Rowena. The contents clinked inside when it was dropped into the dwarf's hand.

Rowena turned to Adela. "This is for her." Handing the bag of coins to the doctor. She pulled out another bag, a velvet bag, and handed it to the doctor, as well. "This is for you."

Adela took the bag for Juniper. "I spoke with the girl while you are your friends were sleeping off the meal, and she agreed to help me around the clinic. She's had some injuries that have healed well. She told me she's gotten some experience treating minor wounds over the years. Tight lipped on the causes, though." Adela smiled. "No matter, she's agreed to work for me in return for room and board. So, you can keep the velvet bag."

Rowena smiled. "I'm glad that worked out."

"I am too. You did well by this one. Your father would be proud." Adela said. She noted the twinkle in Rowena's eyes at the words. "I imagine you and your sisters will be off now?"

"Yes, we heard talk of a war further west. We want to see if they need a hand in the fighting. We'll try to pick up a few recruits along the way." Rowena responded.

"Well, then good luck little cousin." Adela said.

Rowena hugged her cousin. Adela, the eldest child and only daughter of King Charles' uncle, Harold. She had left the court to become a doctor, making her way to East La~Porte in the decades before.

"Goodbye and thank you, Adela." Rowena responded, before joining her fellow mercenaries.

Elva looked to her friend after she mounted her horse. "Off to the western marches?"

Rowena nodded. "The western marches it is."

She was renewed and confident. Her sisters were, as well. Good deed done, coin made, and a new lead for work on the horizon.

The Road of Fame

even years had passed since leaving Lotcala, and success was following her. Too bad she couldn't stop and sit in some lavish castle to enjoy it. Camp life was the only life for her, not by choice. Camps were the places where business was conducted. The tents of the mercenary captains were like palaces, and respect could be gained from showing one's worth within the camps. That respect could be worth more than gold to the right person.

Wars had been fought, and Rowena's company had been called into action, paid well, more times than she could remember. Her reputation was becoming enough to end the war once her name was listed on one side. The sisters now found themselves in the eastern lands of Lomberia, a kingdom on the Southern Continent. Rowena's band had been invited to join the side of the Western Umbero Kingdom against Lomberia. The Umbero Kingdom sent an advance on the payment, totaling one hundred pounds of silver. Rowena couldn't refuse the call.

Two hundred and thirty-three women rode up to the camp, approaching the sentries.

"Rowena of the Sisters, with a call to aid the lord of Umbero." She said, handing over the letter with the request for her support.

The sentry read the letter and told his fellow guards to allow her and her band in.

"Set up wherever you see room. Black Hand is going to want to speak with you." The guard said, handing the letter back to Rowena.

"Black Hand? The Black Hand from The Company?"

"Aye, that's his name. At least, that's what everyone calls him." The guard said, motioning the mercenaries in. "Know him?"

Rowena shook her head. "Just heard of his reputation."

The guard handed back the letter. "Good fortune." He said as Rowena rode her horse into the camp.

Rowena rode up to Elva and Grainne. "Black Hand is here."

Elva looked at Rowena, concern glazed over her face. Grainne was less worried.

"He's going to go where the biggest payday is and that's this war currently. The victor gets total control of the Straits of Good Tides. The safest seaway in a thousand miles." Grainne said. "If he is here, that means The Company is here. The war is all but won."

"They've lost wars too." Rowena reminded her friend.

"Fifteen thousand strong. They don't lose many." Grainne said, stoically.

As the evening darkened the sky and the tents had been pitched, Rowena wandered through the camp. Men and women were hanging about, laughing, drinking, and gambling. A few of the working ladies were plying their trade with some soldiers. The moans echoed in some parts and were drowned out by the boisterous laughter of other areas.

Rowena walked along and finally made it to the main tent. Black Hand's tent. It was heavily guarded by soldiers in lamellar armor and conical helms. Cloth covered their faces, except for eye slits. All carried two handed axes.

"I was asked to speak to Black Hand." Rowena said to the guards that stopped her at the entrance. "The name's Rowena."

One ducked into the tent. When he returned, he held out his hand for Rowena's sword. She gave him her the blade, and a knife sheathed at her side. Another guard opened the flap of the tent and led her in, bowed to the occupants before leaving and resuming his post.

Inside, the tent was decadent. Casks of wine sat around the perimeter, silken pillows covered daybeds, also draped in silk or linen. In the middle, flanked by four elves, was a thin, dark-haired man. A scar crossed his left eye, but that only added to his features. Rowena could tell he was tall, maybe six foot five or more.

"Black Hand?" Rowena asked.

"I am." The man said. He motioned for Rowena to sit on a pillow in front of him. "You're the famous Rowena Carlsdotter. The woman that defeated the mighty Forkbeard in single combat. Brought the walls of Calisba down in a single night. Saved orphans from a sinking ship during the Battle of the Salten Sea." Black Hand sipped his wine goblet. "And then won the battle." He finished with a smile.

"I had help." Rowena said, with no feigned modesty.

"I know. The Sisters. Yet, they would not have done those feats. You did, they helped." Black Hand responded while eating a piece of bread. "I called you here because with your name attached, we should have no problem finishing these stubborn fools off. A winner of many battles, a woman with a taste for vengeance, and the daughter of the mighty King Charles of Lotcala!" Black Hand smiled. "You are indeed a renowned warrior."

Rowena smiled. "You flatter me, sir." She said with a slight bow of her head. "Your reputation presides you as well. They say, just saying that Black Hand is riding to a battle, it will cause the other side to retreat."

Black Hand licked his lips. His companions stayed stone faced.

"Perhaps, but that's the mystique of reputation." He waved off the compliment, then changed the subject. "This situation is unique. Just today, four thousand mercenaries arrived from the south. The Free Companies led by some nobleman." Black Hand responded.

"Marques Reynald du Sale." Rowena answered.

"Know much of him?" Black Hand asked.

"Enough to know that his four thousand will give your fifteen thousand trouble. He and I fought together in the Malqeth War of Succession." Rowena said.

Black Hand slid a plate of dates, olives, and cheeses toward her. He motioned for her to partake as he took some himself. His elf friends did as well.

"We know the Free Companies, but not this du Sale. Not well, at least." One elf said.

"Bastard born." Rowena said, before biting into a date. "Not sure how much of their gold is seeping into the companies, but du Sale himself has the backing of the Cashel Bank. They call on him to collect debts." She reached for another date. "He set himself up well in the

Southern Kingdoms. His Malqeth estate is fairly palatial. I'd have to imagine he uses the companies for protection, and that's costly."

"That's what I need to know." Black Hand said. "Rowena, we have a plan, and your role just got much bigger."

"What do you need?"

One elf handed Rowena a parchment. Rowena unrolled the paper.

"This is diabolical." Rowena said after reading the scroll.

"Rats always return home." Black Hand grinned.

Rowena's eyes narrowed. "This isn't all?"

Black Hand stood up. "I represent a larger faction. A conglomerate of factions, rather."

"The Company." Rowena said.

"Yes, and we have a way to end this war. This stronghold is the key. We'd prefer to take it without a fight and without damaging the buildings, but that's becoming less likely." Black Hand said. "So, we'll play another card. I need the Free Companies out of here. That will take some time, but I can arrange it. After that, it's the queen that will need to be handled."

"That's where I come in?" Rowena assumed.

"Well, yes, but first I'll need your help with du Sale. Once I have a reason for him to leave, you'll need to deliver it. I think he has reason to trust you." Black Hand said, looking at Rowena.

"Do you think so?"

"We hope so." Black Hand replied, his smile faded. "We have one chance. If this Marques rallies the townsfolk, then we are finished here. If this plan works, then that scroll need not be used. The city survives, and we accomplish our goal."

Rowena stood. "When you're ready, send for me." She said, before walking out of the tent.

Back in her own area of the larger camp, Rowena sat down with Grainne and Elva and detailed the meeting for her sisters.

"Black Hand is looking to remove the Free Companies from the fight without fighting them." Rowena explained.

Grainne smiled. "Good plan. I don't know how wise it would be to fight du Sale."

Ingrid approached. "Heard you mention the Free Companies. Reynald coming in?"

Rowena passed a wine skin to her friend. "He's here, or rather, over there." She pointed toward the fortified city. "He's fighting for the Queen of Lomberia."

"She must be getting desperate." Ingrid said. "The Free Companies are not cheap."

Elva scoffed. "Quality isn't cheap, but the queen's brother-in-law paid for The Company."

"What?" Ingrid exclaimed.

Rowena nodded. "Black Hand contacted me, representing The Company. He wants our help in getting rid of Reynald. Our history with him might give us an advantage. I pulled his ass out of the fire during the Battle of Shady Mountains."

"And we helped them with the siege of Palenter." Grainne said.

Ingrid shook her head. "I'd like to get out of this one without losing anymore sisters. Any deal to avoid bloodshed would be fine by me."

The group sat grimly while pondering Ingrid's words. In the past few years, several sisters had fallen in battle. Now of the original eight coming out of the War Academy, only these four were left.

The night went by with little action. Most mercenary camps were uneventful during the sieges. Trebuchets would unleash loads of boulders, but the idea of sieges was to make the fortification submit without an immense loss of life. The pummeling of the walls was more of a scare tactic. It just added to the length of the siege. This obviously meant that the hygiene in the camps and cities would deteriorate considerably. The longer the armies were camped or posted near, the only flowing water meant that the water would not be clean. That would lead to disease.

The next few days were much of the same boring waiting. After a week, Rowena and her sisters were called to lead a raid on a supply route just north of the city. An easy run to scare farmers. Nothing dangerous.

Rowena was being included in Black Hand's meetings, but those didn't amount to more than hurry up and wait strategies. She appreciated that Black Hand treated her as an equal in command. Many still saw a woman first, and not the hardened warrior she had become.

This certainly became a topic for Rowena and her friends. Black Hand would walk over to her encampment, chat with her. Of course, as a captain, her insights were valuable but, their eyes told a different reason for his visits. Rowena's friends would smile to themselves whenever the pair talked. Sometimes in the open, sometimes in private. Never for long, however. Elva, Grainne, and Ingrid were Rowena's oldest friends, and they knew she was a romantic person within. Yet, in the male dominated world of mercenary armies, she had to be tough. This didn't mean that she was a stranger to love. Elva and Grainne each saw that look in her eyes.

Still, the camp was rather mundane to those looking for a good fight. After a month of little to no action apart from trade route patrol, Rowena and her band were growing tired of waiting. It was during one night, thirty-four days after they had arrived in the camp, which things finally turned around for the Sisters.

Rowena, Elva, Grainne, and Ingrid were once again sitting by a campfire when Hadiza walked up to the group. Her bronze skin glistened in the campfire and her dark hair cast a shadow over her war weary face.

"Ro, a messenger is here for you." Hadiza said.

Behind her was wood elf. Darker in complexion than the high elves, but not as dark as the sand elves.

"I bring word from my employer, Black Hand." The elf began. "He has sent word to the Cashel bank on an urgent matter concerning an investment, and they are now calling in du Sale's debts. This is the official dispatch we've intercepted from the Cashel Bank." The elf said, handing a sealed envelope to Rowena. "It must be delivered to his hand, along with this personal letter from Black Hand. The letter from Black Hand can only be delivered once du Sale knows about the bank." The elf handed a second envelope to Rowena.

"Fine." Rowena said. "I'll ride out tomorrow."

"At once." The elf replied.

Hadiza gripped her saber. "You're speaking to Captain Rowena. Watch your tongue, elf."

The elf bowed. "Forgive my bluntness, however, Black Hand is the one that demands haste. Dysentery is setting in throughout the camp. He wishes to end the siege quickly."

Rowena stood. Her frame was just a bit shorter than the elf.

"Fine. I'll ride out now. Elva, Grainne, join me. Ingrid, watch the camp and if I'm not back in an hour, assume command."

"Aye." Ingrid replied, as Rowena and her companions went to ready themselves.

Riding to an opposing camp during a siege wasn't the smartest idea. It was, however, more common than most would believe. Rowena's ride during the night, under a white banner of truce, was no different.

She approached the gates of the outer palisade. A sentry aimed an arrow, Rowena knew that there had to be at least ten more aimed her way.

"I've come to treat with Marques Reynald du Sale!" She called out. Elva and Grainne had ridden with her, but they stopped behind their captain. "I bring urgent news for the Marques." Rowena added.

A few of the sentries ran around behind the wooden wall. A makeshift defensive measure that had worked thus far.

After about ten minutes, the gates creaked opened and a regal looking man stepped out. Several soldiers flanked him. The mud on the ground did little to tarnish the look of pompousness that he exuded.

"Rowena Carlsdotter." Marques Reynald du Sale smiled. "Coming to my camp, brave. You're not armed, I assume."

Rowena grinned. "I'm not, as per the rules of gentlemanly combat. Yet I hardly need weapons to defeat you in battle."

Reynald laughed. "I always enjoyed your wit. You know how to brighten even the dreariest night." He said, motioning to the steady rain.

While many knew the Marques as a formidable warrior, many also knew his charm and charisma. He was nothing if not flattering.

"My lord, Reynald. I've brought urgent news." Rowena said, bringing the topic back to her purpose. Rowena handed the sealed letter to Reynald.

Reynald smirked. "Still sealed. That is a surprise."

"I've not read it." Rowena said.

"And I believe you. However, Black Hand over there has his tricks." Reynald said, before reading the letter. His face turned grim. "A trick?" He whispered. "Where did you get this letter?" Reynald demanded, looking up at Rowena.

"The road coming from the north. Intercepted in a trade caravan, bearing the Cashel arms." Rowena answered.

"You know as well as I what those arms represent."

"The largest bank in the world."

Reynald nodded. "They've called in all my debts. I can't pay until this siege is through." It struck the usually jovial man in a fit of panic. "They'll send the Greymen after me."

"I have this other letter from Black Hand. For you only."

"What?" Reynald said, taking the letter and ripping the seal. "He wishes to negotiate a surrender." Reynald read.

Rowena and her friends seemed confused.

"My surrender, with a payment of gold, if I leave right away." Reynald grinned. "Fine. Tell Black Hand I'll be in his camp within the hour to discuss." Reynald said, before flourishing off back to his camp.

Elva trotted close to Rowena. "That was unexpected."

"I saw it coming. Black Hand is a few steps ahead." Rowena replied. "And he said he wanted to end it quick."

"I like it." Grainne said with a smile to her sisters.

True to his word, Reynald du Sale was there in the camp and alone in Black Hand's tent. After nearly two hours, both men emerged, smiling. They shook hands and du Sale rode off into the night. The next morning, they saw the Free Companies riding out of the town and away from the region.

Rowena approached Black Hand's tent. A frustrated envoy from the city was there, waiting. Rowena was motioned in first.

"Making the envoy wait. Shrewd." Rowena smiled as she walked into the tent.

Black Hand grinned as he ate a grape. He had a goblet of wine in his right hand. "He wants to negotiate terms of the city's surrender." Black Hand sat on a daybed, his shirt flung to the floor.

Rowena was in her full armor of gambeson and chainmail. She noted Black Hand's scarred but muscular form.

"Chilly, isn't it?" Rowena said.

"I have the fire to keep me warm."

"And a few women, no doubt." Rowena quipped.

Black Hand shook his head and smiled softly. "No, not this trip. Not any trip, actually. Business keeps me busy."

Rowena sat down on a wooden chair across from Black Hand. "So, pulling up stakes?"

"Soon, I'll run the city for a while until the king's forces arrive and then my contract is done. Off to the next job." Black Hand offered a plate of bread and grapes to Rowena. "I think The Company has me heading north to the Sile Empire. They've outlawed poppy. We trade in the plant, so I need to open new doors and trade routes within the city of Aran."

Rowena nodded. "A bit of crime then."

"Crime to the Sile Empire, business to others." Black Hand smiled. "It's all about perspective."

Rowena conceded the point. She ate some of the food and enjoyed the warmth of the braziers. She looked up at the man lounging on the daybed.

"How did you get the name Black Hand?" She asked.

"Oh." He laughed. "Family name. My actual name is Gerald Blackhand." He smirked. "I know, I know. It's not very original, nor secret. My father always said that when you are right in front of the world, yet they still can't see you, then you've won."

"Blackhand sounds Gota." Rowena said.

"Long ago, before the conquest. We've lost our family home, literally. I do not know where it was." Gerald smiled. "We kept the name because it sounded menacing. It works, and now my family home is where I lay my head each night."

Rowena thought about it and she had much of the same experience. She didn't have a permanent home any longer. Some of her sisters invested in property, but she didn't. She felt a bond with the man she now knew as Gerald.

"Gerald." Rowena began with a chuckle. "If you're heading north soon, would you be willing to take some letters to Ter Nog for my sisters and I?"

Gerald grinned. "For you, of course."

The two smiled at each other. A short while later, Rowena walked back to her group. They waited for word of the siege's end. That was a celebratory moment. The Sisters roamed the camp, enjoying the festivities, and finding new ways to have fun. Grainne and Rowena collected the gold owed. A few extra pounds were added as a gift from Black Hand. Grainne gave Rowena a wink, but the dwarf princess waved her off.

"Just a business associate." Rowena said. "For now." Rowena winked.

Grainne just smirked. She was putting more tobacco in her pipe. Rowena swore she heard her friend chuckle, but she ignored it.

Later that night, as several Sisters guarded their gold, Rowena took a walk through familiar territory. She had walked that path before, more than a few times. Now, she walked it without thoughts of war or strategy.

Rowena approached Black Hand's tent. No guards this time, but she could see a fire lit within. She strolled in and found him sitting at a table, a goblet of wine in his hand.

"Rowena. A pleasant surprise." He smiled, looking up at his guest.

Rowena took a seat at the table and reached for the goblet. Pouring herself a glass, she smiled. "I'm surprised I've found you with a shirt on, Gerald. Disappointed maybe."

Gerald smiled. "I wear them, at times. You're looking much more comfortable, as well. A linen tunic, gold accents. Nice touch."

Rowena smiled. "Well, as I'm sure you know, in my past life, I was a princess. It's from Biset, tailed for me by the king's own tailor after a successful contract."

Gerald raised his eyebrows in interest. "I love the Diamond Coast, and for King Marius to offer his own tailor is a feat. That man prides his clothes more than his kingdom." He said. He sipped his goblet. He chuckled. "While I enjoy your company during our meetings, why are you here now? You should go celebrate."

"Maybe I am."

Gerald looked confused.

"You're here in your tent alone, and in walks a woman, and yet you want her to celebrate without you?" Rowena asked. She swallowed the last of her wine.

"I'm flattered. I honestly am. I've admired your beauty, but I'm —"

"Busy. Business before pleasure, I know, and I respect that. That's how I've made it this far in life." Rowena said. She stood up and then walked to Gerald and straddled his lap. "But you've won a glorious victory and tonight you deserve some pleasure. And so do I." She said before sinking into a kiss with the man.

Gerald responded in kind. He gripped her from the bottom and carried her to his bed. Laying down, both enjoyed the pleasures until the morning sun came to part them, and the rest of the camp.

Rowena's friends looked at her, walking back to their tents. They smiled at their friend. Everyone was packing the camp and readying the wagons for the road. Part of the mercenary life.

Elva gave Rowena a light shove with her shoulder. "Did the lad enjoy his victory?" Elva asked.

"I'd say so. I did too." Rowena smiled.

Grainne looked at them. "It's about time. You two been making love sick eyes for at least a month."

Rowena blushed. "I thought I was better and hiding it."

Grainne chuckled. "Not from me."

Rowena smiled. She then pulled a scroll from her belt. "Well, it's settled and we're paid up. I'm rested and ready to head off. Grainne, what's our next stop?"

"Off to Samiland." Grainne said. "We've been hired to accompany some scientific expedition."

"Of course, ye'd get us hired by some scholar." Elva quipped.

The group laughed as they journeyed out of the camp and into the open world.

New Worlds, Old Problems

wo more years passed. A couple more jobs came along for Rowena and her sisters, and all the while, their band continued to grow. Now, the mercenaries numbered near six hundred. Not the biggest mercenary band by any means, but certainly one of the bests with a growing reputation. This caught on in the north, where many of Rowena's band were from.

"We take a few more jobs like that last one, and we can think of retiring." Grainne replied.

The previous contract had been their most lucrative by far. Another succession war, however, the king needing to return to his throne, was wealthier than the usurper. Rowena charged two thousand pounds of gold and three thousand in silver. The king paid for it, and Rowena's band, along with several others working under her, quickly went to work in defeating the usurper. It helped that Black Hand sent a few hundred soldiers as a gift. Those soldiers, now back with their true leader, weren't even needed.

Now, they were aboard a ship sailing to Novatera, a small continent on the Western Sea. There, they had to meet with another contact.

"You should think of settling down, Ro. You're twenty seven and with all your gold, you'd have a magnificent castle to grow old in. Find a husband and have little ones running at your feet." Grainne said. "Ingrid did. Last I heard, she was doing well."

Rowena smiled. "Ingrid fell in love and had a baby. Three now."

"Still, having a home somewhere would be wise. At least somewhere to store your wealth and all the trophies you've collected. Keeping it in Adela's cellar isn't a retirement plan." Grainne pointed out.

"My gold is in the Bank of Denos." Rowena answered. "We stop by the Southern Kingdoms so much that I've made my account with them. Besides, they have offices throughout the world."

"Except Lotcala." Elva said from behind.

"I don't expect we'd ever go back. Not unless something bad happens." Rowena said, looking out over the ocean.

Another sister joined them. Severa Harbor, Baron Harbor's youngest daughter. She, too, was Lotcalan, but a year younger than the original eight.

"It's been years since we even stepped foot on the northern edges of the Central Continent. Would we even remember the land?" Severa pondered.

"Aye, lass. We'd remember the land well." Elva grinned. "And she'd remember us with every gust of wind."

"The land or someone else?" Rowena asked, turning to face Elva.

"Aye." The Hardstone woman said. "She'd likely not be as forgiving as the Goddess of the Hearth will be to us."

A shout called out from the crow's nest. "Land!"

All eyes turned towards the view.

"There it is." Rowena grinned. "Our next port, Ostilian."

"About time. I have a duffel bag full of mail to post." Grainne said.

"I have one to send up to Black Hand." Rowena smiled.

"Things going well?" Grainne asked.

"Well enough that he misses me." Rowena chuckled.

Mooring into port and then offloading hundreds of soldiers, supplies, and horses took hours, but by the time the moon was at its zenith, Rowena and her band of mercenaries were on their way into the interior. They had grown much too big to house within the inns of a town, and Ostilian was a small port to begin with. The interior of the continent, however, wasn't as populated by the civilized races as yet. Minotaurs and other beasts roamed the lands.

While not outright dangerous, the Minotaurs were tribal in nature and reclusive. Once more dominant along the southern reaches of the world, now the bulk of the species lived on Novatera. The continent was only known for the past two hundred years. Many speculated about the other beasts that existed there, unknown on the other landmasses.

"We can camp here." Rowena said, stopping the caravan about two miles from the port town.

The night was quiet, but the full moon gave the Sisters more comfort. Rowena walked around the camp, as was her habit, and watched as her band made the most of the warm night. Some drank, others danced, and some played games of chance. Rowena kept an order that was followed, but she also allowed the mercenaries their fun. As long as they didn't get too out of hand, then they had the right to relax from strict rules.

An orc Sister, one of several orcs that had, approached Rowena as they passed each other.

"Captain, the other orcs and I smell a foulness in the air tonight." The orc woman said. "A smell of burning flesh. It grows stronger near our camp."

"Where is your tent, Garosh?"

The orc, Garosh, pointed to the eastern edge of the larger encampment. "There, captain. Along the edge of the forest. We picked that spot for the possibility of a hunt in the morning."

Rowena stood next to the woman. A more remarkable comparison couldn't be made. Garosh, like most orcs, stood over six feet tall, while Rowena was more than a foot shorter. Garosh was lean and muscular. The orcs were a benefit with natural battle prowess and strength, though at first looked at with suspicion.

"We heard tales of beasts roaming these woods. Challenges that would appease Burketh." Garosh continued, mentioning the orc god of the hunt. "But my sisters refuse to enter those woods. Cowards."

Rowena nodded. "Fine, we'll investigate it come dawn. We have a couple of days before they expect us in Arzurvail."

Garosh nodded and bowed her head. "Thank you, captain."

Rowena clasped her soldier on the arm before walking off back to her tent. She gave an update to Grainne and Elva. Grainne cut her hair, while Elva drank from a skin of wine.

"Them orcs always be smelling something." Elva said.

"That's why they are helpful." Grainne replied, snipping her hair while trying to steady her hand in the mirror. "I couldn't even think of doing this on the ship, even though I was tempted."

"Bah, the orcs are going to lead us in a bad way." Elva continued, ignoring Grainne's hair, as usual. She stood and tossed the wine skin onto her cot.

Rowena wasn't so sure. "They've been a great asset."

Everyone knew of the animosity that existed between the orcs and other races of mortals. Most didn't trust them and then again, the orcs didn't care about that. They were warlike, making them excellent mercenaries and soldiers. However, they were often bandits and raiders, as well. This gave them a less than admirable reputation.

"True." Grainne replied. "They're formidable in battle, and their natural instincts help around the camp."

"Bah." Elva repeated before exiting the tent.

Rowena and Grainne shrugged at each other before extinguishing the candles for the night.

The following morning Rowena, Elva, Garosh, and fourteen others rode toward the smell that was on the wind. A haze lay over the area. Even in the sun it was noticeable to see the remnants of a recent fire. A large fire. A few miles away from their camp, they arrived at a burned village. The buildings were rubble, and bodies lay strewn on the ground. The white plaster that had once coated the walls was now blackened and crumbling. Terracotta roofs were broken and burned.

Elva dismounted her horse, followed by everyone else. She turned one body with her foot.

"Gorgon." She said. Elva looked back at the others. "Gorgons!" She said, drawing her sword and running toward the others.

Everyone readied their weapons. They looked around, seeing more dead.

"They're all gorgons." Rowena said, after inspecting a few of the other bodies. "They don't look like warriors, just regular villagers."

A few of the bodies were children and even infants. Most were adults, more women than men, but by the looks of it, no one was spared.

Elva knelt near one. Its body was mutilated with sword wounds and arrows. She recognized the arrow fletching.

"These are from Davenport." Elva said, ripping an arrow from the body. "Blue rapture feathers," she mused.

The women learned how fletchers make arrows at War Academy. Using unique feathers was a sign of skill and wealth. Raptures were rare bird throughout the west, but near Davenport they were bred for feathers and sport. Elva could spot this detail from a mile away. "No ordinary bandits could afford custom arrows." Rowena said, looking at the feathered end of the arrow.

Suddenly, a noise brought her attention back to the rubble of the town. Rowena shushed the sisters. The noise was faint, but she knew she heard something stirring.

Garosh sniffed the air. "Damn." She whispered. "Yarlet, do you smell anything?"

Another orc sniffed the air. "Only dead flesh and burnt wood."

Rowena sheathed her sword. She motioned for everyone else to do the same.

"Come out. We won't hurt you. We just want to see what happened here." Rowena said in a raised voice.

At first, nothing happened. Everyone stood quiet, but then a young gorgon girl shuffled out from behind a plaster wall. She was wearing torn clothes, her face was marked with dried blood, and she was holding a big stick in a defensive position.

"A gorgon!" One orc said.

Elva and the orcs reached for their weapons, but Rowena turned and motioned for them to stop. She then focused on the young girl.

"Hello." Rowena said. "I'm not going to hurt you. I'm Rowena, and these are my sisters. We were travelling nearby when we noticed the smoke and the smell of fire."

The girl tensed up even more than she already was. "They came with swords and axes!" She screamed. "We gave them water and food, but they killed everyone. My family, everyone, they're all dead. I'm the only one left." She sobbed.

"How did ye live?" Elva asked.

The girl looked at Elva. "Mother told me to hide, and I rushed to the woods, but I could see everything."

Rowena knelt down on one knee. "You're safe now. We're here to help."

"Captain. What if it's a trap?" Garosh asked.

Rowena shook her head. "We've seen plenty of war orphans, and here is one." Rowena turned back to the girl. "What's your name?"

The girl lowered the stick to her waist. "Agota."

"Agota, we're going to ride back to my camp. We have food, fresh water, and healers. Would you like some salted pork?" Rowena smiled.

Agota shook her head slightly. "I don't eat meat. Our village doesn't eat meat."

"Okay, then we have fresh fruits and some carrots. Potatoes too." Rowena said.

She extended her hand out and Agota inched closer before taking Rowena's hand. The pair walked back to the horse. Rowena helped Agota on the horse before hopping on behind her.

"We'll be in the camp soon." Rowena said in a comforting voice.

A few hours later, Agota was sleeping on a bedroll while Rowena, Elva, and Grainne discussed their options.

"The scouts say that two other villages have similar scenes. Both east toward the mountains." Elva said. She handed the arrow to Grainne. "It looks like the lord of Arzurvail is fighting against the beastfolk. Another gorgon village, and one with minotaurs. That one had more human bodies."

Rowena sat and poured some wine into her goblet. "That's not what we signed up for. We were coming to help out with a civil war."

"Maybe that's what this is?" Elva responded.

Grainne looked at the young girl. "She's too innocent to be caught in a civil war."

"Most victims usually are." Rowena replied. She turned to the girl. "Find her some new clothes. My cloak will not work forever."

Grainne went to her chest. "I have a cambric tunic. It'll be long on her, but it will be better than the rags she had on."

"A few o' the lasses in the camp are her size. They might part with some items." Elva said, before walking out of the tent.

Agota stirred. Her eyes were still heavy, but she sat up on the bed roll.

"I don't need much. I just want to get to my uncle's village."

"Where is that?" Rowena asked.

"Due east, eight miles." Agota replied.

Grainne handed the girl a cup of water.

"My dear, that village was attacked, too." Rowena said. "Elva reported the scouts found it burned out as well."

Agota began to tear up again.

Grainne sat next to her. "This may be a bad time to ask, but would you have any idea why the lord of the land would want to destroy the villages?"

Agota sniffed. She shook her head.

"I thought so." Grainne stood up. "Ro, step outside with me for a moment."

The two mercenaries left the tent, leaving Agota alone.

"Ro, we need to find out what's going on. I'll ride back to Ostilian with a few sisters. We'll ask around and see why so many of the lord's men are attacking these villages."

Rowena nodded. "Do it, but be discrete. The lord might not take kindly to our presence if he learns we're asking about him. His note to us was that this was to be kept quiet." Rowena paused, looking back into the tent. She turned back to Grainne. "We're used to orders being kept quiet, but not because of murder."

Grainne frowned. "Not like we've ever done that before."

Rowena furrowed her brow, looking up at her friend. "Only to those that deserved it. These villages look innocent, and we know those children were. If these are unprovoked attacks, then that is murder."

Grainne sighed and nodded. "Agreed."

"I think that Ostilian might have more clues." Rowena repeated, getting back to the point.

"I saw minotaurs and centaurs in Ostilian. Not many, but a few. My guess is that there is an open trade market. If their inland villages are in danger, it could get worse for the people in the ports like Ostilian." Grainne said.

"I agree. Find out what you can while we head to Arzurvail. Meet us there as soon as you can."

"What about Agota? She can't go to Arzurvail if they are hunting beastfolk." Grainne pointed out.

"She'll go with you." Rowena said.

Grainne looked apprehensive. "That would be okay in the usual circumstances, but this looks to be a war against her kind. I didn't see any gorgons in Ostilian. Other beastfolk, yes, but no gorgons."

"I understand, but I have to get to Arzurvail before nightfall tomorrow. If not, then the contract is forfeited. We won't learn anything then."

"Maybe that's for the best." Grainne cut in. "we could always cut and run."

Rowena shook her head. "I won't leave innocents to die. We don't even know why. Agota will be safer as far away as possible from the Lord of Arzurvail."

"I agree with you there." Grainne conceded. "Fine. I'll take her. I'll just try to find a hood or something for her head."

"Thanks." Rowena said.

They packed camp up and the two groups split off. Grainne took ten other sisters back to Ostilian to investigate the area. Rowena took the rest to rendezvous with their employer. That trip was a quick one. The way was smooth, and not once was there a sign of any danger along the road.

The entire area looked as if it was being cultivated successfully. Only two generations old and the land was looking plentiful. People were in the fields tending to the crops, herding livestock, and going about their normal chores. The sun was low, but there was at least another hour left in the day for more work to be done. Even in the outer markets of the town, just outside of the walls, the vendors were in the middle of their transactions, hoping to fill their coffers before nightfall.

Rowena split her group as they approached the gate. This was practical. It allowed the town a chance to accommodate fewer people, which used fewer resources. It was a safe guard too. If something happened to Rowena, then the town had an army at their gate already. Rowena kept them there as insurance.

The town's people eyed the dwarf mercenary carefully. Her closest sisters flanked her as they trotted in and rode up to the closest inn. Many of the people turned away from her and hid in their houses. Rowena ignored them as she dismounted from her horse.

A flurry of commotion soon inched closer to Rowena's group. In front of the coming group was an old man, dressed in silk robes and a gold circlet.

"What's this I hear about a dwarf entering my town?" The man said.

Rowena eyed him carefully before speaking up. He looked close to seventy years old, grey haired with a face full of wrinkles. He was old enough to be feeble or very dangerous. There usually was no in-between.

"You must be the Lord of Arzurvail." Rowena said.

The man puffed out his chest. "Yes, ummm, I'm Lorcan van Urbrant."

"And I'm Rowena Carlsdotter."

Lorcan's eyes widened.

"I see." Lorcan said. "Well, I was unaware you were a real dwarf."

Elva raised an eyebrow. "Ye've never heard her called the Dwarven Princess?"

"Uh... Oh... of course." Lorcan stammered. "I just figured it was a nickname because she was short. Or one of those nicknames where you say someone is a dwarf, even though they are really tall. Not an actually dwarf."

"Does it matter?" Severa said from Rowena's left.

"This is a human village. Humans only. Not a safe place for elves, Quarmi, beasts, or stinking dwarves." One of the lord's men said.

Lorcan tried to hush his man from saying anything else. But Rowena took the insult in stride.

"I understand. I only answered your call for aid in some civil war. However, I'm seeing that your fight might not be what I had imagined." Rowena said.

Lorcan looked nervous. "The facts of the war might seem different if you were to know our perspective. A human perspective." He said. "Maybe you're not the right ones to help us out."

"You might be right, but here we are and we will need some gold to cover the expenses of the trip here." Rowena replied.

A few of the town's guards drew their weapons. Rowena's band drew theirs in reply. Rowena gripped her war ax in her left hand, and her sword in her right.

"We don't have to fight." Rowena said. "I see several of your guards shaking already." Rowena gave them a wink. "We're professional soldiers, trained for this. Are your men?"

"You're right, there is a better option." Lorcan said, telling his men to lower their weapons. "Stay the night. We'll pay a tenth of the contract and then you can be on your way in the morning."

Rowena sheathed her weapons. "Agreed. I like it when it's that simple."

"No negotiation?" Lorcan asked.

"The longer I stay, the greater chance I have that my name is attached to something I don't want it attached to. Besides, ten percent is better than no percent." Rowena smiled. "And your men get to go home to their families. I don't enjoy seeing children cry for their dead parents." Her smile faded. "It upsets me."

Lorcan motioned his men away and he followed them to his estate.

Outside the inn, Rowena gathered her sisters around her.

"We'll need to keep our wits sharp. Severa get a message to the camp outside. We have to be ready to fight our way out if need be." Rowena said.

Severa nodded and rushed away toward the gate. The rest of the group walked into the inn to settle in for the night.

Later in the night, long after the moon rose in the sky, Grainne with her band, plus a few more, appeared at the Sister's camp.

"Garosh, where is Rowena?" Grainne said, dismounting from her horse and reaching for a canteen of water. She gulped the water down as hard and fast as she could. "I pushed my horse too hard, but we had to get her as fast as we could." Grainne said.

"The captain is in the town. Things are not good here." Garosh said.

"No shit." Grainne breathed. She motioned behind her. "This is Rosalin." A large form appeared behind Grainne. "She's a refuge from the minotaur village that was sacked. There are a few others with her. We have a couple more orcs too."

Rosalin stood beside Grainne and towered over the woman. Standing at nearly seven feet tall with two massive horns atop her bull shaped head, Rosalin was a unique sight.

"The humans came and attacked us! We've traded with them for years, but now they fight us like enemies." Rosalin spoke with a tone of anger but softened by a sadness.

The others in the camp listened as the minotaur told her tale. Grainne made her way into the town, leaving Agota with Garosh and Rosalin. She had to find Rowena and quickly. Their years together gave her valuable insight into where to look first. Grainne ran straight to the inn.

Rushing through the door, she found Rowena, along with Elva, Severa and a few others sitting by a roaring hearth.

"Captain." Grainne called out. She only used the title in a few situations. "We've got to get out!" She exclaimed, sliding close to Rowena.

The inn was empty, apart from a one or two workers.

Rowena looked at her friend and tried to calm her. "We are in the morning. The lord of the town is going to give us a tenth of the fee in the morning. Then we'll leave."

Grainne shook her head. "No, we have to leave now. He's starting a war with an elder eternal dragon!"

Rowena and everyone around gasped.

"What?" Rowena asked.

Grainne pulled up a chair. "We met with minotaur refugees and others. The lord, Lorcan, came to this place a few years back with the tales of gold and power. He found the place inhabited by humans and beastfolk. He's turning the humans against the beastfolk, but that's not the worst."

"What is?" Elva asked.

"Those mountains along the horizon?" Grainne began. "Just beyond is a civilization of wild Quarmi. No magical bindings like the Quarmi in Lotcala and the north. Wild and aggressive. An elder eternal dragon rules them. The locals call him Vercinex. The minotaurs told me he has been in this land since before the Quarmi. They have a pact to stay away from the mountains, or the dragon and Quarmi will attack. Lorcan believes the dragon is guarding the Far-Off Kingdom!"

The group sat stunned at the thought.

"Lorcan's outnumbered. From what we've seen, he only has a few hundred." Severa pointed out.

"That's why he has brought in mercenaries. Get rid of the surrounding towns, round up any stragglers, and use them in his plan." Grainne said. "The minotaur leader I found told me as much. He wants a war with the dragon, but he doesn't realize that there are probably close to twenty thousand wild Quarmi on the other side of that mountain range. If he does, then he is suicidal."

"Why would he try to go against such odds?" Rowena asked.

Grainne shook her head. "The Far-Off Kingdom isn't a physical place on the earthly plane of Caelus. It is beyond a veiled barrier on the island of Nou Món. He thinks this continent is Nou Món."

"So he's crazy." Elva said.

"We've dealt with crazy before. We'll leave as soon as we have our gold." Rowena said, repeating her earlier plan.

"No, not just crazy. He knows what he's doing." Grainne said. "Lorcan is a low level mage from some other land. He is trying to figure out how to open the veil to the Thin Place. He thinks it is here and he will destroy the land to enter the Thin Place." Grainne saw her friends weren't following. "The Thin Place is a world beyond ours that a magical veil hides, but it is a fragile barrier created by Viri Al Sim, a Quarmi Mage. It was a short time after the old gods fell to Caelus, but before that, magic was much more plentiful. Viri Al Sim used magic to create the Thin Place, but it sapped a big part of power from this plane of existence. That's why only some mortals are born with the skills. Elves are innate with elemental magic as their origins are from the world itself. They weren't affected. The Quarmi are not from the elements, they are magic itself."

"I didn't think magic could create matter." Rowena said, now following more intently.

"Normally, no. However, one form of magic can, and we see it daily with the existence of the Quarmi race. Dark magic." Grainne responded. "Quarmi are proof of the power of dark magic, and of how it can be used for good and evil."

"Is Lorcan a dark marked mage?" Severa asked.

"He'd have to be." Grainne replied. "Quarmi mages can do it all, but humans have to be dark marked to do that type of shit. Even regular blood magic isn't powerful enough. Not without..." Grainne stopped.

"What is it?" Rowena said.

"Sacrifices. It would need a lot of sacrifices for simple blood magic could work." Grainne said.

The look of horror was clear on each face within the inn.

"We have to go now." Rowena said, shooting up from her chair.

Everyone made their way toward the door.

"Wait!" Grainne shouted.

Her friends stopped and then turned to her. Each looked more confused than the last.

"The people here need to be warned. The villagers. Everyone." Grainne said. "Lorcan will use everyone for fodder but he needs as many people as possible."

"How many?" Rowena asked.

"No idea, but for something like breaking the veil it will take a lot of blood." Grainne replied. "I heard rumors of an attempt a few years ago in the far east by a lich but then nothing else."

"Then we have to assume the lich failed, and now Lorcan is giving it his best shot." Severa said.

"Get the word out. Shout it out and be ready for a fight. Severa, you and Grainne get to the camp, gather some sisters, and rush to the outlying villages. Make sure people know." Rowena ordered to her group. "I'll deal with Lorcan."

"Not without me." Elva grinned.

The pair left to find the town's leader while the rest of the group tried to warn the town's people. That wasn't a simple job. Most didn't care about the beastfolk, and a few thought Lorcan's plan was a good one, not knowing how they'd play a part of it.

Grainne rushed as many people away as she could. Others followed her lead.

"We have to get word to everyone down to the port as fast as possible." Grainne said, when she reached the camp and found Garosh.

"What about the dragon and Lorcan?" The orc asked.

Grainne shook her head. "We can't face a dragon that powerful. If it comes for this town, then our only hope is to run. Let's just hope that Rowena can deal with Lorcan before we even have to worry about the dragon."

The sky was dark with the moon hidden in its shadow. The wealthier part of town was quiet, and the streets were clear. Rowena knew that a man such as he would live in the biggest house. He had that look of such an ego.

Rowena stilled herself. The idea that they could have been part of a plot to awaken and battle an elder eternal dragon was enough to chill her blood. She had heard tales of brave knights and adventurers slaying such beasts, but for Rowena, she had rather not fight one if she had the option. Walking through the town, Rowena saw many people running into buildings for safety. She scoffed.

"Run now but not when their lord is killing innocents." Rowena thought to herself. "Cowards."

Rowena and Elva walked up to his front gate, weapons drawn, looking for a fight. A stone wall, around eight feet tall, encircled the house. Outside the gate were the flags of the town. A few guards were posted at the entrance.

"This looks like the place." Elva said.

Before Rowena could reply, Lorcan walked out of his home and down the cobblestone path. Two guards flanked him, one carrying a lantern.

"You should have left earlier. You've lost the opportunity. Instead you and your band of cutthroats run through my town spreading such blasphemy against humankind." Lorcan said, his frown was evident in the lantern's light. "I tried to be reasonable. Just like I tried to be reasonable to the beastfolk."

"Burning villages and killing innocents isn't what I'd call reasonable." Rowena shot back.

"Innocents?" Lorcan scoffed. "Those animals are hiding something. They pray to that dragon and horde the wealth and power of the Far-Off Kingdom!" Lorcan yelled. "By what right is it theirs to hold? They give their own in sacrifice but they squander the gifts. That dragon is the key to opening the gate locked eons ago by the greatest mage that ever lived. He, a true living embodiment of a god, and I will claim that power for myself."

"You'd hurt and sacrifice your own people?" Rowena asked in disbelief.

"I'd sacrifice a million souls! Beasts, Quarmi, elf, humans, it matters not! I'd stop at nothing to gain an ounce of what is hidden beyond the veil. Gifts not given on any but those with magical powers. Yes, I'd kill the world for a small taste!" Lorcan screamed.

Rowena heard enough. She rushed the guards standing on the outside of the gate and swung her sword upward, slicing through the man's heavy cloth gambeson. Elva threw her war axe, splitting the other guard's head in two.

Elva quickly went over and tore her axe from the man's skull, while Rowena slammed her sword down on the gate's lock.

"Let me!" Elva said, doing the same.

The lock cracked open, and the gate creaked wide. Lorcan flustered with his robe before turning and running inside. Rowena bashed her shoulder into another guard, dropping him. She pounced on his chest, piercing her sword into the man's heart.

Elva had similar ease with her next kill. She spotted Lorcan running back into his house.

"He's not a mage." Rowena said, standing up. "If he was, he should have used his power."

"How do ye want to handle him?" Elva asked.

Rowena watched Lorcan slam the door of his house shut. "Find Illiak and Orsima. Show Lorcan what true mages can do with fire."

An hour later, Lorcan's house lit aflame and the two orc mages were fanning those flames higher. Rowena watched it burn. Other mages were helping to contain the fire from spreading, but the heat was becoming unbearable.

The next morning the flames were still crackling, but the fire was not as intense. Soon the smoldering remains would be left, and a lifeless, charred body would be found within. However, by that time the Sisters would be gone. Along with new members, the time was right to venture to new lands. Rowena had new allies. Agota, and a host of minotaurs had joined her band. She was happy in its expansion but thoughts turned her to the north. To a place in-between happiness and hatred.

However, the more she looked, the more she found the world to be a place of hate and spite. How much of that was seeping into her blood, what if she hadn't burned Lorcan? Then others would have burned, but the world forgets that. She worked to save countless innocents. She was a hero. Her sisters, knew it, the villagers were hearing about it. Rowena understood it and accepted her role as a savior to the people. Rowena rode on, knowing that the world will judge her one day, and when that time comes, there would be little she could do about it.

War in the Northern Winter Kingdoms

The Sisters spent another year journeying the world, all in search of wealth and fame. That was what eventually led them to the Mountains of the Copper Moon. The fabled land that bordered the northern lands of the continent that most languages called Kodai-no-ie. The land was known for being cold and inhospitable to most races, but the Quarmi had found it suitable for ages. From that land, several kingdoms grew to prominence.

Rowena accepted a job escorting a large trade caravan to the Quarmi Kingdom of Kiiroi Hana. One of the most northern kingdoms, and the largest on the continent. The Quarmi there, though considered "wild" for not taking the binding oath imposed centuries before, were open to trade with the other mortal races of the world. However, reaching the kingdom had been difficult given the location and the dangers that most trade routes saw. A caravan of a thousand wagons, the largest in Rowena's memory, was sent from four other lands. The Empire of Kesh, the Kingdom of Quis, Ceasarn Free States, and the Republic of Urlanda had sent the large caravan to the northern reaches to facilitate trade in furs, ores, and other mystical riches, including precious gems and stones need by the mages.

Being that these were southern lands, Rowena was the closest and controlled the largest mercenary band in the area. She also included beastfolk in her band, a rarity. That would help in terms of diplomacy, as most Quarmi were open to socialize with the beastfolk races.

The journey, lasting nearly a year, was slow. That gave Rowena and her sisters cause to worry, but such a large host of warriors deterred many of the bandits along the roads. Provisions held, thanks to the hunting and foraging abilities of the Sisters. Though they reached Kiiroi Hana safely, their time had yet to end.

The ruler of Kiiroi Hana, was the Quarmi Queen Joō Sakiko, saw the prowess and skill of Rowena. Not only had she heard the tales of the dwarven princess, her fame growing with each job, but she now saw a woman much like her. Strong, capable, but guided by a path still unknown. Sakiko saw Rowena as a leader but without the experience that many centuries would give her, as that time had given to Sakiko.

The queen, dressed in silks, surrounded by loyal attendants, scribes, and advisors, sat on a golden throne. Rowena marveled at the opulent seat of power as she entered the court. It wasn't gilded in gold, it was gold. Solid gold, with the arms molded to form dragons. Rowena noted the curvature of the beasts that Sakiko rested her hands on. Those were not the dragons of the southern reaches, mostly red or black dragons with two hind legs and vestigial claws on their wings. These were four-legged beasts, without wings. These dragons were of the mythical Maho race of serpents. Dragons that gifted mortals with magic. They lived with a special connection to the Quarmi.

Rowena stopped before the queen and knelt on one knee. Several guards stood at attention, watching her.

The queen smiled. She was radiant. Her beauty was known far across the world, but standing before her was a sight to behold. Her hair was black, flowing in the magical waves around her, like expertly woven strands of silk. The scars on her grey face, born from the magic within her, glowed faintly. Other Quarmi shared similar scars. However, some wore the face coverings of their binding oaths.

"You've come at an opportune time, Captain Rowena." Sakiko said. "I have a need for warriors. We are at war with the kingdom to the south of here, Rōtasu." She motioned for an attendant to hand Rowena a scroll. "In this document, you'll see the task."

Rowena stood, accepted the scroll.

"Sleep on this decision and return in the morning with the sun. We can hear your answer tomorrow. Until then, enjoy my palace as my personal guest." The queen smiled.

Rowena bowed and then backed out of the throne room. The large wooden doors closed behind with a very soft gust of air. Rowena walked back to her quarters, where Grainne and Elva were resting.

"The queen wants to hire us for a yearlong contract." Rowena said, walking into the room.

She tossed the scroll to Grainne, who was lying on her bed roll.

"A full year, with a salary of gold more than we've ever been paid before. Gems too." Rowena continued.

"It's tempting." Grainne said. "A place to rest for a while and call home. A home that isn't a tent is welcomed, too." She handed the scroll to Elva.

Elva looked at the scroll with the details. "This amount of gold and silver would allow you and several of us to retire richer than kings."

Rowena removed her coat and laid it down on her bed roll. She stretched and yawned deeply. "I think that if we stay, it would help to bolster our reputation." She laid back on the bed. "Whatever is decided, we have to make sure that we are prepared for war. The queen said as much. They are fighting other nations here and Quarmi wars typically mean magic."

Grainne sat up in her bed. "Will our sisters want to stay? So many like being on the road."

"I think they would like the steady coin." Rowena replied. "The queen wants to hire a band of a thousand or more. We are at that point now."

"Coming up this far with a band so big and a trade caravan so big gave a lot of pause to the other regions." Elva said. "We look like an invading force."

Grainne gave a soft 'hmm'.

Rowena thought for a moment and then turned to her two friends. "Spread the word. We're being hired on for an extended contract."

It was a simple and decisive measure to ensure that her band stayed whole, but with no more information than what was needed.

A month into their service under Queen Sakiko, the sisters saw very little action. Rowena and her sisters made the best of the new land. Most weren't used to the cold, but the ales did well to warm their bones. Plenty of entertainment existed throughout the realm for the sisters to spend their money on. A few skirmishes occurred, and that was enough to keep the Sisters' bloodlust quenched. everyone was glad to be "bored" with little fighting to be done.

However, all that changed when a delegation from Rōtasu arrived.

Rowena was in the throne room, looking on from the side. She marveled at the glittering robes of the foreign delegation. The air seemed to draw away and waft around the women and men, walking up to the queen. Sunlight from the upper-story windows filtered into the room, reflecting off the gems and jewels woven into the fabric. The colors radiating off of those precious stones filled the already magnificent throne room with more colorful tones.

A Quarmi noble to Queen Sakiko's left stepped down from his dais, knocking his scepter pole onto the marble flow with a clank. "My good Queen Sakiko, allow me to present the royal delegation sent from Queen Ichika to speak on her behalf."

He motioned for the delegation to bow.

Above him sat Queen Sakiko on her gilded throne. She watched the guests offer their reverence and, as each bowed to her, she made a simple motion of acceptance with her hand. Rowena could tell that the queen wasn't feeling very welcoming.

"You've come here to beg for a peace treaty, while my husband languishes in your dungeons?" Sakiko said.

The leader of the delegation, a Quarmi woman, stepped forward.

"You'll have to forgive us if we don't have a great deal of sympathy. Your husband murdered the crown prince."

Sakiko scoffed. "A duel to see whose magic was stronger. Men compare themselves in such ways all the time, and yet here you wish me to offer something for it?" The queen stood. "You'll get no quarter from me, unless you order his release this very moment. I have countless obsidian mirrors for you to speak to your queen back at her palace. Pick one, and we can settle this war."

"I will not." The delegation leader replied. "Your husband will be executed for murder. Queen Ichika demands compensation for the prince's death."

"Your queen will receive nothing but blood." Sakiko drew a knife and slashed her open palm.

Blood dripped from her left hand and dropped to the marble floor. Sakiko clenched her fist and lifted it to the air. Flames rose from the drops of blood. The candles and torches around the room flickered and dimmed. Rowena felt the air grow cold.

The defiant Quarmi woman coughed and knelt on her knee. Blood oozed from her mouth and nose. Soon it flowed from her eyes. The woman tried to scream, but only blood leapt from her mouth. A form took shape from the liquid. Cracks along the woman's skin appeared and her grey flesh tore.

Rowena gaped in horror as a drake formed from the blood and the Quarmi woman's body.

Sakiko motioned to the drake. "Kill the intruders!"

The beast turned and attacked its former countrymen, while Sakiko returned to her throne.

"I will ride this beast back to its home and burn it to the ground." Sakiko announced.

Those in the throne room cheered at the proclamation and at the spectacle. Rowena stayed silent. She wasn't opposed to it, but it was something she'd never seen before. Magic such as that was forbidden it most societies. It was also very difficult to master, and yet the Quarmi could perform it effortlessly.

Rowena and the others in attendance rushed out of the room to their respective posts. Rowena had to gather her warriors for the coming war. She arrived at her quarters, Elva and Grainne already in preparation to leave.

"Did the queen really turn someone into a dragon?" Grainne asked once Rowena closed the door behind her.

"Sort of. More of a baby one or a drake." Rowena answered, looking confused. "You heard about that already? I just left the throne room."

Elva chuckled. "Soldiers and guards have been running these halls screaming it. Greatest magic in years, they're saying."

"If it was a smaller one, then it probably was a drake. Fire drakes are only about ten feet in height where a full grown dragon would be so large it would destroy the throne room. Even a baby would be about twenty feet in height." Grainne continued.

Rowena looked at her friend. She raised an eyebrow. "Yeah, then a drake, I guess. Did you miss the part about her making it out of another Quarmi?"

Grainne snapped her head toward Rowena. "That's their magic. Blood magic. It's natural around here. Difficult but natural for their people."

Rowena nodded softly. "In any case, we have to hurry. The army is moving out tomorrow and we're the vanguard."

"Fuck. Sure, put the foreigners in the front. The expendable soldiers." Elva cursed.

"Or your best soldiers." Grainne countered. "She's paying a lot of money to us. Much of it up front. Why kill your investment?"

"It doesn't matter. The queen has us as the vanguard, and I'm not disobeying her." Rowena said, ending the conversation.

Within four hours, Rowena's mercenary band was equipped and ready to march south. The large army was moving quickly. It came as a sudden realization that Queen Sakiko had prepped most of her force to be ready for the attack. The terrain was rugged and over frozen ground, but that didn't slow the army.

"In Lotcala, we'd have taken the winter season off from war." Elva said to her sisters.

"This isn't Lotcala." Grainne replied with a smirk.

"No, and I get these Quarmi are used to this, but we ain't." Elva shot back. "Frozen earth and heavy snows. It's like being at me uncle's castle in the mountains."

"Fighting in the northern kingdoms will be like this. They have more snow and longer winters. Go up further and we'd see ten months of snow cover, if not more." Grainne said. "Rowena said we'd march until night and then camp just before sunset. The Quarmi will teach us how to soften the earth to dig out some cover for warmth."

Elva chuckled. "That lass has been spending a lot of time with the queen. Riding with her now."

"She's earning her keep." Grainne replied.

"I know, but between her always gone and now a dragon overhead, I'm a'wondering what sort of plan is taking place. She always kept us informed, but now —"

"Listen to yourself." Severa said from behind Elva. "She's our best friend, and our leader." Severa snapped her horse's reins and trotted up closer. "She'll tell us everything we need to know once a plan is made. She might not even know it herself. These Quarmi are secretive."

Elva grunted but conceded the point.

The sun was low in the west when the army stopped. Many Quarmi soldiers unloaded wagons of hay. Hundreds of wagons had been filled with hay and sawdust. One soldier lead two teams of wagons to Rowena's camp.

"Here." He said, dismounting and motioning to a wagon. "Layer a thick amount of the hay and sawdust around the ground. Build your tent over it and the ground will soften quickly." The Quarmi soldier instructed.

The sisters did as he told them and within a couple of hours, they had a livable space for warmth.

"Nice trick." Elva said, sitting on a stool in her tent. "I'll have to take that one back home for trips up into the mountains."

Rowena entered. "The queen has us moving hard and vast. The ground isn't snowy moving south, but it's hard as a rock. Fast movement for quick strikes." She said, pouring herself a mug of hot coffee. She looked at her friends. "What?" She said when she saw their confused faces.

"Yer with the queen practically night and day, and then come to us all business." Elva said.

"You've left our opinions out." Severa added.

"It's the queen's plan. Not mine or ours. We strike at their center hard. The dragon will fly overhead." Rowena continued.

"Our flanks?" Grainne asked.

"Queen's soldiers will charge on the flanks. Led by small contingents of sisters." Rowena answered, looking at Grainne. "Now, Elva, as to my time with the queen..." She began, taking a stool and sitting down. "That's my business." She sipped her drink. "However, as my sister, I'll tell you that my goal in that time is to secure more favorable positions for us. We are the vanguard. That's the strongest point for the best soldiers."

Elva nodded. "Aye, it is. No argument about the vanguard, but ye spend yer wee hours in her salons and throne room. Balls and other functions. Is it our positions in the army ye want to secure, or a position in her bed?"

Rowena choked on her coffee. She chuckled at the thought. The others in the tent also laughed.

"Elva, if I had any chance with the queen, I'd take it." Rowena said, calming her laughter. "We all would. I doubt I'd tell you about it, though."

The others in the tent nodded and chuckled.

"It would be good to have more communication with ye." Elva said, after her laughter calmed.

"Agreed." Severa and Grainne commented.

Rowena put her hand up and nodded. "Fine. You'll have that." Rowena finished her coffee. "However, I think that if we win this war and I survive, I might get more alone time with the queen. She gifted me new armor, and a winter rose."

"A winter rose?" Grainne said in awe. "That's the rarest flower in the world."

Rowena smiled. "I think that my time in her salons is paying off. We're her first choice for the attack."

"And yer her first choice for romance?" Elva asked with a grin.

"Come off that." Rowena tossed her cup at Elva. "We stand to make more gold than ever on this job and I don't want to loss that opportunity for us." Rowena smiled.

The sisters passed the early evening hours talking and sharing tales, as they had done so many times before. Finally, after a restless night of sleep, they woke to see the field. A field fit only for bloody battle.

Rowena donned her new armor. Her sisters wore their usual chainmail hauberks and gambesons. Most had nasal helms, but a few had kettle style helms. Rowena, atop her steed, wore a golden chain and steel plate lamellar armor. Her helm was a conical kegelhelm, with chainmail coming down on the back and sides. A purple plume wafted from the top.

Rowena trotted her horse to the front of the column. The queen sat on her own horse, joined by generals.

"They've amassed a great host of warriors, Rowena." Sakiko said.

The queen was dressed in golden plate armor. She wore silk underneath that was visible at the joints. At her hip was a dao sword. Sakiko looked as regal as any other day Rowena had seen her, but now she looked as deadly as ever.

"Try to come back. It would pain me to be without your presence." Sakiko smiled.

Rowena bowed her head before turning her horse back to her company.

Sakiko raised her hand for her army to see. "Ready the archers." She commanded. A general nearby shouted the order. The sound of thousands of arrows notching onto the bows could be heard on the field. "Loose arrows." Sakiko said, dropping her hand.

Thousands of arrows soared into the sky. The magnitude of the number darkened the daytime sun, yet each arrow fell without striking a single target.

"Closer." Sakiko said. "Seventy-five yards."

The generals relied the command. All the archers rushed forward and took positions.

"Notch." Sakiko commanded to her generals. "Loose." She said again, after the archers were ready.

This time, the arrows flew, and many found targets.

"Fire at will." Sakiko smiled.

The archers followed her commands, sending volley after volley to their enemies. Sakiko looked at a nearby general.

"Give Rowena the signal to charge. Have the others follow in the planned attack." Sakiko ordered.

The general nodded and rushed off. Rowena saw the movement and the flag, signaling her opportunity to advance.

Rowena lifted her spear. "Charge!" She ordered, kicking her horse and leading her rushing sisters, along with a few other warriors, forward.

The Sisters charged forth, some on horse while others ran. The running warriors, led by Elva on the left flank and Severa on the right, took off first. The horsewomen were in a tight formation one hundred yards behind, spears and lances up for the charge, while those running were rushing to the flanks. The minotaur soldiers with Rowena had called it a bull horned charge.

Rowena's force had been supplemented with recruits and conscripts from the regular army and now numbered close to ten thousand. Still, they were charging against a force of fifteen thousand.

Not even a minute and a half of running before the two forces of Sisters crashed into the Rōtasu lines. Within a second or two, Rowena's horsewomen slammed into the Rōtasu mainline of soldiers.

The Rōtasu soldiers carried spear like halberds, usually deadly, but against a charging armored horse whose rider carried a long spear or lance, they were not as effective. Rowena's force ran over the Rōtasu warriors, sending many to retreat. However, their line was so tightly packed that those turning to run were stopped by the warriors behind them. Once amongst the Rōtasu soldiers, those that had their spears broken during the charge were fighting with swords or secondary spears. Within the melee, horses fell from spear or halberd points, warriors were slaughtered in massive numbers. Rowena, with a sword in hand, was slashing down from her horse, hacking at any Rōtasu soldier within her reach. Blood, mud, and entrails flew across the battlefield as the fighting continued.

The fighting along the flanks was just fierce. Elva charged her force, carrying axes and shields, into the left and strongest of the flanks. Elva's strength shined through her warrior prowess. The warriors fighting alongside Elva did their best to keep up with the mighty woman. Hacking at limbs, and any body part visible. Rōtasu soldiers wore a lighter armor made of boiled leather and or iron. Sharpened axes might not cut through the material, but the weighted weapons would still harm the victim. Bones would break from the force of the falling axes.

Along the right flank, typically the weakest flank, Severa broke from the normal shield wall the Lotcalans trained in and instead fought sword in her right hand. Her left held on to a war-hammer, another weapon meant to harm the opponent without slashing skin. Where an axe or sword could slide off a curved portion of armor, a war-hammer would not. It would impact directly, with a force that would drive into the victim's body.

Severa pushed her force further in, driving many Rōtasu back to the center and rear columns. All three forces of Rowena's force pushing hard without letting up their offense. As the Rōtasu soldiers rushed to a hasty retreat, overwhelmed by the onslaught of Rowena's warriors, they fell into the Queen's trap.

A loud roar was heard overhead. Drowned out by the fighting at first, it grew louder. Suddenly, from behind the Rōtasu army, Sakiko's newest dragon appeared and rained fire down on the rear column of Rōtasu soldiers.

Panic set in. Rōtasu soldiers were not equipped, nor were they wanting to fight a dragon. They couldn't fight it. The beast flew overhead, breathing down a scorching breath, melting armor, weapons, and flesh. The Rōtasu mages, at first held in the back as reserve, tried their best to fight back and defend their comrades. Yet, the dragon had attacked the mages first. Sakiko, knowing full well that the mages would be held back, had ordered her pet to strike there first. It was a successful tactic. Now the Rōtasu where trapped within a wall of fire and Rowena's vanguard force. Sakiko sent the remainder of her force in for the kill.

What a glorious fill it was. Nearly twelve thousand Rōtasu soldiers laid dead on the field. Sakiko's army lost two thousand, while Rowena had lost one hundred and seven sisters.

"The capital is just three miles south. March there and sing Rōtasu songs." Sakiko ordered. "Let their people think our army is theirs, returning victorious. Then we attack for the final kill. The last throat to be slit in my empire."

Rowena and the generals nodded. Rowena turned with the generals but Sakiko called her back.

"Captain Rowena, you'll stay with me." Sakiko said. "If they see non-Quarmi, they'll know are deception."

Rowena reluctantly agreed.

"Tonight we will wait for our impending victory." Sakiko grinned.

That victory came and quickly. Sakiko's ruse worked. When the city of Rōtasu, walled and mighty, heard the war songs of thousands of warriors, they gladly opened the gates. Sakiko's warriors rushed in and slaughtered the populace. By dawn the next day, the city was a flame.

Sakiko turned her force back to her own city.

"General Katsu, stay here to regain order and hold the populace until we decide the fate." Sakiko ordered.

The queen left with a small force, Rowena alongside.

"When we return home, I'll have more to discuss with you, Rowena." Sakiko smiled. "Now the war is won. We can rest easy for a while."

Two weeks later, peace and relaxation had returned to Kiiroi Hana. Rowena stayed with her sisters, repairing equipment and seeing to the families that needed to be notified of their relatives' deaths. That was, until the queen ordered her to the palace.

Rowena walked into the large open room where Queen Sakiko performed her divination. The room was stone, as was much of the palace, with detailed stained glass along the high walls. In the middle, the room was domed, with what appeared to Rowena as parents suspended in the air.

"You're never late Rowena." Sakiko smiled. "I like that about you. One of the many things."

Rowena bowed. "I am here to serve. You call and I will answer. That's what we do for our queen."

Sakiko's smile held. "For now you serve, yet I see much of the future. Serving others isn't your destiny."

Rowena perked up.

"Do you wish to know?" Sakiko asked, looking at Rowena.

"Isn't it forbidden to know our future?"

Sakiko's smiled faded. "That's the talk of the mage guild. They'd have all magic users limit their powers for the sake of their own authority. No, it isn't forbidden, but what I see or better yet, interpret, isn't the only path." Sakiko walked to Rowena. She stroked her check gently. "However, I have seen the end. That is usually destiny. The journey to get there..." She paused. Sakiko dabbed Rowena's auburn hair. "That's the fun part."

Sakiko leaned in close to Rowena, cheek to cheek. The queen was at least a foot taller, but she leaned close with ease. Rowena felt the queen's warmth. Sakiko and Rowena turned and their lips met. Rowena knew the touch of a woman, though she preferred men. She preferred Blackhand. Still, she couldn't deny that she was enjoying Sakiko's kiss.

They parted. Sakiko looked down at Rowena and smiled. "I've lived for nearly two millennia and I've yet to kiss a dwarf, let alone a princess."

Rowena returned the smile. "I hope it was worth the wait."

Sakiko leaned in towards Rowena a second time, and the pair kissed again.

"It was." Sakiko replied after their second kiss.

"I've never kissed a queen." Rowena grinned.

Sakiko chuckled. "But you've kissed a Quarmi?"

"No, just humans and elves." Rowena replied.

"I imagine that you have someone in every town."

It was Rowena's turn to chuckle. "No, I don't. That's Elva, actually. She keeps a few lovers spread around." She said.

"You two share a bed?"

Rowena shook her head. "Not something a captain of a mercenary band should make a habit. It's happened, but it's not a good idea." Rowena paused of a moment. "Though she was my first. We're better friends than lovers." Rowena sighed.

"We've spent so much time together. Laughing, talking, flirting, and trying to read each other's ques that I feel maybe we should try being straight forward now. Do you have a love?" Sakiko asked.

Rowena nodded. "I do, but if I ever return home, he'll never be mine. My stepmother will make sure about that. So for now, I'm here in this world without a love at my side."

Sakiko tilted her head, looking at her friend. "That's the journey. This man you love, does he love you?"

Rowena shrugged. "He does when we're together. He seems to, at least for the six times we've spent time with one another. When I'm not around, I don't expect him not to have urges. I do. So if he beds another, then that's his choice, just like it would be, and has been, mine."

"Indeed." Sakiko grinned again. "Yet, he'll be true if you two were to marry?"

"I believe so." Rowena looked up at Sakiko. "I'd be more concerned about life in Lotcala than life as Black Hand's wife."

"Let me reveal what I know of that." Sakiko said. Her smile faded. "Be warned, it isn't all wonderful."

Rowena thought for a moment. "Tell me."

Sakiko brought her arms up. Air wafted around them, Rowena could see the light refracting off of the streams of air. Colors danced around the pair. Sakiko's black eyes sparkled with visions.

"I see a great kingdom in war. Death and despair will follow you until that war. It is imperative that you... lose that war." Sakiko said with a hint of confusion.

"Lose?"

"More war, a dragon dying and stags falling from on high, and a kingdom birthed from fire. A mountain, greater than any around it. Statues of fearsome warriors guarding the entrance to a tunnel."

"A burial mound. A mountain, must be father's."

"No, in the south. Far from Lotcala." Sakiko added. "His tomb is small and forgotten by time. Only the worms and weeds remember him." Sakiko hissed as more magic encircled her. "This mountain tomb is adorned with a black stag. They all have the black stag marking the mounds but only one reaches the sky. Hundreds. All from a great kingdom in the south. A land born through blood and held in the grasp of a dwarven fist."

Sakiko gasped and then fell to her knees. Rowena rushed to her and cradled her close.

"My lovely Rowena, you'll be so much greater if you follow the path laid out before you now." Sakiko smiled and clasped Rowena's cheek. She pulled her in for a kiss. "Stay with me this night. I do not feel like being alone."

Rowena smiled and returned the kiss.

The next morning Rowena awoke is Sakiko's bed. The queen was staring out of the large window.

"You rise too early." Rowena smiled.

Sakiko turned and laughed softly. "I like to see the sunrise each morning." She went back to the bed and curled up close to Rowena. "You call yourself Lotcalan, but that is only part of who you are. Why hide your dwarven traits?"

"Does being a dwarf help me in gaining more gold or respect in the world?" Rowena laughed.

Sakiko chuckled. "No, I heard you in your sleep. You talk about the hatred that the Lotcalans feel for you."

"That's nothing." Rowena said sternly.

"Your people came to this world so many eons ago. Phindoe the Blacksmith hammered dwarves from the stones and the dirt. People look down on your kind but those stones and that dirt are the building blocks of our world. Magic is nothing without this earth." Sakiko said. She stroked Rowena's naked thigh with her index finger.

"You sound like Grainne."

"Does she also try to give you tell you what's best for you?"

Rowena gave a hearty laugh. "They all do."

Both ladies laughed.

"I mean, talking about history." Rowena said when she caught her breath.

"You should be proud of being a dwarf. Phindoe gave the world magic, and he gave the world dwarves. You are connected to this world just as we are. Dwarves walked this world before rivers and streams had names. Mountains sprung up around your kingdoms."

Rowena stayed silent.

Sakiko looked to her and then gave Rowena a kiss on her cheek. "I would be honored if you stayed here with me. I'll make you my queen, and as long as you don't mind me bedding a male to produce an heir then you and I could have a beautiful life."

Rowena smiled. "Did you see that too?"

Sakiko nodded. "I did, but that is not the vision I told you about. That one," Sakiko paused. "That one will only come to pass if you leave at the thaw of spring."

Rowena sat up. "I would have to leave?"

"You will have to face your past to achieve your destiny. To do that you'd have to leave."

"I'm not unhappy here." Rowena smiled. "I could get used to waking up next to you in soft linen sheets."

Sakiko smiled. "And I'd be happy to keep you here, but your destiny isn't with me."

"You want me to stay, but you are turning me away." Rowena said.

"Each destiny has to be fulfilled or the universe will make us pay dearly." Sakiko said.

"The universe?"

"We all have a part to play. A path to walk. If we don't, then forces beyond our control will intervene. I've seen others forgo destiny only to meet with tragedy. I'd gladly suffer that for you but I'd rather you not incur the universe's wrath."

Rowena kissed Sakiko. "The universe doesn't frighten me." She said after breaking the kiss.

Sakiko gave her a grim look. "It does me." Sakiko stood up and walked back to the window. "Two thousand long years, I've seen too much to think that the universe won't have its way."

Rowena stood from the bed and grabbed her clothes. "I understand."

"Rowena." Sakiko said, turning to face her. "I'd never ask you to leave."

"At first thaw." Rowena said, turning to leave.

"That's a month away. Will you join me each night until then?"

Rowena stopped. She turned to the queen and grinned. "Hell couldn't stop me." She winked before leaving the queen's chambers.

Goldwater Rebellion

he Goldwater family fought alone. No banners were called, for none would answer. This was to be their war, and theirs alone. It didn't matter if the Overland, Riverman, or Burg families joined. Little consequence that the FitzRoy, Cullenhun, Redmayne, Mortimer, and the other gentry houses didn't take up arms with the Goldwaters. No. The Goldwaters, Lords and Barons of Antei didn't need their vassals, sworn for centuries to their side. Maybe if Hugo Goldwater, greatest of all the Goldwaters, had still been alive. Maybe if his grandfather, Baron Selwyn Goldwater, had called them. Then they would have joined.

No, this wasn't a baron worth answering, even if he had called. This was Sir Edwin Langley, great-nephew of Hugo. He was the heir, and he was greedy for more. Langley wanted to be a king, and so he named himself one. King Edwin Langley of Antei, the sovereign nation within an enemy kingdom. Yet, Langley controlled the Moon River.

He didn't call the vassal banners because he knew they'd never fight at his side. But that didn't matter. Edwin had seventeen thousand men, several hundred hedge knights, and two thousand Zaragozan pirates.

He started with the lands held by Mortimer. Overran them and then he moved on to the Redmayne, and then Burg lands. In less than a month, half of Antei burned. Edwin Langley of Goldwater was a baron that few liked, but he was a man that could lead an army with efficiency and ruthlessness. He had a host of mercenaries at his disposal. Paid with gold, he pillaged and the taxes from the people he was supposed to protect. Langley pushed through the fields that lay to the north of Antei. The resistance he encountered wasn't enough to stop him.

"What of the other barons?!" King Charles exclaimed to Cullenhun.

His chamberlain was walking beside the king, heading to the council chambers.

"Sir Jakob has said that two barons expressed interest in sending forces, but Elysian forces have mobilized at the border, forcing the barons to stay near their homes. Only Hardstone is sending forces south to Antei." Cullenhun reported.

Charles stopped walking. "Leif is a good man. He'll be the savior of this kingdom if the Creator has anything to say about it." He said before pushing the door of the council chambers open. "What the hell are you doing sitting here?" He yelled to the men in his council. "Get to your homes and mobilize! We have to stop Langley."

The men at the council table looked to the king startled. Lord Blacktower pulled his ledger and began scribbling as the men went on.

"Your grace." Lord Ashe began. "The problem with Antei is more of a centralized army concern, is it not?" Ashe looked to Cullenhun. "And one for the lords of Antei." He nodded.

Cullenhun scoffed. "If you're too much of a coward, then by all means stay here, Ashe, but I am taking my men to fight back. He might be my baron, but he threatens my king. Our king!"

Ashe stood up and began to shout something back, but Chancellor Coldwood grabbed his shoulder from his side, calming the man down.

"You have, what, fifty men here? How many knights, Sir Cullenhun?" Coldwood asked.

He wasn't asking to sound mean, nor was he being condescending. Coldwood knew of the skill of Cullenhun. It was a matter of realistic numbers.

Cullenhun looked to the baron. "Four knights, and fifty-three men at arms with me here. Seventy retainers that made it safely out of Beringridge are awaiting just south of Lowerfield."

"Just over a hundred to fight nearly twenty thousand?" Lord Blacktower, the king's steward, said. "What of the other forces?"

"The ones that could make it out in time made it north to Lowerfield. Sir Jakob is leading my army and will rendezvous with Sir Cullenhun and me in a few days." King Charles was able to answer. "We do not have the accurate count, but just a few thousand is the estimate. Jakob, however, is being called back to Amazon. Their war with Tresha is not going as well as Queen Ophelia would have hoped. She has said that she needs her husband."

Losing Sir Jakob would hamper the Lotcalan forces. He was a veteran of many battles and skilled as a tactician.

"Even with the king's army, you'd be outnumbered. You only have two thousand joined thus far." Coldwood replied. "The last war took too much out of it."

King Charles nodded. "Yes, it did. That's why I'm sending it to hold the border of Antei for the time being. Hardstone will join us with an army around five thousand strong and the remnants of the manor lords and gentry armies will push us to twelve or thirteen thousand. However, we have another army coming from the south, Creator willing."

"Another army?" Ashe asked, his eyes narrowing.

"Sir Cullenhun sent a letter for me a few days ago." King Charles said. "If she responds favorably, then we will see the tide turn."

"Your grace, was that the wisest decision?" Lord Ashe asked, knowing the king's meaning.

Lord Blacktower closed the ledger. The manor lord simply shook his head. "My king, the princess has garnered a bit of a reputation as a villain." Blacktower said.

The king's eyes narrowed.

"Your grace, I mean no disrespect. I am only asking based on the rumors." Blacktower amended his previous statement. Pulling back his light brown hair, he did his best to steady his breathing. "My niece was in Dunhild, in the Kingdom of Coethe, when Rowena's band passed through. She said how she was mixing with beastfolk and other rabble."

The king was about to speak when Coldwood spoke up.

"Aye, I've heard it too." The baron said. "Minotaurs, orcs, and stragglers from other armies. Even rumors of a gorgon." Coldwood said. He smiled slightly. "That's one hell of a group she's leading."

The others weren't sure if he was kidding, uneasy, or impressed.

The king let out a breath of air. He looked to Cullenhun. "Well? You know the most."

Cullenhun, his hair greyed from years of service to the court, grinned. "All true." He said, smiling to the others. "She's taken any that want to join her and has turned her band into a formidable force. Some were outcast or deserters that have become loyal soldiers for the princess. She knows how to lead an army. My daughter Grainne has written to me that they even have the backing of the Bank of Denos, several southern kingdoms, and The Company."

"Cutthroats." Ashe spat.

Cullenhun nodded. "To you and I, but to the rest of the world, The Company is one of the best mercenary and business guilds there is."

"And criminals." Ashe added.

"To some." Cullenhun replied.

Blacktower waved off the argument brewing. "No matter what some mercenary band is or isn't, the fact is that she won't be happy about this."

The king swung his head to his vassal. "Is that of any consequence to me? Am I not the king?"

"Of course, your grace, I only meant to say that the queen is not an ally to your daughter." Blacktower responded.

"Any fool knows that." Coldwood cut in. The baron looked to Cullenhun. "She can lead commoners and beastfolk. Certainly not an effortless task, but can she lead our barons and lords? Nobles are of a different stock."

"I'm certain that with the king's —"

"No, I mean, can she really lead them?" Coldwood interrupted. "The king can name any fool as leader, and we will force the barons to listen. At least for a moment. What we need is someone to gather our forces and rout this coward by taking our men and mobilizing them as one force."

"If you're asking if my daughter can take charge of a bunch of men, then ask it Coldwood." King Charles said.

"Fine." Coldwood sighed, looking to Sir Cullenhun. "Can the princess, a half dwarven bastard sellsword, lead a bunch of noble vassals and their retainers?"

"We'll find out." Cullenhun replied.

* * * * *

Another stop off in East La~Porte for the Sisters, a seasonal occurrence, was a fortunate one. Arriving in the city was always a favorite for Rowena. The vibrant city was a wonder to many. A haven for travelers and merchants. Its market street and square were vibrant in the colors of the stalls. Tarps of every shade hung over common and exotic goods, alike. Voices speaking in any number of languages would be heard. It wasn't uncommon to meet someone that could speak more than two or even three languages fluently within the city walls.

Like most travelers, Rowena and her sisters were always welcomed. Mostly because they brought gold and silver, but in the southern reaches, Rowena was becoming known as a hero. Her tales of victorious battles, slaying of wild beasts, and more than one king owed their lives to her. All fueled her growing fame. A fame she was willing to accept, along with the extra gold.

As she entered the town, flanked by twenty of her closest sisters, the citizens crowded her, giving gifts of food, wine skins, or trinkets. It was like that whenever they arrived; an impromptu parade born out of love and admiration.

When Rowena approached her cousin Adela's house nearly an hour after arriving, a small boy rushed out of the house and ran up to her. The boy practically jumped into Rowena's outstretched arms.

"Noah!" Rowena said. Her voice rang with joy.

Adela and Juniper appeared in the doorway.

"He's been telling us you'd be coming soon." Juniper said with a smile. "He said he could feel it."

Rowena beamed. "He's a bright little boy."

Juniper smiled. "Thanks to you, Ro."

Rowena took the compliment in stride. Her actions years before ensured Juniper and her unborn son's safety, but their success was because of Juniper's tenacity. That and Adela's help.

"Where's the rest of your band?" Adela asked, as the four made their way into the house.

Rowena smiled. "Grainne and Elva are at the tavern with a few of the others. We camped most of the ladies just north of the city."

"What's your number now?" Juniper asked. She was preparing a few glasses while Rowena and Adela sat down in the main room of the house.

Noah was sitting by the hearth, playing with wooden soldiers that Hadiza had made for him the year before.

Rowena had been watching him play. She looked up at Juniper, accepting a cup of spiced wine.

"We're up to a thousand. A few more, actually." Rowena said, sipping the warm wine. "The last war was a rough one. A couple of other companies folded when they lost some of their leaders and a lot of men. We took them in."

"Men?" Adela asked. "No longer the sisters?"

Rowena chuckled. "We're still the sisters, but now we have some help from our brethren. A few wild Quarmi joined up, too. I couldn't pass up on their magic." She said, finishing her wine.

Adela nodded. "It's good to hear your fortunes have been blessed." She sighed and then her eyes perked up. "I almost forgot! You have a letter here." Adela jumped up, scrambling to her study and coming back hurriedly. "It has the royal seal."

Rowena's smile faded. She looked at the sealed envelope in Adela's hand, unsure if she should accept it. Slowly, she took the letter. Her face was grim while reading the words.

Juniper noted the change in Rowena's expression. "Is something the matter?"

Rowena put the letter down. "I'll have to cut my visit short. The Baron of Goldwater has instigated a revolt."

"What?" Adela said. "That's Hugo's nephew, right?"

"Aye, Sir Edwin Langley." Rowena said. "I met him once when I was young. It was his investure to the barony."

"Your father has an army. The barons have armies." Adela said.

"Yeah, why do you need to go?" Juniper added.

"The army was decimated in the previous war and rebuilding has taken longer than father would have hoped. My father is calling me to return to lead his army. Sir Jakob is in Amazon with his wife, Queen Ophelia."

"Brightblade." Adela said under her breath. "I know her well enough to know that Jakob won't return. That queendom will rise in glory under her, but at the cost of many lives. Good woman, but loves war above all else." She continued looking at Rowena. "With no Lord Marshal, what is the king to do?"

"He could lead his men himself, but he wants me instead. Grainne's father could do it, but he is a gentry lord. Father says as a princess, I can lead baronial armies." Rowena said.

"How many men does this Langley have?" Adela asked.

Rowena heaved her chest as she let out a deep breath. "Nearly twenty thousand mercenaries. More expected to come from the south."

"You would have heard, right?" Juniper asked.

Rowena nodded. "I should have. I'll have to ask Grainne. She gets a lot of the notices. Black Hand might have word, but he is still in the north." Rowena thought for a moment. "Last I remember, the baronial armies tallied about twenty-five thousand in total. They can call up conscripts to number more, but those are untrained farmers with poor equipment."

"A good leader can turn an even engagement into a significant victory." Adela said.

A knock came at the door. Juniper went to the front to answer it. Rowena and Adela could hear a mumbled conversation before Grainne, Elva, and Juniper entered the room.

"Ro, some Lotcalan lord is calling for mercs!" Elva said.

She was out of breath as she spoke.

Rowena nodded, holding up the letter. She looked up at her two oldest friends.

"We have to go back. Baron Edwin Langley of Antei has begun a revolt against my father." Rowena said. She stood from her chair.

"Surely, you can stay one or two nights. The day is late, and whether you want to leave now or not, the ship won't leave for a few days when the tides are more favorable." Adela said.

"You're right, my lady." Grainne replied, remembering the proper address for a princess. "I can arrange the passage north, and we can leave for the port once that's handled."

Rowena nodded. "Good." She said, as Grainne and Elva began to leave. "Wait." Rowena said, stopping them. "I need to send a letter north to Aran."

Grainne nodded. Elva looked at Rowena and grinned.

"I'll rouse the sisters and let them know they only have a couple of nights of rest before we leave again. I guess now I'll be able to show them me home back in Lotcala." Elva said before leaving.

Adela looked at her cousin. A decade older than Rowena, but the scorn of the royal court was felt earlier in life. Her father, Harold, was the youngest son of King Erik I and one of his concubines. Harold was a jarl in Gotistan during his father's rule. Adela wasn't meant to rule, nor did she wish it. However, she was wiser than most in the royal court, a court that shunned her when Adora arrived. Queen Adora was King Charles' mother,

Rowena's grandmother. Adora, jealous of Adela, convinced King Erik and Theodorif, not yet the king, to send her away. This also drove Herald back to Gotistan. That divide lingered for years.

Adela looked to Juniper and motioned for her to leave the room.

"I know of your pain, cousin." Adela said, when Juniper and Noah left the room.

"Pain?" Rowena said. Her eyes opened wider. Adela was stoic about her past.

"I too was run out of that very same court. It is our home, the place of our ancestors. The kings of the past are our memories. Our place is within that great hall. To be pushed out by outsiders is a pain that I feel as much as you do." Adela said.

Rowena leaned back in her chair. "We've discussed none of this. Our common past."

"It was never important. Your grandmother pushed me aside for fear of my influence. Ironic that I'm so close to you now. But that has nothing to do with her. It is because I love you as family should. My dislike of your grandmother was for her actions against my father and I. Adora disliked anyone too close to the throne that wasn't her. However, she died before you were born, so you are free from her wickedness." Adela sighed. "I regret to say that I had a hand in that."

"What?" Rowena was unsure if she had heard Adela correctly.

"Your stepmother wanted to secure a place in the royal court of Lotcala, and your uncle wanted the throne. Adora wanted to use your uncle Robert to fight her way back at the expense of your father's life. She came to me, your grandmother did, for help. A mistake. I had heard of Sirie's skill with a blade and sent word.

Sirie killed Adora, and my revenge was complete. Had I known…" Adela paused. "Had I known what that woman would put you through, I would have killed Adora myself and left Sirie to wander the world."

"My father would never believe it."

"No, he wouldn't. He'll send me letters for you and ask for information, but to him and the rest of the court, I'm banished. I have no favor amongst the lords."

"I can return you to court." Rowena smiled faintly.

"I don't want to return." Adela smiled. "I'm happy here. This is my true purpose." Her smile faded. "Cousin, with all my love I wish you well and I will look forward to your return, but they will never accept you in that land."

Pain stung Rowena's chest at the remark.

"So long as Sirie has your father's heart, that bitch will never let you return to the court."

The pair sat in silence for a few more minutes until Adela stood.

Clearing her throat before speaking, Adela's smile returned. "You will always have a place her in my home. You are of my blood, and that is all you need, for you are beloved to me." She smiled her sweet and sincere smile at her younger cousin. "We'll have some food prepared soon. Be sure to tell your friends to join us."

Rowena smiled and nodded. It would be the first home cooked meal in some time. It would be a delightful change of pace, but Adela's words, while ringing true, hung heavily in Rowena's mind.

A few days later, the band of mercenaries boarded twenty one cogs, sturdy sea-going ships. These were the most dependable ships of any navy. Most were built with a stern castle for added protection, but some of Rowena's ships were equipped with fore-castles. These large oak made ships were square sailed, and slow but offered the best protection.

Rowena, Grainne, Elva, and Agota stood on the fore-castle deck of the lead ship. The moon was full above the dark ocean.

"The ocean is deep, with terrors unseen." Agota said, never blinking out into the darkness.

Rowena chuckled. "We're safe on the ship." She said, putting her arm around the young gorgon girl.

Elva and Grainne remained quiet. Grainne puffed on a long, thin tobacco pipe. Her blue eyes sparkled in the moon light. She was far from calm, though her demeanor hid it well.

"Has it occurred to either of you that we are sailing a fleet of warships to our homeland? We'll dock in Ter Nog with a black stag on our flags and shields." Grainne said, then she stops to take a drag of her pipe.

"We're not the invaders, though." Elva replied.

"Perhaps not, but I wonder what sort of welcome we'll receive." Grainne looked at Rowena. "The beastfolk too? Our treatment of the Quarmi is admirable, our alliance with the dwarves is politically motivated, but we're backwards on many things. Will Lotcala welcome Agota and the minotaurs?"

"I doubt it." Rowena said. She took her arm from Agota. "I don't think many Lotcalans will know much of the beastfolk, and that will be a problem for many. Most have never seen minotaurs in real life."

"Aye. The Blue Mountains had legends of bear-men, but I ain't ne'er see a one. Me da' said he saw one in his younger days, but he was ways off, could have been an ogre." Elva added. "There are a few of them left in those mountains."

Agota looked to Elva. "But there might be bear-men?"

"Aye, giant men with the heads of grizzlies but the bodies of hulking men. Furrier than a sled hound." Elva grinned at Agota. "They'd rip a man into pieces and steal away the women, or so the legends say." She winked.

Elva turned back to Rowena and Grainne. "It'll be Yule time when we arrive."

Grainne took another drag of her pipe. "Yep. Cold, snowing, and everyone celebrating the coming seasons of Ymir."

Rowena smirked. "A good time to visit."

The others grinned, thinking of their memories of the fun holiday. Most of the time, spiced wine or mead would be served with roasted meat, cooked over coals. Another treat of the season was the food from the fattened pigs, cattle, and goats from the summer months. Smoke will fill the air with the smell of burning pine logs and spices. Yule was always Rowena's favorite time of the year.

Elva spoke up to her friends on another matter. "We cannae dock all these ships in Ter Nog."

Rowena shook her head. "No, we can't." She smiled. "I sent Severa and a few Sisters ahead of us to secure dock space in Widow's Cape and Greyhold. Docking in the three major ports will give us a chance to meet outside of Ter Nog."

Grainne nodded. "Good plan. Then to Jovag?"

Rowena looked out over the water. "No, then we will ride to Lowerfield. There, I'll assume command of the king's army and the baronial armies."

Elva laughed, but Grainne stayed silent.

"That will be a sight!" Elva continued to laugh. "Ye be the one to lead that woman's army."

"The king's army." Grainne corrected.

"Really now?" Elva taunted.

"She's right." Rowena intervened. "Sirie has controlled that army since Sir Jakob is more concerned with his wife."

"As he should be." Elva said.

"No matter. When I arrive, I will lead the army or we will leave the kingdom." Rowena added.

"What's the pay?" Agota asked.

Elva chuckled. Rowena smiled at the gorgon, but Grainne scrounged her nose.

"What's the money to you, little one?" Grainne asked.

"We have to be paid well to travel so far and risk our lives in another war." Agota said.

"Well said. You've been listening to me." Grainne smiled and patted Agota on the shoulder. "For the sisters, five hundred pounds of gold, three hundred pounds of silver, one hundred new recruits, and five war galleys." She looked at Rowena. "For our fearless leader, a barony, perhaps."

"I don't want it." Rowena smirked. She was lying, of course.

"Ye do, and it's deserved. A place to retire and rest ye bones." Elva said, patting Rowena's back. The much taller woman stood next to her friend. "It ain't what ye truly deserve, but it's the next best thing. Maybe ye'll get it."

"I'll win him this war, and that'll be that. Just another job." Rowena said in a soft voice.

The others stood silently with Rowena. They knew the price of the war to come, and the outcome that might be if they won.

* * * * *

After nearly two months on the open sea Rowena and her mercenary band arrived. Almost three hundred warriors unloaded at the dock in Ter Nog. A bustling port city that was unlike any other city in the kingdom, Ter Nog hosted many cultures, and with the Yule celebrations underway, more people than ever joined in the festivities.

Riding on her horse, along with her officers, Rowena rode through the large city. The citizens rushed out of their homes, children and women waved flags bearing the black stag, Rowena's newly given sigil from the king. The stag was commonly known as the sigil of the Carolyngian dynasty, and for her part and blood, Rowena colored hers black. Others along the streets banged drums, played horns and flutes, all in celebration of the noble warrior returning home. Rowena's exploits, though some controversial, were known far and wide.

Riding through the city, Elva looked to Grainne. "Wearing the wolf on yer breast?"

Grainne looked down at her armor, and then at her friend. "Next to Rowena's stag. I'm coming home. The people should know that I'm a lord's daughter."

Elva smiled. "Ye are always about being proper."

Grainne sneered. "We are noble born, and we're in our homeland. Just because we are more than willing to spend our days trudging through muck and swamps, sleeping on the hard ground, and eating days old gruel does not diminish who we are. We're still noble born, no matter how we live our lives."

Elva nodded. She along with the others wore Rowena's sigil of the black stag. Most painted it on their shields or surcoats, if they had a surcoat. Many others tied flags with the sigil onto the spears.

Severa Harbor, daughter of Baron Henrik Harbor, another noble born from Lotcala, also wore the stag beside her family's sigil of a kraken.

She was in Greyhold, where another three hundred warriors docked and unloaded. Severa watched as the warriors of the company unloaded from the ships and started preparing a wagon train of supplies. An old man approached her.

He was withered with age and years of toil. The salt air left its mark on his worn face. He looked up to Severa atop her horse.

"*Ër di där kvin med Rowena Karlsdetter?*"[1] The old man asked, in a broken form of the old Gota tongue.

Severa looked at the man. "*Aye, vid ër.*"[2] She replied with an enormous grin.

The man looked back at the large force of warriors unloading from the boats.

"*Ër dü viss ikar ik inntrëngere?*"[3] The man asked.

---

[1] Are those the women with Rowena Carlsdotter?
[2] Yes, we are.
[3] Are you certain they are not invaders?)

Severa looked confused. *"Jør dü ik se di blekkspruten pa min brust?!"* Severa responded angrily. *"Ja stadig Rektor Henrik detter! Ja er detter a härd."*[4]

The old man looked to Severa and shook his head. He pointed to the woods to the north. *"A häxaskov séd e stur hord fra syd. A häxa advare mod Rowena."*[5]

Severa shook her head. "Listen to witches and you'll burn with the other *hedens a elden gottin.*"[6]

She snapped her horse's reins and rode to the head of the column, leaving the old man behind.

In Widow's Cape, nearly four hundred more warriors landed on the beaches and the docks. The Moray family welcomed them, having been informed by Hadiza a week prior.

The three forces left for the western outpost of Barron Hill, the seat of the Alban gentry family. There Rowena's force would converge and then march to Lowerfield where her father was waiting.

However, in her plans was another three thousand hedge knights coming from the north. Her dear friend, and sometimes lover, Gerald Blackhand would supply those soldiers. Known to the world simply as Black Hand. Those knights, were not a cheap investment, though Black Hand wouldn't dream of extorting Rowena. Sure she loved him, but he also knew that she wasn't the type to take such an offense lightly.

---

[4] Do you not see the kraken on my breast? I am still Baron Henrik's daughter. I am the daughter of the hearth.

[5] The witch of the woods saw a great horde from the south. The witch warned us against Rowena.

[6] heathens of the old gods

Besides, having her, and her sisters as allies was good for his business.

Ter Nog was nearly two thousand miles from Lowerfield. That meant it would take almost three months for Rowena's army to reach the town where her father's force was staged. The travel was easy going on the king's road. All along the route, villagers and others would rush out to meet the princess and her warriors.

"While I'm not at all disappointed by the attention, we're getting from the commoners, I am wondering where the lords' armies are." Severa said, riding up to Rowena. "It bothers me."

Rowena looked to her friend and smiled. "The lords that aren't in danger from Langley won't venture out to fight him. They would risk their own lives when they feel it doesn't concern them."

Severa wasn't so sure. "I met a man in Greyhold. Older than most in the town. He said a woods witch had warned the people about you." Severa looked into her friend's eyes. "Nothing specific but he said she warned the town about Rowena bringing a horde from the south. It was old Gota, maybe I heard wrong."

Rowena's smile faded. "Old ramblings in old tongue from an old man." She sighed. "I suppose that our force could look like an invasion. Most of the warriors aren't northern and their skin is darker in complexion. We aren't here to conquer, though, and most of our kin will know that."

"I know, Ro." Severa said. She turned back toward the road. "Still, we should watch for arrows aimed at our backs. The lords staying away while we march through their lands is an odd reaction."

The others looked around. The countryside stretched for miles, fields blanketed with snow, and rolling hills along the horizon.

"Severa is right. I too think we should have heard the tale of soldiers moving west." Elva replied. "They won't really shut their borders to Antei, would they? This isn't about nobles but about the people."

Grainne shrugged. "It's possible. Maybe all these years away has changed little for the kingdom. The lords are probably still squabbling."

"Then that would mean one thing." Rowena said. "They'd want to get rid of Langley, get rid of the Goldwater family and take Antei for themselves. They'll just wait until it looks like he is beaten before joining in."

"To the winner goes the spoils." Elva said.

Severa looked to Rowena. "If none of the other barons or lords show up, then that will be you Ro." She smiled. "Even with our fucked up politics, they can't deny a claim won in battle."

Rowena nodded. She didn't want to smile. Mostly she didn't want to get her hopes up, but the prospect was compelling. However, she felt something new as she rode through the kingdom, her kinsmen bringing her flowers, gifts, and waving her flag. She felt a pull from their love. Rowena knew that her heart was changing, and the throne was her destiny.

The winter months were new. In another couple of months, about the time Rowena and her force would arrive, the snows would increase and the temperatures would dip below freezing even during the mid-day. Waging a war would be nearly impossible. Yet, Rowena wasn't afraid of the possibility, nor was she inexperienced at the task.

War was often a spring or summer pastime. Few were foolhardy enough to march warriors in the winter, but Rowena still knew the land well enough. She knew the game that she'd could hunt and the copses of trees to fell for firewood. A siege camp wasn't the best plan, but an attack could be. It would have to be fast, and precise. There was no room for error. Too long in a frozen camp and the soldiers would begin to revolt, but a quick victory would encourage them, while hurting the morale of the rebels. It was a risky plan but a good one. It didn't hurt that Rowena's reputation was well known.

Safely away in Lowerfield, King Charles watched the roads daily. Scouts had come in, his and Rowena's, reporting that her army was marching close by. Another host had come from a northern border town in the Moray hold. Black Hand's knights, led by the Company's agent under Black Hand's orders, had also arrived and were only a couple weeks behind Rowena. That agent was known only as the Iron Prefect. He was a ruthless and fanatical mercenary, carrying a reputation for winning wars at any cost. Rowena wasn't thrilled to have him near, but she couldn't deny his success.

The fateful day arrived when King Charles looked out over the hills and saw a host of warriors getting steadily closer. A mass of black, the color of their armor, grew closer and larger with each moment. He could soon make out his daughter's sigil of a black stag, the one he had given to her. His heart leapt for joy at the sight. His beloved daughter was home at last!

"Fetch me meat, wine, and fetch me pine logs for a great fire! We'll roast the fattest pig we have!" Charles ordered with more enthusiasm than he had spoken in months.

Servants ran off to gather the items that the king had ordered.

"Prepare a table in the castle. My daughter is home. This is an occasion for a feast!" Charles said.

The king rushed to his horse and rode out to meet her along the road. He kicked at the flanks and snapped the reins. The king's horse burst into a gallop. Sir Cullenhun and a few guards followed the speeding king closely. Crown Prince Alfred stay behind at the castle, not as eager as his father.

A short time later, the smiling king was riding alongside Rowena and her sisters as they entered Lowerfield. Laughter filled the air during their approach. Tales were surely being passed around.

"The castle will be your home until we finish this damned rebellion." The king said, as they reached the front battlements.

Rowena smiled to her father. She looked up to the castle, large for the size of the town. It was built for another king a hundred years earlier. The castle was grand, and certainly still fit for a king, even after all these years. Rowena had stayed in it once before when she was young, and the memories of its grandeur contrasted the current state as a military garrison. However, once inside, Rowena and her closest companions, found the castle to still be as hospitable and regal as it had ever been.

By the time that Rowena and her officers were settled within the castle, joined by Agota, the feast had been laid out. Each of the women took their places among the hall. Rowena, as the princess sat at the head table with her father and younger brother, Alfred.

"Sister, we've missed you these many years." Alfred said, as the dinner was being served. "Shame you couldn't have come home to visit at least once."

Rowena smirked to her younger brother. "Business has been going too well, I'm afraid. Of course, Adela was happy to take my correspondences Alfred. Although, I don't remember a letter coming from you."

Alfred, not one used to being spoken to in such a manner, did his best to let the dig slide. "Ah, cousin Adela. How is our banished and disfavored cousin getting on these days?"

"Well, she's an elder in East La~Porte, and her clinic is very successful." Rowena grinned, cutting her meat on her plate. "Father?" She said, turning to Charles. "I trust the queen is well?"

Charles stammered while trying to finish his mouthful. "Oh yes, yes. I'll tell her you've asked of her."

Rowena nodded, taking some bread and dipping it in the sauce served with the pork. "And your other ladies? They're doing well too, I hope?"

Charles stayed silent at first. "I suppose they are doing well too." The king said, finally.

Others had been looking on. If it had been anyone else to ask such a question, a head would have rolled. But it was Rowena, and that was the saving grace. For Rowena's part, she wanted to put Alfred in his place for perspective. He'd be an idiot to think that he only had two siblings. Rowena worldly, and having further details from court officials, knew better.

Rowena ended the night with her closest sisters in the spacious apartments of the castle.

"Playing it dangerously with the crown prince, aren't you?" Severa asked, as she was readying herself for bed. She combed her hair. Severa was one of the few sisters to keep it long. "Might be good to have him on our side one day."

"I'd rather be gone from here." Hadiza said. "Too cold, as was the welcome from this heir." She spread her blanket on her cot and laid down.

"That heir is my younger brother, and he is as spoiled as he is clever." Rowena smiled. "Colder than most. I'm sure he is cruel to his attendants, but he isn't our employer. The king is, so count us lucky for that."

She was lying on the bed, looking to her sisters. A few others occupied other rooms, and most were camped in the town, Rowena was joined by a select few in her apartment. Elva, Severa, Grainne, Agota, and Hadiza were in Rowena's chambers.

"He'll find war often when he is king, I'm sure." Grainne said. "Men like him invite it."

"Most men do." Hadiza said.

"Yes, they do." Severa concurred, sitting on her cot. "These nobles are either too aggressive or too passive. Never anything in the middle."

Rowena pondered that thought as she went to sleep.

The next morning, Rowena walked out on the balcony of the castle's tall watchtower. Her father was standing near the crenellations along the wall. He was wrapped in a wool blanket to protect from the cold air.

"There is breakfast in the great hall." Rowena said, catching her father's attention.

Charles looked back and smiled as she walked up next to him. He returned his gaze to the landscape beyond the castle.

"Our home is that way." Charles said, pointing to the north. "But before you get to Jovag, you'll reach the City of the Ancients."

Rowena knew of the place. It was the necropolis that housed their ancestors. All the dead kings, queens, and other royals going back to Theodorif I, the first king of Lotcala, were buried in large burial mounds in the City of the Ancients.

"The place we all end up." Charles continued. "My mound will pale compared to Theodorif's, even to my father's."

He sounded sorrowful at the prospect.

"Your tomb will be much greater than you think, father." Rowena reassured him.

Charles smiled. "No, I've seen nothing but rebellions in my time. My own reign has been squandered among banquets, war, and laziness."

Rowena placed her hand on her father's back. "You are too hard on yourself."

Charles shook his head. "Perhaps your tomb will be greater than all others."

Rowena grinned. The only way she'd have a tomb greater than a king's was to be a queen. A true queen, not a regent nor consort. She shook the thought from her head.

"I'll be happy to be given to the western winds, to return to the land of our fathers." Rowena said.

Charles looked down to his daughter. "Gotistan. *Lanid a oker furfedra.*".[7] He said in a soft voice, speaking the Lotcalan dialect, adapted from the Gota language. "When our people came to this land, they

---

[7] The land of our ancestors.

came not simply to conquer but to settle. We've succeeded in that task, but our old blood of war still pumps within us. This war could break us, bring out old blood feuds."

"You're the king." Rowena answered. "You're the one that can resolve such disputes. All the kings and chieftains of the past did so."

Charles nodded to her, accepting her counsel. "Come, let's eat our breakfast before the cooks yell at us for letting it get cold."

The breakfast meal went smoother than the dinner had the evening before. Mostly because the crown prince hadn't shown up. Rowena was happy for that. She loved her brother and would loyally fight for him, though she had little confidence in him as a commander. She also did not like his disdain for non-nobles, or those he felt weren't noble.

After breakfast, Rowena rode out with Elva, Grainne, King Charles, and several of his council. They rode close to the border with Antei, just a few miles south of Lowerfield. From that landscape, Rowena and her group could see the massive keep breaking through over the horizon.

"A new keep?" Rowena asked.

"Built up over the last decade." Sir Cullenhun replied.

Rowena pulled a spyglass from her side pouch. Others looked at her. She felt their glances.

"A little trinket I picked up from Caisa, in the eastern lands." Rowena said, holding the eye piece up. "Let's me see great distances. It works like how water spheres magnify things on paper for the sages. Just without water and instead uses glass."

Coldwood trotted his horse close by Rowena. "I've heard of such tools."

Rowena handed him the spyglass and the older lord peered through it.

"Magnificent!" Coldwood said. "I can see the town battlements and even the outlying farms as if they were only feet away!"

Other lords took their turns.

"We have to make these!" The king said when he looked through it. "Have the sages work on it right away!"

"Grainne?" Rowena smiled.

Her sister trotted up to the king and bowed her head.

"Your grace." Grainne said, presenting a spyglass to the king.

King Charles smiled and handed Rowena's back.

Rowena returned the smile and then turned back to overlooking the area.

As the council met on the coming plans, Rowena knew of the difficulties.

"It's a frozen ground of snow cover. A siege would be nearly impossible. They won't expect it, so that's our fallback plan." Rowena said.

The king had prepared a tent and table for the council to sit in. It was a comfort that Rowena wasn't used to in planning an attack. She knew Langley would be used to the same comforts, and that was something she'd use against him.

"We could use more of the lords' armies." Rowena said. "Still, we'd have to get Langley to leave his castle to beat him, else we'd be held up in Lowerfield for the season."

Coldwood looked to the princess. "The other lords won't commit their soldiers until the final thaw. Even then it's unlikely. Most will not let their forces be commanded by a dwarf. They feel it's beneath them."

Rowena rolled her eyes. "Typical. Nice to see that the kingdom hasn't changed too much while I've been away."

Elva cursed their lack of support and spat on the ground.

Coldwood turned to her. "Hardstone is sending a force, however." He turned back to Rowena. "Lady Catherine is leading them while Leif is in the north fending off orc and dwarf bandits."

Everyone knew that the winter was an active period of banditry in the Blue Mountains.

Rowena nodded. "We'll be happy to have her. Any idea of her numbers?"

Cullenhun answered that one. "Twenty-five hundred infantry and five hundred archers." Cullenhun smirked. "Most of the infantry are thought to be levy and conscripts."

Elva stood up. "All due respect Sir Cullenhun, but Hardstone levies are just as fierce as any regular from a baron."

"I have no doubt." Cullenhun said, putting his hands up to show defeat.

The planning went on further into the afternoon. None of the lords could agree on the best plan. All that they could agree on was that no one wanted to press a siege.

"We fought in the northern winter kingdoms over the last couple of years." Rowena said. "We can fight in snowy pitch battles. That's not a concern. What is concerning is bringing them from safety."

"We need a ploy to entice Langley." Grainne pointed out. "Is there something that we can offer?"

The king bristled. "He is seeking recognition for being an independent kingdom."

"What if we give him that recognition?" Rowena said.

"What?" The king sneered.

Rowena put her hand up to calm the atmosphere in the tent.

"A ruse to make him come out for the sake of diplomacy. Then we kill him."

"That's criminal." Lord Blacktower spoke up.

"Is it?" Rowena shot back. "He is trying to usurp a throne that doesn't exist. What claim does he have to make Antei a separate sovereign nation?"

Blacktower huffed. "Well, it is dishonorable."

"Just as well. He is a usurper." Cullenhun replied.

"So we kill him and cut the head off the snake. The rest will retreat?" Coldwood asked.

Rowena nodded. "That's the hope. We kill Langley, and his mercenaries should lose heart without their employer."

The king nodded. "Do it."

* * * * *

Early the next afternoon, Rowena, Coldwood, and Cullenhun rode out under the banner of truce. The trio made a fine entourage as they rode to meet with Langley. The usurper baron, for his part, was commendable as he rode to meet them. At his sides were several men at arms. One, his second in command.

"I see the king sent his two war dogs, and his forgotten bastard bitch to treat with me." Langley taunted.

"There isn't a need for that, Baron Langley." Coldwood replied with a sneer.

"King." Langley corrected.

"Not quite." Rowena smirked.

"If you've come to offer a white peace, then I accept and welcome you to get the hell off my land."

At her hip, concealed within the folds of her tunic and cloak, was a throwing knife. One that was light enough to fly at lightning speed, but strong enough to piece most padded clothes and even cheap chainmail.

Rowena discreetly slid her hand down her right side. She knew that there would only be one chance to successfully throw her blade. She gripped the short, thin handle. One toss with expert precision would sail the blade into Langley's uncovered throat. She gingerly held the blade. Just waiting for her target to give her the right opening. The two other knights with her were ready for the moment. Veterans of battle, they were calm and not letting any sign of the plan to show.

Langley turned to flash an arrogant grin at Rowena. She did not know why, nor did she care. It was her moment.

The sun's light gleamed for a split second as the sharpened metal weapon flew from Rowena's hand and directly into Langley's throat. The force of the knife pushed the man back. He didn't fall from his horse, but the beast reared up from the force of the projectile. Langley gurgled. Blood oozed from his mouth, his hands instinctively reaching for his neck, but the blade was too deep. His campaigns rushed to attack, but Coldwood and Cullenhun had been ready, and cut down two of Langley's soldiers.

The second in command of the Antei force cursed in Zaragozan.

"This will be the death of you!" He pointed. "Long live Edwin Langley II!" The man shouted before rushing off, turning back to the castle.

"A son?" Rowena asked.

* * * * *

"That was a fucking disaster!" Alfred yelled. "You made him a martyr!"

"To whom?" Rowena shot back. "A bunch of mercs?" She looked around the tent. Not everyone shared her younger brother's anger.

"We did right in killing Langley." Cullenhun said. "Who knew he had a son?"

"Must be an infant or we'd have heard of such a birth. He styled himself a king, and a son would have just made him more brazen in his claim." Coldwood added.

Rowena grabbed a pewter cup and poured herself some wine.

"Then we siege the keep, starve out the army and kill the son." She said after taking a sip.

"An infant?" Alfred questioned. His voice dripping with disgust.

"We can't leave any doubt of the true liege." Grainne pointed out. "And a pretender is a liability."

Grainne's father, Sir Cullenhun, shook his head. "Southern politics." He chastised.

"We'll make it quick." Rowena said. "Like in the south, a red cord around the neck."

It was a realization that everyone knew was the truth but not what anyone wanted to accept. The tent grew quiet until the king finally spoke.

"We have to hurry. Winter is setting deeper and soon the northern snows will engulf this barony." Charles pointed out.

Rowena nodded. "We'll set to work straight away. Black Hand's force will join us in the coming week. We'll be outnumbered, but we'll have something that the usurper doesn't have."

"What's that?" Alfred scoffed.

Rowena smirked. "Me, little brother. Me."

Grainne and Elva grinned.

Elva stood from her chair. "I'll get the girls to work digging us in."

Grainne also stood. "We'll need stores of supplies. Father, can you give me a hand with some requisitions?"

Sir Cullenhun nodded and then the three took their leave.

King Charles looked to his daughter and son. "Coldwood and I must return to the capital. Do what you can, but be careful."

"Easier said than done, father." Alfred replied with his arms crossed.

Charles looked at Rowena. "I'm trusting the future of this kingdom to you."

Rowena hugged her father. "Don't worry, I'll win this war."

"I mean Alfred. He is the future." Charles correct as the pair broke their hug.

Rowena felt stunned and a burning in her chest at the slight. "He'll be safe with me." She said in a soft voice.

Charles returned the hug. "I know."

Beginning of the End

or the next week, Alfred strutted around the camp as others were preparing for the siege. Rowena had her mind set on a quick siege. That wasn't disagreeable to Alfred, but he also wasn't one for sticking around while work was to be done.

Rowena, on the other hand, wasn't as averse to the labor of setting up a camp. She spent enough time in her younger days building camps, break them done after the campaign, and simply trudging through the worst conditions. All for the sake of victory, fame, and, of course, gold. That was what set her and her sisters apart from Alfred and the king's army. Even the baronial armies weren't of the same stock. Rowena and her Sisters were professional, hardened warriors. They fought in every terrain imaginable, fought for and against almost every culture on the planet, and against odds that would break weaker men and women. Setting up a camp on the hard, cold ground wasn't a chore. It was routine.

None of the preparation kept Rowena away from her other duties as the commander of the offensive. She stood atop a newly formed earthen mound to look over the land. She could see the keep in the distance, just over a two miles away, she reckoned. Between the keep and Rowena stood the city of Antei. A shell of its former glory, the city kept one thing from its past, its stone wall.

"We have seven mangonels that Queen Sakiko gifted us." Rowena said. "Set those as close as we can to the city walls. We need to bombard those walls. The gate is the strongest part."

"Then we move down toward the dockyard along the river." Grainne suggested.

Alfred walked up, hearing the conversation. "Of course we move to the river. We can use pontoons to make a flotilla."

"That'll take more time than the weather is going to give us." Elva said. "The mangonels and any covered ram can knock that part of the wall down in a matter of days."

Alfred sneered. While his plan would be good in the summer months, time wasn't on his side at the moment.

Grainne nodded. "I can give the order."

Rowena grinned. "No." She said. She turned her back to the city. "The gate is the strongest. We know that and they know that. It's reinforced with timbers and iron beams. Twelve-foot-thick at its thinnest point. Filled in with loose sand, rock, and timbers. That gate is the strongest part of that wall and the builders of the city made sure of that."

"Which is why we are going to the riverside." Alfred said.

"No. We mount our siege here, gate side." Rowena corrected.

Elva and the others looked confused. "Ye just said it was reinforced."

"The gate is. The wall connecting to it isn't. Four feet thick, and nothing to bolster it." Rowena walked back to the encampment. "We'll hit that wall. They'll think we're going for the gate or that we know nothing about tactics. Either way, the usurpers will underestimate us, and then we'll breach the city."

Elva stood with Grainne and Alfred. "She's going to win this war by supper."

Grainne laughed, but Alfred huffed before storming back to his tent.

"Piss-ant of a boy." Grainne whispered to Elva.

Within twelve hours, the mangonels were in place and being loaded. Scouts had ridden from the north, bringing news of Black Hand's force. It turned out that Gerald Blackhand was riding at the head of his eight thousand men-at-arms and knights. His arrival was expected within a day or two.

"Hedge knights?" Alfred scoffed. "No better than sellswords." He said while sitting with his personal entourage.

Rowena and her officers were also with him at the strategy table, set up with a map and pieces, showing the military movements.

"Mercenaries will often enough tip the scale, your highness." Rowena said. "I've counted and the barons only sent a few hundred men. The king's army is barely around four thousand." Rowena pointed to several wooden pieces on the map. "My force is sitting at thirteen hundred while Black Hand is bringing eight thousand. We sell swords make up the bulk of this army."

Alfred gave another of his so common sneers.

Grainne looked at the prince. "We should note that we are also fighting an army that is primarily mercenaries. Helps to understand the opponent."

Several of Alfred's group nodded. Not all of his men were as prejudiced as the prince. Some had been at the war academy with Rowena, Elva, and Grainne. All noble born since Alfred would accept nothing less.

Alfred feigned a smile and nodded. "Let's rest for the night. It's been a long day."

Rowena and her companions bowed and exited the tent. They did not oppose ending the meeting. They knew who'd be in charge on the field and they knew the plan down to the least important detail. That least important detail was still a detail worth practicing a thousand times.

Rowena looked to Elva and Grainne. "I wish Liam was here." She sighed. "He was always my favorite."

Her friends laughed. "Too bad he isn't the crown prince."

"It is too bad. He'd make a better king than Alfred. Liam always enjoyed being among the people. Not stuffed up in a castle with attendants or yes men." Rowena replied.

The three walked to their tent.

"So when Black Hand comes, Grainne and I will have to shack up elsewhere?" Elva grinned. She sat on her cot. "Let ye and he have some time to catch up?"

"Damn right." Rowena said, laying down on her bed roll. "I've been missing him."

Grainne was removing her coat. Throwing it on her cot, she walked to the middle of the tent where the heating stove was. She knelt down and put a few more sticks in to add to the warmth.

"Will you tell him about Queen Sakiko?" Grainne asked before standing up and walking back to her cot.

Rowena smirked, looking up to the roof of the tent. "Probably. He gets it. We both do." She rolled over to face her friends. "Let's be honest, he's a damn handsome man and probably has had many lovers over time. Maybe a bastard or two. I'm surprised I don't have a wee one myself."

"Ye never really took many men for lovers." Elva said.

"Neither did you." Grainne pointed out.

"And ye-self?"

"I'm not much for sex or love. When I decide it's the right time, I'll have a child with a good man, but this idea of courtly love doesn't fill me with any more emotions than paying my taxes to some higher born baron." Grainne replied. "I just don't have that sexual desire that many of our sisters do."

"Fair enough." Elva responded. "Back to ye, lass, and Black Hand." She said, looking back at Rowena.

Rowena grinned. "He is different. I feel different when I'm with him. Creator willing, if I ever have a permanent home, I'd want him there with me."

The trio continued talking into the night before falling asleep in the early morning hours.

As the sun rose, a cloud of dust rose from the north.

"Black Hand." Rowena smiled, looking to the north. She turned to her officers, again all atop the earthen ridge surrounding the city. "Launch the attack." She said.

Elva looked out over the army below the ridge. "Fire the mangonels!" she yelled.

Hours passed as the mangonels shot large rocks, some covered in oil and lit aflame, toward the city walls. At that time, the soldiers representing the Company entered the encampment, bringing five covered rams with them. As expected, at the head, atop a black horse, was Gerald Blackhand.

He dismounted and walked towards Rowena before embracing her. Rowena and Black Hand shared a kiss and, as they parted, each smiled.

"I've missed you." Black Hand said.

"And I you." Rowena smiled. She looked at her lover and gingerly touched his face. He had a recent scar on his left cheek, close to his eye.

"A present from a Hun warrior." He said, clasping Rowena's hand. "Nothing worth telling."

"I'd say fighting Huns is a story worthy of a campfire." Elva said from behind Rowena.

"Then later tonight, Elva." Black Hand grinned. "It is good to see you and Grainne as well."

Grainne nodded. "Gerald." She looked at many of the warriors filling the camp. "You brought plenty of help."

Behind Black Hand were his warriors. Clad in lamellar or ring mail, bearing large axes, kite shields and or spears. Most have conical helms with face plates. All looked hardened and fierce.

"Northern huscarls mostly. Heavily armed warriors that prefer two handed axes to swords. The Sile Empire has been inviting many Gota and Eire warriors as guards and regular soldiers. I figured it might work for me, too. I have western hedge knights too. More traditional fighters." Black Hand said.

"Happy to have experienced fighters on our side." Rowena grinned.

"Fill me in on the plan?" Black Hand said, looking back at Rowena.

The pair discussed the ongoing siege, already in motion, while sharing some mulled wine.

"Had I known these were Zaragozans, I would have brought more men." Black Hand said, sipping his wine. "Or more gold."

"I don't think we'd be able to buy these off." Rowena responded. She poured another cup for herself. "They are fighting for a lord, the son of the previous duly installed baron."

"So, the kid has the proper claim?"

Rowena nodded. "For the barony, yes, not as a king."

"Did anyone ask if the kid would renounce his claim?" Black Hand thought for a moment. "Or if his mother would do it for him, given the kid's infancy."

Rowena shook her head. "That wasn't an option. I killed Langley and then they pronounced the son king."

"And your father wants him out of the way." Black Hand finished. "Clean and simple."

"As it all should be." Rowena smiled. "I plan to take this barony for myself, as payment. I'm already speaking to the lords about it. Coldwood and Cullenhun seem to be supportive. I would be the rightful baroness but, you know, I'd need a baron. This is still a kingdom run by the men."

"You mean to make an honest man out of me?" Black Hand smirked.

Rowena chuckled.

"You don't need a man to rule at your side. You certainly don't need me to help you rule. You're all that you or any realm needs." Black Hand continued.

"Thank you, but here in Lotcala, that isn't the way."

Black Hand looked into Rowena's eyes, clasping her hand. His face grew grim. "Then make it the way. Don't let this place suffer because they can't see your greatness."

The next morning, Elva and Severa were waiting for the pair to emerge from the tent. The sun was just beginning to crest over the eastern horizon.

"Ye think they plan on joining the war today?" Elva asked.

Severa grinned. "She hasn't seen him in over a year. Maybe we should give them more time to get reacquainted." She sighed. "We know the plan well enough."

"That wall is breaking today." Grainne said, walking up to the pair, eating a hardtack cracker. "She still in there with Gerald?"

Severa looked at the older sister. "You never call him anything but Gerald."

"That's his name."

Elva looked over. "Everyone else calls him Black Hand."

"I'm not everyone else." Grainne said, taking a bite from her hardtack.

Just then, Rowena and Black Hand emerged from the tent. Rowena fixed her chainmail with surcoat over her gambeson. The surcoat was embroidered with both the Rowena's black stag and the Lotcalan brown stag. She held a nasal helm at her side. Black Hand was dressed in a northern hauberk mail and already had his helm on.

"Yer not wearing yer new armor from Queen Sakiko?" Elva asked, raising an eyebrow.

Rowena shook her head. "I'm representing the king here, so I figured I'd wear his sigil." She explained. "Are we ready to storm the city?" Rowena asked, putting her helm on.

"Shortly." Grainne replied. "The walls are in a sorry state. However, that keep will be an issue. They built it with loose stone and a sand mud mortar mixture. The mortar can melt away and soften. Hitting it hard enough and we'll bring it down."

"We don't have to bring the entire keep down, just bring the occupiers out." Black Hand said.

"We might have a few sisters that can help with that." Severa pointed out. "The orc mages having been working on some fire spells. I've seen them liquefy some smaller stones."

Black Hand's eyes grew. "That would turn the tide of many battles."

"It's not a simple task, but they can try it. At least work on something that could make it too hot for those inside." Severa continued.

"I've also been working on something that might help." Grainne said. "Something I found in an old scroll from the desert kingdoms. A mineral compound that makes a fire that burns five times as hot as a forge fire and water won't put it out." She looked around. "We have all the ingredients locally, but we'd need to be careful. It's said to be highly unstable."

Rowena nodded. "Get the orcs ready and look for whatever you need, Grainne. However, right now, let's get the wall out of our way and the city subdued. Then we'll take the keep."

A rider approached. It was one of Rowena's scouts, a Quarmi named Nanami.

"Troops approach from the north. Bearing a standard of a brown bear on a green and blue field." The Quarmi scout reported.

The sisters smiled.

"Lady Catherine!" Elva exclaimed.

A short time later, Lady Catherine arrived in the encampment. Hardstone soldiers followed her. Most were conscripts with lighter armor and weapons, but their numbers would make up for their lack of professionalism.

"Ye lass have things underway, I see." The Hardstone lord said, walking up to Rowena and Elva. "Those years fighting have taught ye all well." She said, looking over the landscape.

Below them, the ground was being torn apart by the siege. Boulders being thrown from large mangonels, fires fueled by pitch and burning tar covered hay, and the remnants of farms spread out before the Lotcalan army.

"This will be a hell of a place once it's over." Catherine said. "Such a shame."

"It has to be done." Rowena replied.

"Aye." The elder woman turned and motioned for her soldiers to begin their own work. "Me warriors are here to do whatever ye be needing, princess. Just put them to use."

"And where will you post up?" Rowena asked, looking up at Catherine.

"I'll be sticking near you. I plan to do some fighting before I had back up to Hollerton."

Lady Catherine was always eager for a fight. Most Hardstones were, and she had eagerly volunteered to lead the Hardstone warriors south, not a usual task for the mountain folk.

Most Hardstones liked to stay in the northern reaches, where there were always bandits to fight. Often, they'd be asked to venture south to fight in baronial conflicts. However, the south was a different country culturally, and that didn't always sit well with the Hardstones. Still, for Rowena, every Hardstone was happy to send a force to fight for their favorite royal.

Suddenly, a loud crash sounded. All of those along the earthen ridge line turned toward the city. The noise was loud enough that Alfred came out from his tent to see what the sound was. They all saw the same thing, and a jolt of excitement rushed over everyone.

The wall surrounding the city of Antei was broken and burst open with a dramatic crash, leaving an opening large enough for warriors to rush through.

"Send in the vanguard under Hadiza. I want her carrying our banner." Rowena ordered.

The Fall of Antei

he thousands of soldiers all fighting in the king's name rushed toward the city. Many hundreds had already burst into the city through the newly created opening. Others were running, trying to get there as fast as they could.

The fighting was fierce as the Lotcalan army reached the city walls. The Zaragozan force was reinforced with armed citizens and others from the surrounding areas. Fodder and shields. Still, standing against the king's army was a crime punishable by death. Lotcalan warriors surged in through the breach, storming the gatehouse. A wise tactic used in many battles of the past.

Rowena sent out the order to take the gatehouse, and open it, allowing more warriors to pour through. Most of the opposing mercenaries fell back toward the massive keep. Just beyond that keep was the second wall protecting them from the sieging force. That left the citizens of the city to fend for themselves. Rowena's force had little trouble against untrained farmers and merchants fighting for Langley.

"These are our own countrymen." Alfred said to Rowena.

The two rode into the battle scene together, followed by their retainers.

"My sisters know that if the townspeople surrender, then we'll show them mercy." Rowena responded. "However, if they attack us, we have to defend ourselves."

Alfred accepted the answer. There wasn't much he could say, after all. Rowena held the command even though he was the crown prince. The king had made it clear it was her army to command. The one positive spin for Alfred, the only positive spin, was that it was her battle to lose as well. Alfred ordered his men at arms to follow Rowena's. Rowena knew that, if nothing else, Alfred would feign support for her.

Rowena saw her force charge through the city. A great satisfaction rose through her seeing the well-trained army dispatch, even the hardest of Zaragozans, with little trouble.

Hadiza did her job in leading troops. Most of Rowena's force was armed with spears, swords, and kite shields. Standard of the time. All wore chainmail hauberks or chainmail shirts with gambesons over the mail. Hadiza rode on a black mare, Rowena's black stag embroidered on flag attached to a lance. She shouted orders, leading troops further into the city.

The fighting was desperate for the defenders. Many using axes or hand-me-down swords. Others with spears. Most without armor apart from padded heavy cloth. Her soldiers made quick work of the opposition. Most were simply cut down or impaled with spears.

"This is madness. A massacre," Hadiza shouted, her face burning red and crumpled in anger as she rode beside Severa. The Lotcalan woman shook her head.

"They've turned their back on the king. They can run or stay away from the fight." Severa replied.

Hadiza stayed quiet, watching the violent scene unfold. She sighed in frustration.

"This is not honorable." Hadiza commented. She looked to Severa. "Take half the force and make for the western approach of the palisade. We need to work on the outer battlements of the keep." She pointed to the area with her lance.

Severa saluted and signaled for the force to split in half and follow her.

Atop the ridgeline, Rowena watched with her brother as the fight progressed.

"Even the baronial force that Coldwood and Cullenhun left us is keeping up with my sisters. Rowena turned to see Alfred's grimace. "Having trouble watching the battle?"

Her brother rode well in tournaments, fought in mock battles more times than he could count. However, this was different. Here he was amid the battle, seeing bodies falling along the ground. This was a mock battle. This was war and people were dying.

"I never knew it would be such a... it's bloody and chaotic." Alfred stammered.

Rowena smirked. "Spending too much time in court and you'll never get used to this. This is the life we lead to protect our family's throne. People will always want to test their limits of our power, of what we will tolerate. It is our job as the royal family to enforce the order and to keep everyone in line. No matter the cost."

She left nothing for Alfred to interpret differently. Rowena was stern in her lesson. She wanted her brother to understand that rebels were nothing more than criminals.

Alfred nodded. Rowena accepted his response and snapped her horse's reins. She rode forward, drawing her sword to be ready in case of an attack.

However, the bulk of the fighting was moving closer to the keep. Most of the city was under Rowena's control by the time the sun passed its zenith. The mangonels were positioned closer to the keep, trying to break through the outer façade. Rowena's and the Hardstone mages cast as many fire spells on the fortress as they could send. Some worked with the boulders being fired from the siege engines. Sending flames rocks hurtling at great speeds, crashing into ramparts or crowds of defenders.

Those defenders, staunch in their fight, shot arrow after arrow down to the Lotcalan army. Severa led charges for Rowena's force. The outer palisades, defended by hearty Zaragozan fighters, were proving to be more difficult than the town had been. Severa was an experienced commander, however, and she led with bravery.

"Break through to the right flank!" Severa ordered. Her spear raised in her right hand, and a kite shield in her left. "We'll burst through this time or the next." She grinned.

Severa watched her force and Lady Catherine's army follow the order. She was proud of their resolve, and for a moment, she lost sight of the battle. A brief moment was all it took. Severa lowered her shield just a few inches. An arrow from the keep's battlements found Severa's barely exposed neck. The famed commander fell. Three of her attendants witnessed the shot and covered her with their shields. One urging the attack onward.

"Take her to the back. She needs a healer." One attendant said.

"Too late girls." Severa spurt out. Blood mixing with her words. "Leave me on the field and fight on." The arrow was still protruding from her neck as blood flowed from the wound.

"Nay, my lady." The attendant said. "We have to get you to the healers."

Her loyal soldiers carried Severa back a safe distance to where Rowena, Alfred, and Grainne were standing, watching the battle.

"Severa!" Grainne yelled.

Grainne knelt down next to her friend.

"Lay still." Grainne said.

Rowena called for a healer before kneeling next to her as well. Agota dropped across from Rowena, beside her friend.

"No time, captain." Severa whispered. "I have to get back to the fight. We've almost got this battle won." Blood poured out of her neck. Severa's face was turning pale. "Just a moment, maybe, is all I need."

"Rest here." Rowena said. She cupped her friend's head and cradled her close, trying to keep some pressure on the wound. Grainne knelt next to Rowena.

Alfred was standing in shock, hovering over the scene.

"Give me water!" Rowena roared to an attendant.

Severa tried to laugh. "It's just a flesh wound."

Rowena and Grainne both tried to smile.

Severa looked up at Alfred. She noted the terrified look on his face.

"What's the matter, boy? Ain't you ever see a warrior die before?" Severa coughed, spurting more blood from her mouth and nose. She looked at Rowena. "It's a hell of a thing. Ro, tell my father I died for the king, I died for the kingdom we..." Her voice trailed off as her final breath eased out of her lungs.

Rowena placed her hands on Severa's eyes and gently closed them.

Rowena lowered her friend softly to the ground. Standing up, Rowena's eyes burned in anger.

"Find that archer. I'll have his head before nightfall." Rowena said to the attendants.

Alfred tried to stammer something, but his face turned as pale as Severa's. Rowena and Grainne looked at him.

"What's with you?" Grainne asked.

"I... I... got to leave. Retreat!" Alfred called out.

He rushed to his horse, mounting the steed. He turned the beast around and rushed toward his men. Urging them to follow him in a retreat, many did.

Elva ran up, after hearing the news of Severa, just in time to see the prince beat a retreat.

"Where the fuck is he heading?" Elva asked.

"The coward is bolting back to the encampment or further." Grainne answered, still looking at Alfred riding away with his men.

Rowena turned toward the keep. "Send in everything we have to the castle and bring it down. Fire, stone, anything that will topple it. I want every stone torn from that keep."

Grainne and Elva saluted their captain and rushed off to follow the order. Rowena stood next to Severa's body and watched as more of her force pushed toward the castle. The army gathered and charged again. This time, the mangonels threw more boulders, flaming with pitch and tar. The orc mages, along with other spellcasters, hurled as much fire as they could muster. On the western approach of the keep, Black

Hand's battering rams pounded the battlements. The ground shook from the force of each pounding boulder and slam from the siege.

Further back, Rowena watched. Her sneer left little to wonder of her intention. The keep was crumbling and if she had her way, nothing or no one would be left alive within. Behind her, the city of Antei burned, revenge for turning against her father. Though it wasn't the decision of the barony, the baron's choices would fall upon the land's head.

She had forgotten her brother's cowardice. She only thought to the sisters she'd lost, the memories of their years together. All in some attempt to prove something deeper. Rowena never turned her gaze from the keep, bombarded from multiple sides by the strongest siege engines that she could bring. Walls and battlements toppled to the ground, along with any warriors unfortunate enough to be present.

Rowena grinned as the mighty keep, poorly built as a sign of Langley's power, fell to the ground in a mound of rubble and fire. She would show little mercy to traitors, nor would she let up on her attack. There was a baron within that had to be removed. In a swift maneuver, the battle and the rebels would see the end with the crumbing keep.

Scorned

ntei was destroyed. The barony was in ruins and all that was left of the baron's former estate was the ancestral home of the Goldwater family. A manor house on the motte. The people were left in shambles but alive.

As for Charles, Sirie, and Alfred, they were celebrating the victory in the king's hall, his throne room. All but one member of the family. Princess Rowena was missing from the festivities that included many noble families. However, that was to be corrected shortly.

Rowena was still in Antei, ensuring the victory that her brother, Alfred, had failed to accomplish, and she had been excluded from the celebration. Alfred was awarded the barony, given his tale that he had commanded the siege to great effectiveness. His flight from the battle, and then the ensuing news of the victory, allowed him to reach the king first. Alfred's lies and timing were beneficial for him but a curse for Rowena.

Word reached Rowena two weeks after the battle, after her brother fled north to Jovag, of his appointment to Baron of Antei.

Rowena rushed to the capital with several of her closest friends and officers. Once at the palace, she stormed into the throne room during the first official court being held for the peaceful kingdom. She passed lords and ladies congratulating her younger brother Alfred sneering at each.

"I should be Baroness of Antei!" She roared to the king, sitting upon the throne.

Charles looked up and everyone in the room turned to regard her. Rowena's eyes were a blaze with anger and pain.

"You?" A voice came from behind Rowena.

The princess turned to see Queen Sirie walking towards her.

"My son won the battle. Why would you assume you'd take the baronial title?"

"He ran after he failed to take the keep. My company and I took that damned keep and clasped Goldwater's widow in chains and did away with the child." Rowena said, turning to the queen, and motioning to her brother. "He fled at the first sign of resistance. I won that battle."

By now, her company officers had made their way into the throne room. Among them, Elva came to stand with her friend.

"Funny, that's not what Alfred said. He said you and your company failed to take the town and he was forced to fight his way through the baronial army to take the keep." Sirie replied. "He said you were killing innocent people." Sirie smirked. "That's a criminal offence punished by death."

"He didn't even make it to the keep before he turned and ran." Rowena smirked. "He was a coward." Rowena scoffed. "We only killed those that attacked us. Your son could barely hold his stomach. He isn't made for war. You made him too soft!"

"How dare you!" Sirie shouted.

"I've never run from a battle. I've fought in many battles and all victories." Alfred boasted.

"Others won those battles for you!" Rowena countered. "Me or another competent general, while you take all the credit."

Elva stepped forward and knelt before the king. "Beggin' yer majesties' pardon, but Princess Rowena speaks the truth. I was there with her. I saw her fighting. I fought alongside her. I, and me sisters, we saw the prince take his army and flee."

"Lies!" Alfred cried out. "She is lying for her friend. They want to usurp my place! Criminals after my crown!"

The crowd gasped at the accusation.

"Your crown?" Charles finally spoke up. "I'm not dead yet, boy." Charles rose from his throne. His knee strained from the pain of a long ago battle. "You'll get this crown when I say you can have it, and that's when I'm cold and buried."

"Father, I only mean..."

"I know what you mean, and you fear her." Charles said, cutting his son off. He pointed to Rowena. "You're scared that she'll be a better monarch than you, since she's a better warrior. She's my daughter, after all, so you are right, she would be a damn good ruler."

Rowena approached her father. "I only wish to have what is entitled by my birth. I'm your firstborn. I've never asked for it, but I know I've earned the right to be your heir."

Charles looked at his daughter with tears welling in his eyes. "I can't."

"You can, no one else can but you, father." Rowena said, almost in a plea. "I should be your successor."

"See! See, she wants the crown." Sirie shouted.

"Of course, I do! I'm the firstborn, and it is my right by the laws of our Gota heritage." Rowena answered, turning to Sirie. "I've fought and bled for this kingdom. I've never asked for more than to survive. I never sought the crown, but after this war, that changes. It is my right by birth and honor!"

"Honor? You're nothing but a killer." Alfred said.

"If I wasn't a killer, then an assassin would have murdered our father, the king, years ago!" Princess Rowena reminded the court. "Yes, I'm a killer, and I'm also the rightful successor as the first born."

"You're a whore's daughter and lucky to have what we have given you." Sirie countered.

Some lords and ladies in the hall nodded softly, trying not to be noticeable to the king. Others, more than a few, murmured disapprovingly at the queen's words. Sirie looked around and scowled.

"I trained you to be what you are, and this is how you repay me?" The queen said, angrily. "Guards, take her and Elva away!"

Several guards moved in as Rowena and Elva drew their swords. The members of the court from Hardstone also drew their weapons and stood near Rowena and Elva.

"Stop!" The king yelled. "You will not touch my daughter or Lady Elva! Get back! Get back now!"

The guards did as ordered by their king.

Charles glowered at Sirie. "I've given you leave to say more than you should concerning Rowena, but you'll do well to remember that this is my kingdom."

Sirie curtsied to her husband. "As you wish."

Charles turned to his daughter. "I can't make you my successor, but you have my love. I will make a new title for you and any children you have." Charles pleaded with his daughter. "I'll make you a gentry lady, within the barony you fought to take. It will take some time and if you're found innocent of the charge of killing innocents. Of course, the lords will have to agree to it, you being a dwarf."

Rowena scoffed. "I'm no murderer and my blood is just as royal as yours. Father, I am destined to be queen or nothing."

Charles walked down from the dais to his daughter and clasped her hands. "I can't."

Rowena stifled her tears. "You can, you're the king."

"I won't." Charles replied. "I won't put a half human woman before my son. It would not be proper for a dwarf to come before a human."

Rowena pulled her hands from her father's. Her pain was masked by a burning rage. "Then I must go. Lotcala is no longer my home. Not until I'm sitting upon that throne." Rowena motioned for her officers to follow her as she walked out.

"You can't expect me to just name you heir." Charles said. "You're a bastard. I love you, but make no mistake, that's what you are. No one can fault me there, not even you. You'll see when you are calm. And then we can deal with the allegations of you murdering innocent citizens. It was war, after all." Charles said with a slight shrug.

Rowena ignored his insult. "It was war. It is war." Rowena whispered to herself. She turned and looked at her father. "You were wrong all those years ago, father."

Charles looked at Rowena, confused.

"You said that sometimes, the cause of something isn't what's important. Only the outcome." Rowena sneered. "No, the cause of this rift is just as important." She pointed to her father. "You stole from me my birthright over your own cowardice. You let her taint my childhood and placed weaker men before me. Now you insult me to my face with lies and talk of my heritage being less than Alfred's." Rowena roared. "Remember, you caused this and everything that will happen here on out is on your head. This kingdom's blood, until this wrong is corrected, will be on your hands. No amount of water will wash it away. History will remember me as a warrior, but you'll be the man that drowned this kingdom in a sea of blood." Rowena turned and left the hall, ripping the royal sigil from her cloak.

Outside, her officers were mounting their horses alongside the Hardstone barony members.

"Where to?" Grainne asked Rowena as she was mounting her horse.

"Antei." Rowena replied, coldly. "We have something to finish." See looked at the others. "Leave now if you don't have the stomach for it, but I will show this kingdom how I deal with betrayal, starting with a barony of traitors."

The others alongside nodded, and some even grinned. Rowena kicked at her horse and they rode off to the south.

* * * * *

A force of five thousand and seven hundred trained warriors were still camped outside of Antei. Others, prisoners from the Zaragozan mercenaries, were sitting in chains awaiting their fates. Rowena rode her horse hard, making the trip that would take a week normally in a matter of four days. She had to reach the barony before the news of Alfred's accession.

Lotcalan law of accession was much like the old Gota traditions. The eldest son inherits the bulk of the lands. Often fathers would give smaller portions to younger children so they'd have something when the eldest came to rule. However, that wasn't always the case. Rowena originally hoped, more accurately, she'd pray that her father would grant her something for her loyalty. A barony for her role in securing his kingdom, her brother's future. That was all that she'd asked for. Rowena was sure her father would grant such a boon. She was wrong, and now she was going to make everyone else pay for it.

Rowena and her entourage rode up to the gates of Antei. The siege camp was still operating as a headquarters. Black Hand and Hadiza approached.

"How did it go with the king?" Black Hand asked.

The grim look on everyone's faces gave away the answer. Rowena dismounted, but never looked at the two. She simply walked to a water bucket so she could quench her thirst and ease her parched throat.

"The king said that Alfred is the lord of this land. They've branded Rowena a criminal for killing the townspeople." Hadiza asked. "This is the soil that we buried our sister in. It is land we fought for!"

Rowena turned to regard Hadiza. "We will have this barony, and I'll have my father's throne." She said, angrily.

Black Hand and Hadiza stood in shock.

"The throne?" Black Hand spoke up after a moment. "That wasn't the plan."

"The plan has changed." Elva said, walking up to the group.

Others joined her, some to be involved in the conversation. Others for water.

From their left, Lady Catherine walked over. She had noticed Rowena arrive, but she hadn't heard the conversation.

"What's the word from the capital, lass?" Catherine asked.

Black Hand turned to her and shook his head.

"They denied Rowena the right of conquest." Grainne said. She took the cup from the water bucket and drank deeply. "We rushed back as fast as we could ride." She gasped. "I've never pushed a horse so hard."

Lady Catherine spit on the ground. "That's a sacred right from our oldest traditions! No one has earned this barony more than ye, lass."

"Thank you, my lady." Rowena said. "I'd appreciate your help in the coming days."

Catherine gave Rowena a confused look. "What are ye planning?"

Elva stepped up beside Rowena. "First, we'll conquer this barony and rip it from Alfred. Then we're taking the throne of Lotcala for Rowena as the heir." She said. "It's her right as first born."

Catherine scoffed. "If only ye'd been born a Hardstone or yer da' was one. We'd hold no legitimacy over ye." The older woman clasped a firm hand on Rowena's shoulder. "I cannae raise a hand against yer father. It's not the way of Hardstone to fight the king. Even in their most terrible, we are his vassals. However, yer his daughter and I love ye as kin. I will allow you the use of my warriors. If ye need a place to rest, then Hollerton welcomes ye."

Rowena smiled and nodded. "I thank you, my lady."

Lady Catherine bowed and excused herself from the camp.

Rowena stepped back and looked to Black Hand. "How many men can you spare me?"

Black Hand was less enthusiastic. "This can't be a company endorsed action." He said.

Rowena's eyes narrowed. "How many?" She said. "My love, this has to be done." Softening her tone.

Black Hand sighed deeply. "I know. I have to leave and return to Aran. Plausible deniability." He grinned sheepishly. "I'll leave all but fifty warriors. Transferring their contracts to you is simple enough, and if you wait until I can reach Elysia or Panyakuta to declare war, then I can feign some diplomatic response."

Rowena touched his hand and whispered a quick thank you to him.

"Hadiza, tell me how our prisoners are doing." Rowena said, returning to her sisters.

"They're being carried for. Thinking of adding some to our ranks?"

Rowena smiled at Hadiza. "How many are there?"

"Nearly six thousand." Hadiza said.

"We'd double in size." Grainne pointed out. "Still outnumbered, without support from any barons."

"That's if the barons enter the war." Rowena replied.

The rest of the day and evening went by quickly. Lady Catherine and Black Hand both rode out with very small entourages, leaving the promised forces. Rowena appealed to as many of the Zaragozan mercenaries that would hire on. Most did. The others were moved away in chains. Rowena's only idea for them was to use them later on.

As for the town's people, Rowena had a plan already in motion. Antei was stripped clean of any valuables. Gold, silver, copper, iron, and steel were all taken. Weapons, food, animals, anything that could be sold for more gold or used to fuel the army. Elders and representatives to the crown were beheaded, their heads placed on pikes outside the city gates.

"Impale the prisoners that refused to join us." Rowena order.

Grainne and Elva both hesitated at the order.

"Captain?" Hadiza spoke up. "That's never been our way."

Rowena looked at the woman. "You're right." Then she walked away. They all knew that leaving bodies strewn across the landscape would show the king that she would not go silently. There was nothing more for her to say.

"Is killing fellow mercenaries the right choice, though?" Grainne asked. "I understand the choice for the leaders, like the mayor and bailiff. But some of those mercenaries are friends with ones we just hired."

"Grainne is right. It could cause a mutiny." Hadiza continued.

"Any other ideas? Taking them with us will be a burden on our supplies." Rowena replied.

"Then leave them here." Elva answered.

"Leave them?"

Elva nodded. "Leave them to fend for themselves. The mercenaries will know justice, might even get a few more for our cause. Antei will see the price for siding against us, and the king will have more than just used to worry about."

"It could cause banditry, which we could use as a distraction. A short term advantage for us." Grainne agreed.

Rowena smiled. "Then do it. Let us make those preparations and leave this waste of a city. I want to raze Estan before month's end."

* * * * *

Hadiza walked up to Rowena two days later. Her look told Rowena that she carried ill-fated news.

"Captain, the kingdom is refusing to pay for the campaign." Hadiza motioned to two men at arms that had come on behalf of the new baron, Alfred. "They say that since Alfred won the battle, he will claim the price."

"It doesn't work that way. Not even if he had stayed to see the end of the battle." Rowena answered. Her anger was growing. "Tell them that his highness will pay what was promised."

Hadiza walked back over and after a few moments of shouting, the two men brushed her off and walked up to Rowena.

"You are a cutthroat and nothing more!" One said. "Our lord refuses to deal with criminals who slaughter innocents like you did!"

"Innocents? Those traitors? I only did as the king, my father, commanded." Rowena replied sternly. "Alfred has no claim to what they owe to my sisters and I. Yet, he refuses me and insults me for winning this barony for him. He was a coward during the battle and a coward now to refuse to face me!"

"How dare you! Dwarven swine!"

The first man at arms reared his hand back as if to slap Rowena. However, she was faster with her blade. The man's hand dropped in a bloody mess onto the frozen ground. The man dropped to his knees. Rowena sheathed her knife. The other man at arms looked on in disbelief, watching his friend wail in agony.

Rowena stood in front of the crying man. She pulled her war ax from her belt and plunged it into the man's skull, splitting it in two and silencing him.

"Kill the other and send Alfred their heads back." Rowena said, looking at her fellow mercenaries. "Place a note with them." She pulled her ax out of the first man.

"What should it say?" Hadiza asked.

"With love, Princess Rowena." Rowena said.

Her bitter voice left a chill with her sisters, but they knew their leader. They trusted her. That is why they did exactly as they were told. Drawing straws to see which two sisters would take the heads to the capital, knowing they would likely be executed for it.

"Prepare the army. We'll raze this city and then move to Lowerfield." Rowena ordered, mounting her horse. "Creator willing, Estan after that."

After going through and convincing many of the Zaragozan mercenaries to join Rowena's cause, she mounted an offensive against the city of Antei.

"This is my brother's seat. His throne?" Rowena said, overlooking the city. "Let it be his cemetery." She finished before turning her horse. She looked over at Elva. "This will be bad if we don't force the king's hand."

"I know." Elva replied.

"Grainne has promised to see this through, knowing what it could do to her family. She thought about staying behind, returning to her father's estate. However, she is going to ride it out with us. For that, I am grateful. I hate to make any of you choose. You don't have to go along with me. You don't have to suffer if I fail." Rowena added.

"No, I don't, but I will. Yer my sister, not just because we grew up together, but because ye have bled with me. I'd die for you, and I know ye would for me." Elva responded. "If ye find yerself in front of the gates of the underworld, waiting for judgement from Wohd, know that I'd be right next to ye. Nothing will cause me to leave yer side."

Rowena smiled, her eyes watered. Throughout their youth, the pair had been through everything the world could throw. Now, in Rowena's greatest hour of need, Elva was unflinching in her loyalty to her sister.

Rowena gave Elva a nod before the pair rode off to lead their army.

What lay ahead of the army, now totaling nearly nine thousand, was a kingdom that was ripe for plunder. Rowena wasn't as interested in just taking Antei. That ship had sailed. Rowena was about to make Antei an example. Her goal was to claim the inheritance of the kingdom.

Rowena and Elva caught up to Grainne a short while later as the army marched north. Lowerfield wasn't a great distance away, and with no outer wall surrounding the city, it would be an easy battle. However, the goal in Lowerfield was to plunder the winter stores and supply Rowena's army for another month or two.

The plan was as simple as any other that Rowena could organize. Raid the towns held by her father, brother, and stepmother. Leave the other baronies alone unless they attack first. Hardstone, she knew, would stay out of the fight. Rowena also counted several gentry and manor families that would remain neutral or maybe even join her. She never dreamed of leading an attack on her father's lands, so she never thought of gathering allies in greater numbers. She had only ever remained close to the Hardstones. The Coldwood family also held her in high regard, but she knew that the best she could hope for with them was neutrality.

Winter was a tough time to march an army, therefore the priority was to keep supplies well stocked. It was even harder with a full supply train. Elva was assigned to the rearguard. The army had to be protected, therefore it had to keep moving. It was the only plan, but not the best plan. However, holding out in a keep or barony would not allow Rowena and her force the ability to restock. She had to stay on the move.

Lowerfield proved to be nothing more than a minor skirmish when Rowena's army finished with it. The keep was well provisioned, and many of the king's valuables were left inside from his recent visit. Rowena ordered the keep to remain standing. Thinking of the pressing time but also needing lands in the future.

Grainne walked through their camp on evening, passing campfires, blinding her to the darkness. She made her way to Rowena's tent. There the princess had set up a makeshift court, already calling herself Queen Rowena.

"Your grace." Grainne said as she entered.

Rowena scoffed. "That will take some getting used to."

"You wanted it." Grainne replied. She poured herself a goblet of wine. "This will take the chill away." She said before sipping. "Is there a new destination? Jovag?"

Rowena looked at a map. "No. Pern."

"Pern?" Grainne asked. "Ironhand holds Pern."

"Yes, they do, and they've been called to fight against us." She handed Grainne a rolled up scroll.

"Accepting the honor of fighting. Will attack the southern flank." Grainne read aloud. "Then we turn and attack Pern. Reasonable. We'd never be able to siege Jovag."

"Not yet." Rowena countered.

"Is Elva safe?" Grainne asked, thinking to her friend, who was riding in the rear column.

"I hope so." Rowena said.

Her voice was soft, and Grainne recognized the compassion that was for her friend.

"She'll be here soon." Grainne replied before hugging Rowena.

* * * * *

Along the rearguard of Rowena's army, Elva marched slower to give the bulk of the force a chance to move on to a more secure area. She knew that the Ironhand family was fiercely loyal to Queen Sirie, and to a lesser extent, the king. Elva watched and waited for a sign of an attack. She could feel something in the air. The road was quiet and empty. That didn't seem right to Elva.

"The damn Ironhands will watch this road." Elva said to one of her sisters. "Gunnar Redhorn holds an estate near here, and he'd never let Antei encroach on his lands or his lord's."

"You think they'd attack?"

Elva nodded. "Aye. They'd attack knowing what happened in court. That news has to have reached the lords by now."

The Ironhand family was one of the oldest families in Lotcala, coming over from Gotistan with the three brothers two and a half centuries before. Thored Järnhand (Ironhand in old Gota) took a large swath of land along the western mountain range south of Jovag and north of Amazon. Over the years, the Ironhand family integrated themselves within the royal family, marrying a daughter to King Charles' grandfather. Being cousins, the Ironhands were willing to fight and die for the throne. That meant that any of their banners would do the same. Redhorn would be a threat.

Elva knew that desire to remain on good terms with the throne and was keeping an extra careful eye on the forest edge. She was keenly aware of a possible ambush. She kept her horse steady as she trotted along the dirt road. A light appeared ahead, but the night hid the torch's holder.

"Er det Hårdsten med en svart hjort?"[8]

"Yer old Gota is as broken as yer face, Redhorn." Elva replied. "Yer putting too much emphasis on the wrong syllables." Elva smirked. "To answer yer

---

[8] Are you the Hardstone that rides with the black stag?

question, aye, I am indeed a Hardstone, and I ride with the Black Stag."

"Förrädare."[9]

Elva's grin turned to a grimace. "Ny, lojal mot Rowena."[10] Elva said in the old tongue. "The true heir!" She shouted.

The man, Gunnar Redhorn, laughed. "She'll never be our queen." He turned his horse and led it back into the forest.

Elva watched as the light faded. She felt what was coming next.

"Shields!" She shouted just as the twang of bows launching arrows echoed through the forest.

Her warriors were quick to raise their shields, but some weren't quick enough. While some fell to arrows, others did their best to fire arrows back into the forest. Elva was atop her horse, her shield up, ordering the counter attack.

"Damn bastards ambushed us in the dark of night!" Elva laughed. "Cowards!"

A yell burst out from the edge of the forest, just before a hundred spearmen ran out.

Elva saw the new attack. She turned her horse toward the action. "Shieldwall!" She ordered.

The warriors did as ordered, forming a line, interlocking their shields together. From the second line, spear-women and men leveled their weapons toward the charging soldiers.

---

[9] Traitor
[10] No, I'm loyal to Rowena.

That charge ended in a crash against the Sister's shields. This was the warfare that the Sisters excelled at. Standing their ground along a wall of shield and spears, fending off an oncoming army. Even outnumbered, a shield wall was an advantage. However, Elva and her army weren't outnumbered. The Hardstone woman knew as much, and she ordered her force to push forward against the rush of Ironhand soldiers.

"Hold! There's only a handful of 'em!" Elva shouted out to her warriors.

The Sisters were steadfast in their defense of the line. Not only were they holding the line, but they could push the Ironhand force further back toward the forest. Some of the Sisters fell in the fray, but not as many as their opponents.

Gunnar Redhorn looked on from a safe distance among the trees.

"Sound the retreat." He said. "I've seen enough of their force. I'm needed in the north." Redhorn finished before turning his horse and riding away.

The horn blew. Instinctively, the Ironhand men knew the time was right to leave the battle.

Elva knew that sound as well. The Redhorn family horn was famous in Lotcala. However, she had never been in a battle where she heard the retreat called.

"Keep yer guard!" Elva shouted.

The retreat was as disjointed as the initial charge was. Elva wasn't sure if the retreat was real but she knew that at the very least, Redhorn was testing their strength. Possibly attacking to judge them, and keep them from getting too close to Ironhand lands.

Either way, Elva knew that a second attack would be with a larger force and would not be so easy to defend.

Elva turned to her warriors. "Keep moving, carry the wounded, and anything else worth dragging along."

"And our dead?" One minotaur sister asked.

Elva sneered at the thought that came into her mind. "Leave them be. We have to make haste to the north. We need to meet up with the main force quickly."

No one, including Elva, liked the answer, but it was the only one that made sense. Creator willing, they'd be back to burying their fallen friends, or they'd ask for forgiveness in the afterlife.

Two Stags

hree weeks after the scene in the throne room and Rowena's attack on Antei, the barons, manor lords, and all the gentry lords met to discuss the future. It was a clandestine meeting that no one, not even the king, was privy to unless they were in attendance. Each lord brought one son or other designated heir. The stage was set for something that had never happened in the two centuries of the kingdom; determining the right to rule the Kingdom of Lotcala.

Standing on a hill, near the site of an ancient battle within the Barony of Coldwood, the men gathered around stone altar. The area was partially within the ruins of an old castle. Its name lost to time and memory. Ancient battlefields dotted the kingdom's landscape, yet so many laid largely forgotten, and most people only knew them for their modern names. Legends spoke of the days before the conquest, and even before the Yendis people. Some songs still harkened back to the days of yore, brighter, and full of magic wafting through the air unseen but felt by the world.

Directing the meeting was Baron Henrik Coldwood II. He, much like his predecessor, was a stern-looking man. Aged in the last twenty-odd years since he had taken the mantle of baron. His once black hair was fading to gray and his eyes constantly looked heavy. With him was his son and heir, Robert. Another stern looking Coldwood.

"We will speak freely on this night. My son, Robert, will act as our scribe and tally any votes we have." Coldwood began. "The question is of succession. Do we acknowledge the son, Alfred, as designated by the gold stag upon his sigil or the daughter, Rowena, as seen with the black stag?"

Murmurs began throughout the crowd.

Manor lord Uffeson spoke up. "What if our choices are not the same?" He asked, looking around.

"We will have a chance to debate but I fear we all know what the true consequence will be if a vote is not unanimous, or close to it." Coldwood replied. He looked out among the gathered men. "I'll hear from the barons first, and then the manor lords. Last, the gentry can speak." Coldwood added. "Lord Canton, please begin. What is your vote?"

Baron Theobald Canton stood from the stone he claimed as his seat. "The Canton Barony knows no other heir than Alfred, the golden stag. The true successor!"

Although many cheered at the bold statement, others showed their opposition through silence.

Baron Baldwin Harbor was next. "I respect Rowena for what she has accomplished until recently. I also respect her for her care with my daughter. Rowena has a place in my heart." He paused, emotions becoming too much. "However, I must vote with my head. My family is there only by the grace of Charles' vengeance against the Seabanes who were once in my place. I, too, will fight for Prince Alfred."

Harbor was followed by all the other barons until finally Leif Hardstone was called upon. He was the final baron to speak.

"We Hardstones have always been loyal to the crown and Charles is me king. However, I cannae in good conscious follow the boy Alfred. Rowena has proven herself the better of the two. She is intelligent, and an excellent commander. We Hardstones cast our lot with the princess!"

"You call yourself loyal?" Manor Lord Ashe shouted. "You're not fit to call yourself a baron!"

Others joined in the jeering, while Hardstone's vassals jumped up to defend their lord. Ashe's vassals did the same. Shouting soon filled the air. The lords closed in. Hardstone starred down Ashe, but the younger manor lord kept shouting. Soon the scene reached a fever pitch.

Baron Coldwood had heard enough.

"Silence!" Coldwood shouted, standing from his stone. "This is a place for us to speak freely! Lord Ashe, you will respect Baron Hardstone's opinion, and hold your tongue until it is your time to speak." Coldwood sat back down as the area calmed.

He knew the lords were tense and fickle. They had just seen the effects of a minor civil war with the rebellious Goldwater family. Now Coldwood was trying to stave off another clash.

Baron Coldwood sighed before continuing. "This is a time for peace. War could be upon us. Rowena and her supporters have decimated Antei. Some of you lords are from Antei. Those that are here were loyal to the crown, and you were spared her wrath. Still, this may be our last chance to safeguard our homeland. We have little time, and none of it should be spent squabbling."

Many of the lords nodded in agreement or gave claps to show their support for the baron's words.

"Yer the Lord Chancellor Henrik. What say ye?" Hardstone called out to Coldwood.

Baron Coldwood stood back up. "I've watched Rowena grow from a baby to a fine warrior and leader. I have no doubt that she will be blessed in command. She deserves the crown for her skill alone, but I can't go against my king. He placed Alfred as his rightful heir, and I will respect that. I cast my lot with Alfred, the golden stag."

The baron sat back down. The manor lords rose to give their say. Much like the barons, the manor houses sided with Alfred, while Hardstone's manors voted differently.

"We in house Strongmotte will fight for the black stag, Rowena!" Lord Henry Strongmotte proudly proclaimed.

Lord Malcolm Loach rose next. "As a loyal vassal of Hardstone, I will follow my lord. Princess Rowena is the true heir and our next queen."

The final manor lord to speak was Lord Sweyn Highwind. "This is a war that is brewing, and ye lords might not see the entire picture of it. We along the Blue Mountains feel it, though." Highwind stood. "As a march-lord, 'tis me duty to guard the border. This war will pit a human against a half dwarf. Do ye not think that the king of Panyakuta is watching our discord with interest? What do ye think he'll do in response to treatment over one of his own kind? The Highwind family will remain in Highwind. We chose not to pick a side other than protecting our border." As Highwind sat down, many of the others jeered him, but that did little to change his mind.

Baron Coldwood stood up and looked at Highwind. "My respect to you, Lord Highwind. As a fellow march-lord, I understand your reasoning. I only hope that the victor does as well." Coldwood then turned to the gentry lords standing in the back. "Sirs!"

He called out. "What say you? Should you choose the golden stag, come to the right." He said, motioning with his right arm.

Most of the gentry lords moved as he directed.

"For the black stag, to the left." Coldwood yelled out.

The remaining lords, apart from the houses of Whitehall and Bluestone, both vassals of Highwind, moved to the left. Those two houses each stayed out of a war, in favor or protecting the border with their liege house.

The last to move was Sir Duncan Cullenhun. "I'm an Antei lord, formerly loyal to the Goldwaters and still loyal to Lord Overland, yet I don't agree with my liege lord tonight. I cast my lot with the Black Stag. Long live the queen!" He said, moving to stand with other Rowena supporters.

The sides were not even, mostly along older family lines. Rowena supporters were outnumbered nearly two to one, and none of the barons or manor lords apart from the Hardstone lords had sworn to support her. The bulk of Rowena's support was from the gentry class.

Something about the split was also familiar. Previous wars had been fought among many of the same families in the same position, on opposing sides in the past. Old wounds were going to be reopened.

* * * * *

Rowena left Antei a scorched and broken shell of its once former glorious self. However, she did her best to spare the people of the city and those around the barony.

That was then, but now, after being attacked by Ironhand forces, she had little choice but to fight. Her plan to move on Estan was brushed aside as she led her army to the plains south of Jovag.

Rowena sat around a tent warming stove the night Elva returned to the main army. She was with Grainne, Hadiza, Agota, and Elva. They were discussing their next move.

"Scouts are reporting movement along the western reaches. Hardstone riders intercepted messages being sent to Fe, Amazon, and Tresha." Grainne reported.

"Amazon." Rowena said in a low voice. "Father is reaching out to Sir Jakob."

"He'd be a fool not to." Grainne replied. "Tresha is too far to pose a threat, and I would not count on Fe joining. However, the Amazons are as close as siblings. As close as we are to their border, we have to be careful not to provoke them."

"Would they attack us?" Agota asked.

"To keep us from running south, probably." Elva replied.

"I know little about your politics here in Lotcala, but in the desert kingdoms, when a king dies, the sons and daughters fight to rule. Often whoever gets to the throne first, then they kill the others." Hadiza interjected.

"Things aren't always so different here." Rowena replied. "Our kings of the past have typically been the stronger sorts. A few exceptions, and when you're an only child, then sometimes you get a pass for being weak." She stood from her chair. "The court has always been a treacherous place for anyone brave enough to play its game." Rowena paused for a moment. She thought about Adela's story. "It has cost countless lives, within and out. Alfred is clever and devious, but is he strong enough to endure the court? I don't know."

"That's why we Hardstones stay in our own lands." Elva added. "We'll come when the king calls, but we don't mix with the political machine of the court."

Grainne stood and walked over to Rowena. She put a hand around her shoulder. "I told my father that becoming the king's chamberlain was a curse. He didn't want to believe it."

Rowena nodded, knowing the meaning. "I'm glad Severa isn't around to see this. None of our other sisters who started in the academy are. I'd hate to make them choose a side."

"No way, she'd side against you." Hadiza said.

"I don't know. I don't like to think of it." Rowena responded.

Just then, a scout entered the tent and knelt in front of Rowena.

"Captain, your grace." The scout said.

"Up." Rowena motioned.

"I have a message sent by Baron Coldwood." The scout said, handing a sealed scroll to Rowena.

"The Coldwood seal." Rowena observed. "Not the chancellor seal?"

"Unofficial." Grainne remarked.

Rowena broke the seal and read it. She scoffed and chuckled. "It's a tally of the noble families. All one hundred and three families."

"A tally?" Hadiza asked.

Agota marveled. "So many families."

"We have more than we need." Grainne said, looking at Agota. She turned to Rowena. "What's the tally for?" She was sure she knew the answer.

Rowena looked at her friends. "A vote of who they side with. Seventy-one families recognize Alfred as the heir and twenty-six proclaim me as the rightful heir."

"That's only ninety-seven families." Grainne counted.

"The other six, Highwind and their gentry, are neutral. Staying along the mountains to protect the border." Rowena said, reading the scroll.

Elva spat on the ground. "Cowards."

"Smart." Grainne countered.

All looked at her, confused.

She noted their eyes. "If the dwarven king gets word of this war, he might use it as a pretext to invade. Humans fighting a dwarf, half dwarf even, could be cause enough to defend their heritage."

"A heritage I know nothing of." Rowena replied.

"Doesn't matter. Not to the people of Panyakuta. You could be a source of pride." Grainne added. "And it would be Highwind's land that they encounter first."

"A march-lord." Rowena reasoned. She remembered her father's lesson of the duties of being a march-lord.

"He's worried that the dwarven kingdom will use you as a symbol. At least, that's what makes the most sense." Grainne reasoned.

Rowena tapped the scroll on her palm. She thought of the possibility. It could mean an ally, legitimacy even. However, it was just a theory. She didn't know the first thing about being a dwarf. She didn't know her mother. Rowena had lived in Lotcala since she was barely walking. This was her home, her heritage. Lotcalan, Gota, which was her culture.

But she didn't look like everyone else. Of course, she was shorter, but there was more than just that. She was darker complexion. Sure, Lotcala had seen more people come and settle that were different cultures and looked different. Several notable families, originally from foreign lands, had taken the reins of the gentry. One was the Holts from the southern isles, a land known for much more diversity in complexion than the northern kingdoms. Sir Alain Holt, whose grandfather had been the first of the family to own the land they held, was the first man who Rowena had ever seen with dark bronze skin. Others had come in more recent years. Now many were willing to stand against her.

She looked at her hands. The dim light hid her own skin. A deep amber tone, which she'd never given much thought to. She just knew it as a trait from her dwarven mother. Her red hair was a Lotcalan trait.

"Who am I?" Rowena said aloud.

Her friends turned to regard her.

"What do you mean, captain?" Hadiza asked.

"Who am I?" Rowena repeated. "A dwarf? A human? I know little of who I am. I only know what my father and stepmother pushed upon me." She continued. "If Panyakuta ever wants to use me as a pawn, then they'll have to recognize my claim, but I will not be a simple puppet." She said sternly. "No matter what others whisper behind my back, I'm a princess. My father may not have given two shits for my mother. She might have been a smoke skin bar wench or a camp girl working for coin. It doesn't matter. What matters is that I, Rowena, am here to claim my birthright. I am Rowena, Princess of Lotcala, and that is all that matters."

The others stood up with her. They each smiled.

Rowena turned to them. "Send a letter to Black Hand. I need more soldiers and I'm willing to give him all that he asks for." She said. "Tomorrow we march on Pern. I want to see Ironhand grovel before me. I've known him to be a good man and loyal, but he will regret signing his name under the golden stag."

* * * * *

A few days later, Hubert Ironhand was called to the battlements of his fortress, alongside the borders of his city, Pern. Across the field, he saw an army setting up a siege camp.

"She wouldn't." Ironhand said softly. "Not in this weather."

He was sure that the coming snow, just flurries for now, would turn Rowena away. However, he could hear her drums.

"Dwarven bitch." Spat Rodrik Longpine.

Ironhand looked to his gentry-lord and shook his head.

"She's nothing more than a nuisance, my lord." Longpine said with a smirk.

"Then you'd be willing to go out there and fight her in the open field." Ironhand said. He noted Longpine's silence and lack of eye contact. "I didn't think so." Ironhand turned back to look at the camp. "Make no mistake, Princess Rowena is not an amateur, nor is she a nuisance. That woman was trained by a formidable warrior, and harden through years of combat. She's brought an army of humans, elves,

Quarmi, and beastfolk. No ordinary person could do all that."

Longpine huffed but was not agreeable. "She's just a cutthroat."

"Sir Longpine, I'm sure you're needed elsewhere." Ironhand said.

"My lord?"

Ironhand looked to the manor-lord. "Get the hell out of my sight."

Longpine bowed and did as instructed.

Ironhand walked off, ordering his men to prepare for the siege.

* * * * *

Rowena, using her spyglass, saw Ironhand on the battlements. She knew and respected the man well. Rowena also knew that he held some respect for her. He had told her as much a few years back. She would be lying if she said she did not feel a bit of apprehension. Ironhand was a skilled tactician and defender. However, Rowena knew that if she was to march anywhere, she'd have to deal with him now.

"Once the mangonels are set up, begin the siege." Rowena ordered, turning from the fortress.

Her warriors saluted and went to work.

Rowena walked back to her tent, a short distance from the center of the camp. As she approached, she noticed the banners of the Cullenhun, Ironsmit, FitzRoy, Strongmotte, Gilcomgain, Fairhair, and Redwaters families. As she looked, two more Hardstone bannermen rode in, Murray and Highwall.

Rowena bowed to the two leaders of the latest families.

"My lords. I bid you welcome." Rowena said.

"We thank you, your grace." Sir William Murray said. He dismounted and clasped Rowena's hand. "I've brought you three hundred levies and forty-seven men at arms. Five knights." He finished.

"Happy to have everyone." Rowena smiled. She needed more.

"Your grace. We've never met, but you knew my father. I am Gerald Highwall." Sir Gerald Highwall said, introducing himself with a bow. A young lord, but with several scars from recent skirmishes on his otherwise handsome face.

Rowena bowed her head. "I knew your father. A good man."

"He would have supported you. He was always speaking kindly of your grace." Highwall said with a smile.

"I remember talks of a marriage." Rowena grinned sheepishly.

"Your stepmother put an end to those discussions."

"She did, indeed. She'd couldn't have me marry such a handsome man."

Highwall blushed. "It was the Creator's will. I have a wonderful wife and two babes now."

Rowena smiled at the news. "I'm sure they want us to be done with this war soon, so you can return."

"Creator willing." Highwall replied. "They know I must do my duty to you first. I have two hundred levies to join, but only twenty men at arms. I'm the only knight."

"Highwalls fight like ten men, so that maybe the edge we need." Rowena said.

She motioned for them to join her in the tent where the other banners were placed. Once inside, they found the other bannermen that joined Rowena's army.

"My lords, you all honor me." Rowena said, taking a seat with the lords. "I saw the tally from the scroll. I was happy to see such friends."

"Nine of those noble families have joined us here in camp." Sir Cullenhun said. "More to come."

"I am grateful." Rowena said. She tightened her lips before continuing. "Ironhand is here in his fortress. We can take it, but it won't be easy. We are also open to an attack from the north and south."

"Jovag has yet to send troops. Your father won't hear of it." Cullenhun said. "However, the queen rules Canton, and she can order them to march without your father's consent."

Rowena scoffed. It was that sort of practice she despised. A baron could send an army marching to attack another noble and the king had little to no say against it. That was the feudal world of Lotcala, a holdover from Gotistan.

"We need to break from the old ways." Grainne said, knowing what Rowena was thinking. "The monarch needs to have more control over the noble families."

"I understand how it hurts us now, but those old ways have worked for us for generations." Lord Strongmotte said. Charles Strongmotte was a manor-lord under Hardstone, and one of Rowena's staunchest supporters. "As for this fortress, I'll leave my siege machines to aid you. In the meantime, I'll ride north and patrol the trade roads. If Canton comes, then we'll hold them off. I think that with my five hundred men at arms, we'll stand a better chance of delaying an attack." Strongmotte stood. He motioned for Sir Ironsmit to stand. "I'll take my vassal Sir Ironsmit, and his men with me, to bolster the defense. By your leave, of course."

Rowena stood and nodded. "I'll be grateful for your protection, my lord." The two hugged.

Once the pair had left, Rowena turned to Elva. "Reach out to Loach. I need his men here as well. He swore to our cause."

Elva stood and saluted before leaving the tent.

Rowena looked to Hadiza. "Any word from Black Hand?"

* * * * *

Over the years since his meeting with Rowena, Gerald Blackhand rose higher in The Company's ranks. Now he was the second in command of the Northern Region, and in a position to help his friend Rowena. He had done that once during the Goldwater Rebellion.

Now that he had been successful, he was on his way home. There was still much for him to do in his daily role as the second in command on the northern sector.

His headquarters were entrenched in the Sile Empire capital of Aran, hundreds of miles to the north of Lotcala. Rowena's second letter asking for help was received at an opportune time. Gerald had yet to leave from Ter Nog. The baron of the area, Harbor, was gathering troops, and Black Hand was watchful of the movements. He was accompanied by only a handful of housecarls. He was careful.

A scout from Rowena's army, without her sigil, rode up to the inn near the docks of Ter Nog and found Black Hand. He was in the midst of planning a quick exit.

"She needs more mercenaries?" Black Hand read. "I can put a call out, but it would be tough given the timing and the distance. The season doesn't help any either."

"Any help would be appreciated." The scout replied.

Black Hand looked at the woman. "I'm not sure how much you've learned in the past few weeks or what you've seen, but things are not looking good." He took a piece of paper and a charcoal stick. He wrote out something on the paper. "The barons took a vote, along with the other lords. They're merging their forces to attack Rowena and defend the kingdom. A few are on her side, but not many. Not enough."

The scout sighed. "Rowena is right in her claim."

"Perhaps." Black Hand replied without looking up. "However, the numbers are what's important, not right or wrong. It's simple math." The mercenary leader finished his note. "I have some contacts close by. I'll see what I can provide." He handed the note to one of his housecarls.

Black Hand looked at the scout as she was getting up.

"However." He said. The scout turned to look at him. "We should always have a contingency plan."

"A way out?" The scout scoffed. "Rowena would never abandon us."

"Perhaps, and knowing her, you're probably right." Black Hand responded. "Yet, knowing her, she'd make sure you all were with her as she left." Black Hand smiled. "I have one contact here in Lotcala that might provide a way out of the kingdom, should things go bad."

Black Hand took out another piece of paper and scribbled something on it. Once he was finished, he folded the note, sealed it, and handed it to the scout.

"Tell Rowena that I'll provide any help I can. However, give her this note and tell her it is the best help I can provide. It is worth far more than gold."

The scout took the note and nodded.

"Oh, and one more thing." Black Hand said. "Tell her she can count on this contingency plan. He owes me. Like I said, worth more than gold."

The Stag War

ern was not an easy nut to crack. Even with the new siege equipment, Rowena was having a hell of a time breaking the walls. Ironhand only counted two thousand soldiers, mostly men at arms. However, that was Rowena's advantage. The mercenary princess brought over ten thousand warriors to the battle.

The siege, however, was only part of the battle. Once the walls broke, she would need to lead her force inside. That was another aspect, however, it was one that she was very skilled at. She just had to get within the walls.

Pern had a massive eastern wall, built during the wall with Hardstone two centuries before. A war that sowed the seeds of hatred between the two families. Now, that hatred was being used as fuel for Rowena's war. She could count on every man and woman from the Hardstone barony to help her break every stone from the fortress wall. It would just take some time.

Sun had long set on the siege. Smoke from the fires, long blocking out the sun, was now blocking out the full moon. An auspicious omen for those in the fortress. Rowena did not take stock of such superstitions. She used the cover of night to send small detachments of sappers toward the wall. She wanted to find its weak points and exploit them.

Rowena had other methods at her disposal, as well. She still had the orc mages, known for their fire magic skills. Other mages, mainly from Hardstone, had joined her as well. Any expert mage would have been skilled with the use of fire magic. Rowena knew just how to use those skills on the wall. That was where her newer recruits would come in handy.

Minotaurs were strong and resilient. Rowena needed tunnels. Minotaurs could dig quickly, haul more dirt loads, and withstand the conditions better than humans. While the work atop the ground was focused on levelling the wall, below ground no fewer than ten minotaurs were inching closer to the base of the wall.

"We could use towers." Grainne pointed out during the night. She and Rowena were looking out over the rampart of Rowena's siege camp. "We have the numbers."

"And no time." Rowena said in agreement. "Elva is trying to get word to Loach. They're the carpenters and they'd build the towers."

Grainne frowned. "I can only see two reasons why they aren't here. They ran into another army or they betrayed us."

Rowena shook her head. "Loach is loyal to Hardstone more than any other lord. He would never fight against him."

Grainne shrugged. "It's a possibility, but I agree, far-fetched." She paused. "They'd have to march through Canton."

"That would explain the lack of enemy presence in the north." Rowena added. She looked at a guard nearby. "Send word to Strongmotte to investigate the trade roads north to the capital and towards Canton. I want him to find out what happened to Loach."

The guard saluted and rushed off.

"If Loach encountered Sirie, he likely lost that fight. She commands nearly five thousand. Loach is a manor-lord with a few hundred men." Grainne pointed out.

Rowena remained silent.

Elva approached from behind the pair. "I sent riders to Oak Hall. We should know in a few days what has become of Loach."

Rowena smiled and filled Elva in on the possibility of an attack from Canton.

"Aye, the queen's lands are close by Loach's." Elva responded.

The three watched as the mangonels and other siege machines launched boulders and flaming payloads toward the city.

Rowena turned. "We should rest. The morning promises to be a long one."

The friends went to their tents. Grainne walked into hers and found her father there.

"Da'." She smiled. "I figured you were with your men."

"I was." He smiled. "I thought I'd come here and talk a moment."

Grainne looked at her father. "Of course."

Donovan Cullenhun was just a gentry-lord, a sir, but he was as respected as a baron. The king, bowing to pressure, never elevated him to a higher station. However, Cullenhun had never held it against the king. He was loyal until the moment he signed his name under the black stag. Even then, he did not turn on the king, only choosing to side with Rowena as the heir.

"It is time I made preparations in case things do not go well for us." He said.

Grainne handed him a goblet of wine. He sipped the warm drink. He could feel the cold air leaving his body.

"I have given it a lot of thought, and while I trust your brothers well enough, they aren't you." Cullenhun continued. "I've trained you since birth, and out of all of my children, you are the closest to me in personality and mannerisms. You're stoic, like me." Cullenhun smiled. "You don't need anyone and yet you're there to support others." Cullenhun handed Grainne a sealed scroll. "This is my will. Signed and sealed, naming you the heir to my holdings and all the titles with it."

Grainne was shocked. "Father, I can't."

"The king has also signed it. His last act for me as his chamberlain." Cullenhun said. The sorrow in his voice was clear. "He then wished me luck and good fortune."

"Good fortune?"

Cullenhun tried to smile, but he couldn't. "He asked that I do what I could to protect Rowena." He said with a nod. He pointed to the scroll. "That will protect you as a noble born lady. However, don't think Alfred will simply allow his father's words to hold true. You need more to ensure your survival if you're ever put in front of the king's justice. Something that will insure our family's future."

"A child." Grainne reasoned.

"Aye, a child, or at least expecting."

"I didn't have a notion of having children." Grainne said.

"No, but that's the way of the kingdom. They won't execute a mother with a babe on the way or nursing one." Cullenhun said. "The rights of the mother prevail. Even the queen will adhere to that. She might be a hateful woman, but she is a mother and respects a mother's rights."

Grainne nodded. "I suppose there is little choice if things go south."

Cullenhun stood up to leave. "I understand this wasn't part of your plans. I'd never even suggest it, but I can't stand the thought of a world with none of my children." He said before leaving the tent.

Grainne sat and thought about her options. She looked at the scroll and wondered. Her life was not sitting in a castle as a wife. Her father knew that, but it was the last resort for a desperate father to protect his daughter.

"Dammit." She said to herself. She sat in thought and then scrunched her lips as she got an idea. "I think I saw that lout Bowen Leckey around earlier. A Hardstone retainer would make for a decent mate and he owns a patch of land in the barony. If his lord is agreeable, then I can at least get a landed man for a husband." She said before tossing the scroll onto her satchel and getting in her cot.

* * * * *

Dawn came, and Rowena was already watching the siege continue. Grainne and Hadiza stood with her.

"If Loach does not come with those towers, we'd have to scale the wall with ladders." Grainne said. "I wish Elva would hurry back."

Hadiza shook her head. "Without the towers, we'd lose many good warriors on that wall. Still, we have to try."

"I will be the first up the ladder and over the wall." Rowena said. "If I die, then I die."

"Captain." Hadiza spoke up. "I can't let you do that. I'll take the force up the ladders and occupy the south wall." She gauged her captain's response. "We have the numbers and the equipment, not counting the towers, to take the walls." Hadiza said. "Give me the word and I'll lead our force."

Rowena looked on. She pulled out her spyglass. Looking around, she spotted the area the minotaurs were digging.

"Keep to the southern end." Rowena said. "Soon we'll send the fire casters into the tunnels and burn the beams."

Her plan, one that had worked in other areas of the world, was to burn out the tunnels that were dug under the fortress walls. Tunnels that had been stuffed with wood beams, hay, pig lard, and flammable pitch. The fire, burning out the beams, would burn away the support, bringing the heavy stones down.

"Once the wall is burned down, I'll lead the rest of the force through that breach." Rowena finished.

"What I wouldn't give for a few more months or more." Grainne said. "I'd rather starve them out."

"No time for that. We're up against the snows and a larger army that could be on our ass any week." Rowena replied.

Rowena nodded to Hadiza to begin her assault. The lieutenant saluted Rowena and Grainne before turning. She rushed off to where the warriors waiting for the advance on the wall were stationed. She grabbed her helm, securing it on her head. A nasal helm trimmed with gold accents and a gold chainmail neck guard. Hadiza was successful in her long mercenary career with Rowena. The gold in her new helm was evidence of that.

Hadiza gathered her force, several hundred warriors, and instructed the leaders among them of the plan. Position the ladders along the walls, archers would fire arrows up to the battlements while other warriors would scale the wall. Reaching the top would be dangerous, but if the archers could provide cover, then those climbing the ladders might have a chance. Hadiza gave the order to charge with a yell. Her soldiers followed as she ran down the rampart of the siege camp. Some that carried the ladders rushed with the long ladders in one hand and a raised shield for cover in the other hand. The run was a short one, only about a hundred yards, but it was under the heavy volley of arrows and stones. Once at the wall, the warriors raising the ladders, hooks at the top of each ladder secured it to the wall. Almost immediately, the mercenaries started their ascent up the twenty-foot-high wall.

Hadiza, sword in her right hand and raised shield in her left, stood on the ground shouting orders to the warriors climbing the two dozen ladders. Her force, armed in chainmail and gambesons, was proving skillful in the attack. Ironhand soldiers shot arrows, to a limited effectiveness along the wall, and tossed large stones, weighing eight to twelve pounds. Those stones were deadlier than the arrows, yet slower to toss. Hadiza rushed her soldiers onward. Faster meant more warriors to the top of the wall.

The first warriors to reach the top of the wall found Ironhand soldiers waiting with swords and axes. The two armies went to work battling each other. Hadiza's force mostly carried shorter war axes, some with spatha swords, fit for fighting in narrow spaces. The wall's walkway was such a narrow space. The fighting was fierce as men and women on both sides fell to the ground, either died from weapons or from the impact with the ground. Axes chopped limbs and at necks, blood sprayed on the grey stones. The wall's walkway was slick with blood, bile, and entrails. A dangerous fight was becoming more and more dangerous with the consequences of the battle. Hadiza's warriors kept climbing up the ladders as few Ironhands stood on the walls. Most moved to other defensible locations, giving up the southern wall. Within two hours of hard fighting, Hadiza's force had fully stormed the wall. Hadiza stood atop the wall's crenellations and waved her sword and shield, signaling to her captain that the wall was theirs.

Suddenly, a great explosion was heard and felt around the battlements. Rowena was monitoring the fighting along the southern end of the wall. Happy that it was going as well as she could have hoped, Rowena saw her flags being raised higher and higher, until the wall was surmounted. She turned to Grainne and gave her the order to ignite her trap.

"Send in the casters. We need those walls to burn." Rowena said.

Grainne saluted and rushed off to follow the order. She rounded up the fire mages, and other mages that could control spells. The tunnels had been dug, beginning in the siege camp, traversing the many yards to the wall. It wasn't exactly a guess at the distance, but measuring the length of the tunnel compared to the wall wasn't a straightforward task. Grainne had figured the distance by seeing the amount of time it took the sunlight to move from one point, the tunnel entrance, to the fortress wall.

Grainne led the casters down through the cramp corridors. She held a torch out, pointing the direction for the casters.

"Get deeper in. We have another hundred yards to go." Grainne said. The minotaurs were walking out of the area after having unloaded the last of the flammable materials.

"It stinks in here." One of the Quarmi mages said.

A minotaur woman smiled. "That's the pig fat we stuffed down at the end."

The other minotaurs chuckled.

Grainne sighed at the Quarmi's confused look. "Pig lard is highly flammable. It burns hotter and longer than pitch." She pushed the mage further down the tunnel. "Let's keep it going. Time is against us."

A few more yards and the first signs of the wicks and igniters.

"Here, cast the flames here, and then run the fuck out." Grainne said.

"Why use casters and not flint stones?" One mage asked.

Grainne looked at her. "Simply put, your flames are much hotter and quicker. Flint stones take too long."

The mages with Grainne accepted the answer and nodded.

"Let's get on with it, then." Grainne said before taking a few steps back.

The mages began their litany or rituals to cast the spells. Soon enough, the tunnel was brightly lit with flames. Grainne turned and rushed out of the tunnel, the mages behind her. All knowing that within a moment, the entire area would be engulfed.

The explosion rocked the entire fortress and the ground surrounding it. The portion of the wall directly over the blast crumbled to the ground in a smoldering pile of burning mortar, stone, and the remains of the soldiers.

Rowena watched as the wall fell. She smiled at the success of her plan. Donning her nasal helm, she walked confidently to her army. Joined by Grainne, Rowena signaled the charge toward the broken wall. In that instant, hundreds of armored men-at-arms, mercenaries, and hedge knights rushed to the breach. Rowena's plan to bring down the wall, soften by mangonels, then attacked at one end, finally broken by fire, worked as well as it had been planned.

Rowena ran alongside her army, her spatha sword in one hand and a kite shield in the other. She wasn't the first to the breach. Her shorter legs made her run seem slower, but once there, she wasted little time in cementing herself as the fiercest of the warriors.

The fighting was difficult. Though Rowena's force was stronger and well trained, the occupants were not willing to give up the fortress without defending their lord and his homeland. Ironhand was a skilled tactician and warrior. As Rowena's force charged into the breach of the broken wall, Baron Ironhand was there to lead his own men. He must have known that they were outnumbered, that his chances of victory were slim, but Ironhand didn't let that shake him.

Baron Ironhand stood across the rubble from Rowena. He raised his sword to her. It was a personal challenge for her alone.

"Your fame has led you to me. Your skill has become the stuff of legends!" Ironhand yelled to Rowena, who was walking to him.

Others moved past the two. None wanted to get in between the leaders.

"I've seen you grow from that little dwarf whelp into a fine warrior. I hate to stand against you now." Ironhand continued.

"Then stand aside, my lord." Rowena said.

Ironhand smiled. "Keeping the proper respect even now." The man admired the respect she showed. "It would be an honor to be defeated by you should the Creator will it."

"Not the Creator." Rowena said, raising her sword. "He is staying out of this war."

Ironhand nodded and rushed toward Rowena, his sword held high. He swung down, but Rowena dodged the blow with her shield. Swinging her own sword toward the older man's body. Ironhand deflected it with an expert parry.

Rowena stood up straight, her sword held tightly in her right hand. She nodded and charged at Ironhand. He was ready and parried her strike again. But Rowena had extended her entire body in the strike and could take the parry with ease, pushing her shield into the man. Ironhand stumbled again. Rowena charged in again, but used her shoulder to knock him on the ground.

Baron Ironhand landed with a hard thud, the wind being forced from his lungs. Rowena stood over him, her boot on his chest. She pointed the end of her sword at his face.

"Yield the fort." Rowena said.

Ironhand gasped. He turned to see his men failing to hold back Rowena's force. Around them, many of his own soldiers were dying or surrendering. The walls had been overrun with Rowena's force. He knew the battle was lost.

"If you promise my men mercy, then I yield." Ironhand answered.

"So be it." Rowena replied.

* * * * *

The areas and towns surrounding the fortress, including the city of Pern, fell within two days of heavy fighting. Rowena's force of nearly eight thousand had suffered fewer causalities than Grainne and Rowena had expected. Ironhand was shackled, though he was allowed to be kept within the interior of his fortress. Longpine was not so lucky. He was placed in the stocks with the courtyard square of the fortress, awaiting execution. Though Grainne tried to convince Rowena to ransom him, Hadiza offered to be the executioner.

Rowena sat on the steps of the keeps entrance, eating an apple and drink ale.

"Hadiza, come here, please." Rowena said.

Grainne was standing next to her on the steps. She stepped down to the ground level and motioned for Hadiza to stand directly in front of Rowena, who tossed her apple and stood up.

"You have stood beside me for over a decade. You have led my soldiers, and you honor me in battle." Rowena said. "Please kneel."

Hadiza knelt as instructed. Others gathered around their comrade.

"Let it be known that in my power as Princess of Lotcala, rightful heir to the Carolyngian Throne and rightful Baroness of Antei, I name you Lady Hadiza Orkenbay, Knight Banneress." Rowena pulled out her sword and tapped Hadiza's left shoulder once before sheathing her sword. "This honor gives you the right to carry your own standard and sigil. You can also hold lands in whatever kingdom I hold, passed down to any children that you might have." Rowena smiled down at Hadiza. "Stand and embrace me, sister."

Hadiza stood, tears in her eyes, and hugged her dearest friend. Grainne stood, smiling. She hugged Hadiza next. Cheers went up around them.

Just as everyone was celebrating, Elva rode in on her massive horse. The woman was bloody and exhausted. Elva dismounted and went directly to a soldier with a waterskin. She grabbed the skin and gulped it.

"Elva!" Rowena exclaimed. "What news of the north?"

The warrior woman gasped after she finished the waterskin.

"Loach is dead." Elva began.

"Dead?" Grainne asked. "The Queen's force attacked?"

Elva shook her head. "Not entirely. It was Cleves and Pavia leading the Canton forces." She breathed. She grabbed another skin of water and emptied it. "They ambushed Loach and destroyed his force. Hung the lord up on an oak tree. His son too. That was me da's liege lord. Fucking crime to do to a lord. Just as I was about to come back here to warn ye, Lords Robin and Smitlan came with the full might of the Hardstone forces. We joined in once the Hardstone banners came into view."

Elva caught her breath. She walked over to her horse and grabbed a bloody bag that was tied to her horse's saddle. She dropped the contents on the ground. The heads of lords Selwyn Cleves and Roger Pavia rolled on the ground in front of Rowena.

"I made sure to get revenge for Loach and any others. We left a field of bodies there along the trade road north. Ramsey was there, but he ran off. No doubt to the capital." Elva finished. She looked around the fortress. "I see things were successful here. What of Ironhand and Longpine?"

Grainne motioned to the stocks. "Longpine is there, while Ironhand is guarded in the cellar."

Elva looked over to Longpine. She rushed over, drawing her sword, ready to strike. The others ran in to hold her from dropping the sword on the captive man's head.

"What are ye stopping me for?" Elva asked, her eyes burning with rage.

"He is a prisoner!" Rowena yelled.

"Aye, and we're in war!" Elva replied. "I'm not in the habit of letting my enemies live to come back and stab me in me arse!"

"He is our prisoner, Elva, and he will be ransomed." Grainne responded.

"Bah!" Elva spat. "Ransom Ironhand. He'll fetch more coin. Let this one be the example. They didn't ransom Loach or his son. This is a new war. Nobility means shit!"

Hadiza shrugged. "It's a good point." The others looked at her. "We ransom the baron and make more coin, but the lower noble isn't worth as much in gold. But others might be more inclined to surrender if they think they'll die like him."

Rowena sighed. "That's not the memory I want for these lords."

"Ha!" Longpine snorted. "You'll be remembered for nothing but this foolish war. No lord will follow you." Longpine spat blood. "You're just a disgrace. No lord wants a darkened stump of a girl to be their queen."

Rowena grabbed the man by his hair and pulled his head upward. He couldn't look at her directly while in the stocks, but that didn't stop Rowena from pulling his head up anyway. Even as painful as it was, the man hid it well.

"If the lords don't want to follow me, then that's on their heads. Two have already fallen to our blades. You will be three." Rowena let Longpine's hair go. She looked up at Elva. "Do it."

Elva nodded as the others backed away. Elva lifted her sword and swung it with expert precision, the blade slicing through with one swing. Longpine's head rolled on the ground.

"He wasn't well liked, but he was a lord." Grainne said. "We'll need to prepare to reprisals."

Elva scoffed. "We're rebelling. Of course, there will be reprisals!"

Grainne shook her head. "I mean others joining Alfred's cause. If we start killing local lords, then others might see us as tyrants."

Elva spat on the ground and shrugged. Rowena pursed her lips before walking back to the keep. Grainne sighed and clasped Hadiza's shoulder.

"Come, let's discuss your banner." Grainne said.

"So, Rowena made ye a banneress?" Elva grinned.

* * * * *

The fortress outside of Pern was just a steppingstone for Rowena. Within a week, she had moved her army north, leaving the fortress lightly garrisoned. Now, she was intending on relieving the Hardstone army that had stayed behind to guard the road between Jovag and Hardstone. Effectively blocking the Barony of Canton from any movement and keeping the king and queen blockaded in the capital city.

That trade road was the key to victory for Rowena, as well as for the king's army. Whoever controlled the trade road leading to the capital controlled the western half of the kingdom. That would cripple Jovag without a siege. However, Rowena knew that would leave Ter Nog, controlled by Baron Harbor, at her back. It was a risk she'd have to take.

Ending the Ironhand threat helped. Antei was subdued, and many of its strongest noble families fell in with her. Rowena was confident that taking the road was the best move available to her.

Rowena positioned her force along the border between Jovag and Canton. It was a crossroads, with an inn and several small trade depots. Rowena acted quickly, taking control of the depots and securing the supplies. From there she had her army build palisades and earthworks ready to defend any incoming force.

"This is the road we have to hold." Rowena said to her friends. "We hold here and then we can choke Jovag without a fight."

"Aye, and if Black Hand comes through in Ter Nog, we can end this without any trouble from Harbor." Elva pointed out.

"If Black Hand's force can hold Harbor and Baron Leif can hold Coldwood, then we're all set to negotiate." Rowena responded.

Grainne puffed on her pipe. She wasn't as confident. "Lostwood is still out there. Canton's forces might regroup with Sirie at the head. If our two allies do not win, and Lostwood marches toward us, then we are trapped."

Rowena nodded. She knew the words to be true. "Any suggestions?"

Grainne tapped her finger on her chin. "We have to keep Lostwood out of the war and we need more allies. I think we need to send envoys to Eylsia and Fe. Tresha too, but being that they're engulfed in a war with Amazon, it'll be a lost cause." Grainne puffed on her pipe again. "I think we also need to be mindful of Prince Liam. The scouts report that he has returned from Denos."

The tent went quiet. Everyone knew the implications and the impact it had on Rowena. It was known that Rowena and Liam were closer than either was to Alfred. Still, Rowena held no illusions that Liam would join her. Liam was loyal to the king, his father. Then his sister.

Retaliation

iam was everything that Alfred wasn't. Alfred could fight when backed into a corner, and he was literate in the ways of war. However, he wasn't professionally skilled in tactics or with a sword. No amount of instruction his mother tried to heap on him could change that. Liam, however, was naturally gifted in the deadly arts and warfare. Like his sister, and like his father.

The youngest child of Charles and Sirie had spent the last three years away from Lotcala, in the southern lands of Denos, on a diplomatic mission. His skills in speech craft were almost as formidable as his skill with the sword. A skill he further honed while away from Lotcala.

Liam landed in Ter Nog and rode with great haste to Canton. Once he arrived at the keep in Kirkhaven, he met with his mother and brother. There the pair had been trying to discuss strategy, while King Charles stayed in Jovag, refusing to fight against his favorite child. Liam approached the pair and scoffed after overhearing Alfred's lackluster plan.

"I'll take an army of soldiers from the loyal baronies and ride to Rowena's camp." Liam said as he walked up to his brother and mother. "I want to parley with my sister."

Rowena's rebellion had gained some support from the southern noble families and their vassals, as well as within the Hardstone Barony. However, no baron, other than Leif Hardstone, threw in any support.

Liam knew this. That's why he based his plan on leading the baronial armies into battle. However, first he wanted to convince her to stop the rebellion.

Queen Sirie gave her approval of the plan for a parley, but not to lead the baronial armies. Alfred refused that role, and Sirie gladly took that honor herself. Alfred was also against Liam being involved in the war and meeting with Rowena. It wasn't up to him, and though Sirie did not like the idea, she knew of Liam and Rowena's connection. That was a weapon she could use. While Liam would meet with Rowena, Sirie would merge her forces to attack Rowena head on. Liam would be nothing more than her pawn to distract Rowena before the queen could crush her.

Liam rode out that same day with a force of housecarls from the Canton barony. He had several personal men at arms alongside him for added protection. Rowena's camp was only twenty miles away from Kirkhaven, and Liam did not want to waste any time getting there. Something felt off to him.

Five hours later, Liam approached the outskirts of the camp under a white flag of parley. Sentries rushed up to the prince.

"I'm here to speak with my sister, Princess Rowena. Tell her Liam comes to greet her." The prince said.

One sentry rushed off into the camp while the others stayed behind, watching the prince closely. The prince's men stayed further back.

After a few minutes, Rowena rushed to the gate alongside the sentry.

"Liam!" She exclaimed, running to her brother and wrapping him in a hug.

"Ro!" Liam smiled. "I had hoped to find you in Denos, but the steward at your estate said you had just left." He said once they broke their hug.

"I had to push north to treat with a contact in Marselai." Rowena replied.

Liam looked down at his sister and nodded, knowing her meaning.

"How is our dear cousin?" Liam asked.

"She's well. Though Alfred seemed to care less than you do." Rowena answered, leading her brother by the arm to her tent.

Liam chuckled. "Alfred is like that. He wasn't thrilled to see me. That's why you and I always got along so well. No jealousy."

Rowena scrunched her nose at the remark. "How do you mean?"

The pair entered the tent where Grainne, Elva, Hadiza, and Agota were waiting.

"Nothing bad. Just to say that as the second-born son, I get nothing unless father gives me a holding of land or title, and as a recognized but illegitimate daughter, you get..." Liam trialed off.

"Nothing." Grainne finished. "She gets nothing, except through a marriage."

Liam nodded and tried to flash a smile. "Direct as always, Lady Grainne." Liam grinned wider to her. "Your father is well, I hope?"

Grainne returned the smile, though hers was much less cordial. "As well as a traitor to the crown prince can be."

"Yes, about that." Liam turned to his sister. "I've offered to broker a peace. A peace that will see everyone allowed to return to their estates and be vassals again."

"Offered? To whom did you make such an offer?" Rowena asked.

Elva scoffed. "Ye know."

"Now, Lady Elva, I know your distrust of my mother and brother, but I'm here as Rowena's brother and I want all of this war to be done with."

"Too late I think." Hadiza replied. "In the past few weeks, the lords took a vote on the succession. We've defeated two armies and taken Pern."

Liam looked at the woman. "You've also burned and raided innocent villages." Liam paused and waved it off. "I'm sure reparations can be made, however." He said. "I'm sorry, I don't know you or your sigil." He said, looking to Hadiza's black dragon."

Rowena stepped up to Liam. "You'll have to forgive me. I forgot you haven't met everyone. This is Knight Banneress Hadiza." She said, motioning to the woman. Rowena looked to Agota. "This is my ward, Agota."

Liam smiled at both. "It is a pleasure to meet Rowena's trusted companions. May I?" He asked, motioning at a nearby chair.

"Please." Rowena smiled.

Everyone in the tent took a seat while Agota served wine to the occupants.

"It is a terrible thing, this war." Liam began, before sipping his wine. "This whole thing is out of hand. You did a great service defeating Langley, and that certainly deserves a reward."

"Aye by right of conquest." Elva interjected.

Liam frowned. "That's an old way, yes, but not the way it's done outside of Hardstone. What you're talking about is more in line with trial by combat and letting the gods decide. We established long ago that this kingdom, though it allows for multiple faiths, believes in one God. One all knowing, all powerful true God."

"Bah." Elva snorted.

"Whatever your belief, Lady Elva, it still holds true to the rule of law." Liam turned to Rowena. "You won a significant victory and at a cost. The lords know who won the battle, no matter what lies Alfred spins. However, the rule of who takes the barony still falls to whomever father deems right." Liam took another swallow of his wine. "He feels Alfred needs experience in ruling and the Barony of Antei will set a precedence on future crown princes."

"Bullshit." Rowena retorted. "Do you believe all that?"

"No." Liam said frankly. "However, I have to plead their case. They do offer something." Liam took a scroll from his coat. "Here is their new offer."

Rowena took the sealed scroll and cracked the wax royal seal open. She was not happy with what she read.

"Do you know about this?" Rowena asked.

"I haven't read it, but I was assured it was fair."

Rowena tossed the scroll to him to read.

"Exiled with two thousand pounds of silver and a pardon for all my soldiers except for thirty of my choosing. Those thirty will be executed in my stead."

Rowena said. "I'll be branded an outlaw and exiled on pain of death. Signed by our father."

Liam read and re-read the scroll over and over. "It can't be."

Rowena shook her head. "They've used you to get to me."

"Ro, I'd never knowingly betray you." Liam said, dropping the scroll. "I thought…"

"That you could trust them? I know." Rowena said with a light smile. "I did too." She stood up. "Liam, you are a grown man. A fine man with a bright future. I love you more than this world and I hope to never see you across the field of battle. But the die has been cast. I have to finish this."

"What about your life?" Liam said, standing to approach his sister.

Hadiza and Elva both shot up, but Rowena motioned for them to sit.

"I love you as well. You are my sister and I'd give my life to protect yours." Liam continued.

"Then leave Lotcala and don't come back until this is all over." Rowena said.

"I…" Liam began, but stammered short.

"I know." Rowena said. She clasped Liam's hands in hers. "I wish you well in this war, brother. God speed and may the Creator protect you."

Liam nodded and kissed Rowena's hands before leaving the tent and camp.

Hadiza spat on the ground. "They set him up."

Rowena nodded. "She did. To weaken me."

"What now? He will be much more formidable than the barons." Grainne said.

Rowena sniffed back her tears.

Grainne wrapped Rowena in a hug. "War is hell. Sirie taught us that, and now it is our turn to teach the same lesson to this kingdom."

* * * * *

Dawn came quickly, and Rowena's army marched north toward Kirkhaven. Her scouts told her that Sirie was waiting for her there and there was little chance of moving further east without first facing the Queen. Rowena and her closest friends sat upon their horses atop a ridge, watching the army march past.

"We'll see Sirie's force soon, and then we'll have to face her." Rowena said. "She won't be easy to defeat, and I'm certain that she'll bring more than just Canton forces alongside her."

Grainne agreed. "She'll have Estan as well, and that means most of Greenfield if the baron lets her."

"He won't stop her. She's the queen." Elva pointed out.

"Half of Hardstone is with us now. No one left but Lady Catherine to stop Coldwood and Harbor." Grainne added.

"Harbor is staying out." Rowena announced. She pulled out a scroll from her pouch. "In memory of his daughter, Baron Harbor won't raise a sword to us, but he does publicly back Alfred."

Pillars of smoke rose from beyond the ridge.

"She's there, waiting for us. Estan is just twenty miles in that direction." Rowena added, pointing toward smoke. "Her final test for us is just a few days away."

"Good. I've wanted to see that bitch in the dirt for a long time." Elva said.

Grainne wasn't so sure. "It won't be easy. Even without Harbor, she's bringing the rest of Canton's force, Estan, which does indeed mean Greenfield. He would never refuse the queen. My question is what of Coldwood."

"If Leif can't stop him along the western road, then Coldwood is there." Rowena guessed. "She'll want to finish this in one fell swoop."

"His loss then." Elva said.

Rowena grinned.

"Or ours." Grainne replied.

"Why?" Elva sighed. "Why must ye always be such a pessimistic bitch?"

Grainne turned to her friend. "Because I rather not ride to my death, like I have nothing else to lose." Grainne looked at Rowena. "I'm sorry, you're my sister, and I'd do anything for you, but I have to tell you the truth." Grainne sighed. "I've taken a lover and I'm pregnant. Bowen Leckey and I have conceived a child."

Rowena and Elva looked shocked.

"When?" Rowena asked.

"Is that really important?" Grainne asked. "I... I rather not implicate him any further, but should I be allowed to keep the titles of my father, he and I will wed to make it binding and legal."

"And me uncle's word?" Elva asked.

"I am a lord's daughter, and my father brokered the deal." Grainne answered. "It is all well and good. Settled."

"Brokered the deal." Rowena scoffed. She shook her head. She sighed.

"Aye." Grainne grinned. "As archaic as it is, our kingdom still pushes this way of male dominion. Either way, I've missed my time. By more than a fortnight. The healers checked me and say that I'm carrying."

"Congratulations, Grainne! I support it. However, I can't help but think why." Rowena said with a beaming smile.

"You know why." Grainne said. "I'm not a warrior like you two. If I'm captured while carrying, then I'll be spared."

"And if ye die?" Elva asked, genuinely concerned.

"No, I won't have it. Ride to your home and wait there." Rowena's voice left no doubt of her concern for her friend.

"I will not. This is my choice." Grainne shot back.

"And if you die in battle?" Rowena asked.

"Then it won't matter in the least." Grainne replied with a smile. "I'll die in the service of my best friend. Either way, it will be fate."

Rowena nodded. Still unhappy, but accepting the answer. "Then let's meet fate together." She snapped her horse's reins and rushed forward to the head of the army. Her friends following close behind.

* * * * *

Armored horses and riders charged and crashed into one another along the plains north of Estan. The fertile grasslands, known for rolling hills and bountiful soil, was stained with blood from thousands of brave warriors. Lotcalan mounted men at arms and knights, armed with heavy spears and lances, rode their beasts into Rowena's line of lighter but quicker riders. The mercenaries rode coursers, faster horses than the larger Lotcalan breed of destrier, but not big enough to hold as much armor. It was only a matter of time before a headlong charge into the Lotcalan cavalry would break Rowena's own formation.

Rowena, riding in the front of her army, commanded the movements with ease. She knew that accepting that charge would be their death. Gripping her steed's reins, she pulled him to the left, her warriors followed her. They were more agile, and the Lotcalan riders were left behind. Rowena tugged her horse's reins again, pulling him to the right now, and into the Lotcalan flank. The Lotcalans did not have the room, nor the time to turn effectively. Rowena's cavalry slammed into the flank, spears piercing horses and men alike. Carnage on a scale that hadn't been seen in years ensued. Beast and men both littering the battlefield as Rowena's riders were able to get the upper hand in the fight.

Elva blew her horn, signaling the infantry to charge in. It was their turn to take over. The Lotcalan army hadn't brought as many infantry as they did horsemen. That would be a mistake. With the riders unable to move around, Rowena's foot soldiers would be more effective.

Many were wearing chainmail hauberks or chainmail coats, carrying shorter spears and kite shields. While not any lighter than a Lotcalan soldier, they had the advantage of not being pinned down or thrown from a horse. These were also not conscripts, but professional soldiers. There was no fear or hesitation. They knew their role and how to implement themselves within a battle. The Company had brought in one thousand hedge knights from a group called the Black Watch. This was a boon for the princess. While she had hoped for pikemen to help hold off the cavalry, she was happy with the success of the knights she received.

Her time was short. She could hold the advantage in the short term in most battles, but on the whole, she was outnumbered. Hardstone and the remaining Loach forces, led by Leif and Lady Catherine, were tied up in battles with the Coldwood and King's armies at the Hardstone border. Those were led by Prince Liam. Rowena's scouts had reported that the fighting was fierce for Hardstone. The news wasn't encouraging either.

Queen Sirie watched from a safe distance. Her former student was now making easy work of her famed army. She wasn't worried, or at least if she was, she never showed it. Sirie watched as the armies clashed. She lifted her right hand, held in a chainmail mitten. She flicked it up, signaling to her commander to send the newest order.

"Archers!" He called out.

Signalmen waved large flags, and a thousand archers rushed forward, prepared to do their duty.

"My queen, won't we hit our own soldiers?" One commander asked.

"Conscripts and a few men-at-arms." The queen replied, unfeeling. "We'll record their sacrifice. For the greater good." She turned to the signalman. "Loose."

The man waved the flag and the order echoes throughout the valley, followed by the twang of a thousand bowstrings snapping back. A mass of arrows darkened the sky.

Elva and Rowena saw the approach with a second to spare.

"Shields!" Rowena and Elva both called out.

Many of their soldiers were quick enough, but Sirie's force and some of Rowena's couldn't react in time.

"She's killing her own people!" Grainne said.

She had been sent to the rear. Her earlier announcement kept her out of the main fight. However, she was not out of the full battle.

"Send in a force of riders from the north! Signal them now!" Grainne ordered.

A sister waved a flag and from the northern edge of the field a cloud of dust kicked up.

"Send them toward the archers!" Grainne yelled.

It was a desperate plan. If nothing else, the riders would scatter the archers. However, the hope was that they would kill many along the way. Grainne watched the riders rush toward the archers. It was her only idea to give Rowena's force a reprieve. Just as she watched, thinking that the force was enough to break the archers' line, something caught her eye from the north.

"No! It can't be!" Grainne exclaimed. "Mount a charge!" She ordered. "To the northern ridge!"

To the right flank along the north border of the field, Baron Harbor's force burst through the tree line and slammed into Grainne's riders. Three thousand fresh, and heavily armed soldiers entered the battle.

Grainne ordered a full charge. It was the last ditch effort. Rowena watched from the field below as the chaos unfolded out of her reach. She saw the kraken sigil waving above the new force charging in. Rowena knew the deception. Harbor had lied about staying out of the fighting and instead took up arms with the queen.

"Grainne, retreat!" Rowena called. She kicked her horse to reach Elva. "Blow the fucking horn!" She yelled. "Signal a retreat!"

Elva saw Rowena rushing towards her. She knew the meaning. Elva gave the horn a long, steady blow, signaling the retreat. Their mercenaries broke from the battle as best they could. The two friends watched the ridge above where Grainne had charged in to intercept Harbor's force.

"Harbor lied!" Rowena cursed. "He tricked us to make use vulnerable."

Elva gazed in silence as she watched the Harbor force emerge.

"That woman will never let us have our peace." Elva said in a low whisper.

Both kept their eyes on the ridgeline. There they spotted their friend. She turned her horse to face them. Grainne waved them off, motioning them to retreat south. She blew a kiss with her hand before turning back to the charge and then disappeared into the melee.

"Grainne!" Rowena yelled out. "Grainne!"

Several sisters came to Rowena.

"Captain, we have to go! We're being overrun by another force from the east!" One orc sister said.

Elva looked out and saw the Coldwood banners coming into view. Her heart sank.

"Uncle Leif?" Elva said in a hushed voice. "Where is he?"

Rowena turned. "Dammit!" She looked to Elva. "If Leif isn't here, but Coldwood and that bastard lying Harbor are, then that means the barony is defeated."

Elva sneered. "I'll kill them both!"

"No!" Rowena shouted. "We have to leave."

"Never! I'll never leave my family behind." Elva's eyes burned with hatred.

"You're not." Rowena replied. "You're leaving with your sister. We will return."

Elva let out a growl. "Fine."

Elva rode off with the remaining force. Rowena stared up to the ridge and saw Sirie's banner. She pointed her spear toward her stepmother. Even from that distance Rowena could swear she could see the queen's smirk before turning and retreating with her army.

* * * * *

Snow fell in the Hardstone barony as the sun was setting. Lady Catherine was sent back by her baron to guard the borders. Her force held out with Leif, but in the end Leif saw the need to send her away. He had to safeguard his homeland.

Lady Catherine was relying on the reports of the aftermath of the great battle between the remainder of Hardstone forces and the Coldwood army. However, other reports told her that Harbor was moving his force west to attack Rowena directly. She knew the meaning. Her brother most likely had lost. Now only she remained as a buffer to Rowena. The king's force would not let a Hardstone stand at the backs, fearing an attack. It was then she saw a small contingent of riders approach. Rowena would have to fight to reach Hollerton or the Hardstone Barony, and that was a fight she'd lose.

Lady Catherine's sentries told her that Prince Liam was approaching her gates.

"Leif has failed." Catherine said in a whisper. She was sitting in her chair, at the head of her great hall. "Then it is left to me." She sighed.

Lady Catherine walked down to the main gate to meet with Prince Liam, dismounting from his black warhorse. His surcoat was bloody.

"You're hiding rebels, Lady Catherine." Liam said as he walked up to the gates of Hollerton.

"*Nej.*"[11] Lady Catherine answered, shaking her head. She walked out and motioned behind for the gate to be closed. "I'm not. Hollerton is neutral." She lied.

"There is no neutral and your brother was just defeated by mine and Coldwood's force. Creator bless Baron Coldwood, who now rests within the earth." Liam said.

Catherine stood silent and stoic. "Gods protect him. He was a good man. What news of me, brother?"

"Alive along with his son, and being taken to Jovag as a prisoner but taken care of as a noble."

Catherine nodded. "Thank ye for the news."

Liam smiled. "Others wanted heads on pikes. Many still feel the hatred for Hardstones from two hundred years ago."

"Ye were the one that kept them calm then?" Catherine asked with a raised eyebrow.

---

[11] No.

Liam nodded. "I was. Rowena hasn't been so noble. Many highborns have lost their lives to her. Towns have been razed by her warriors. Antei, Lowerfield, Frosthall, and Starkwind. All reduced to rubble and their inhabitants massacred."

"It's war boyo." Catherine said.

"But in war, even nobles are spared for ransom. She doesn't." Liam countered. His fist clenched.

"And ye have spared us nobles in your glorious victories?" Catherine asked, her voice sounding more sarcastic than concerned.

"I have, but some have died in battle. Sir Cullenhun fell in yesterday's battle."

Catherine winced. That name was important to the rebel leadership.

"His sons?"

Liam shook his head. "A significant loss for the kingdom, but they made their choice." Liam sighed. "I'd love to see them in chains, rather than a mass grave. Word is Grainne will assume the role of Lady now in her father's place." Liam shook his head. "I would rather take nobles hostage than to execute them."

"Then yer mercy is somewhat misplaced." Catherine's voice dripped with an accusation.

"This is a war that shouldn't have happened."

"That we can agree on." Catherine looked around. "Did ye come alone?"

"No, but only with a handful of retainers."

"And I'm to trust that? When Harbor lied, and yer queen sent you into yer sister's camp to lie?"

Liam sucked in air at the accusation. "I was an unwilling party to that farce."

"And yet here ye are."

"I'll be gone once I know the rebels are not here." Liam answered. "I'll say you cooperated and that you're still loyal."

Catherine sighed. "It isn't true, though. Me being loyal. At least not to Alfred. King Charles, yes. Princess Rowena, always." She said, drawing her famed sword, *Svikarar Bölva,* from its sheath. "But, to yer brother, never. It has to be here that it is decided."

"It does." Liam smiled. "You're the most famous sword-master in the kingdom. Everyone says that there is no better fighter. Yet, I'm never talked about except to say I'm Rowena's little brother. I've trained with the best swordsmen in the world, and I've led many men in battle. I think my name deserves a bit more respect."

"Jealous?" Catherine quipped.

"No. Just tired of being compared to you and Rowena." Liam replied, drawing his own sword.

"Then... let's put an end to it. I win, yer men leave. Ye win, and ye have a search of me town."

Liam nodded. "Then ready yourself."

Liam lunged at Catherine, but the elder swordswoman dodged his attack. Parrying his blade with a simple flick of her own sword. She stepped back from the fight. Catherine raised her enormous sword, a bastard sword that could be used with one or two hands in her right hand. Liam held his spatha in his right but drew a dagger with his left.

Catherine smirked. She kicked some snow in Liam's face. Using that distraction, Catherine rushed him. Swinging upward at Liam, the younger man barely had time to deflect her blow. Catherine was quick to rebound and brought her blade back down towards Liam's shoulder, but the blade scrapped, painfully, across his chainmail. Liam jumped back and held his own sword out to keep Catherine at a distance.

Catherine chuckled at the prince. "Just a scrape." She said, adjusting her own chainmail hauberk.

"Kicking the snow is cheating!" Liam shouted.

Catherine smirked. "This isn't a tournament. This is war. No such thing as cheating."

Liam yelled and ran with his sword held high. Swinging down and Catherine, she parried his first blow, and dodged his second. The third, she could block, but the pair locked swords, pushing against each other. Catherine kicked Liam away.

"Enough playing boyo." Catherine said.

Gripping *Svikarar Bölva* with both hands she took a swing at Liam. The prince parried her swing, but she was quick with another. Each swung their swords, Catherine pulled back while Liam didn't. That left the prince open, and Catherine drove her sword through the prince's chainmail and into is belly.

Liam staggered, blood seeping from his mouth. He fell into Catherine's arms. Trying to speak, nothing but gasping noises came out.

"Don't speak boyo. You fought brav..." Catherine said but her own voice was cut short.

She looked down to Liam, a smile across his face as he fell dead. Catherine dropped his body and looked to her left side. Liam's dagger was still in his hand, sticking out from beneath her chest. Catherine gurgled blood, before falling back.

The gates to Hollerton opened up and Lady Catherine's men-at-arms rushed to her side. Several of Liam's retainers did as well, but they were cut down by the force from Hollerton.

Catherine reached up to one of her men and pushed her sword into his hand. She struggled but could breathe out the name, Elva. Her soldier took the blade and nodded.

"Get the prince and his men inside. Burn their bodies." The soldier said. "Take Lady Catherine to the great hall!"

The men did as ordered and sat their lady upon her seat within the great hall. There each of her men paid homage to their fallen leader. The great swordswoman was gone to Ymir's Great Hall to feast among the ancestors and heroes of old.

* * * * *

Rowena and her force didn't stop to camp. They kept marching. Grainne's sacrifice kept the queen's army away and slowed them down. However, Rowena was done. Her army had been destroyed, and she'd lost nearly three-quarters of her warriors. All that was left was to keep moving south. They had a small force near Pern, but that force was at risk of being attacked by Lostwood. The King's Road south of Jovag was key to keeping Lostwood and Greenfield at bay. Now, that road was open to an attack.

"What's our numbers?" Hadiza asked as she rode up to Rowena.

Rowena sighed. "Three thousand, maybe." She looked back to the marching force. "Probably less than half of that in fighting condition." She looked to her friend. "We can rebuild, but we'll need help. Hopefully, Black Hand can offer that help."

Rowena pulled a small scroll from her saddle bag. It was a note from Black Hand with an important contingency plan. One she was saving for later, and had yet to read.

She took out the scroll and read it.

"Shit." Rowena said.

Elva rode up next to her. She gave Elva the scroll. The Hardstone woman cursed and spat on the ground.

Rowena grimaced. "We have one play left. We need to go and meet an old friend."

Birthright

er a dead man, Paul." Elva said calmly. "Why should I not shove this sword through yer gut?"

Paul gulped back his breath. "I can help you, all of you. I can help you leave Lotcala."

Rowena eyed her former friend. She shook her head. "We trusted you once."

"And it was well founded." Paul replied.

"You betrayed us!" Rowena roared back.

Paul pulled his head back. "I... I did what I had to for survival." He stammered.

"Survival?" Elva scoffed.

Paul nodded. "Everyone knew I was different. I was scared they would send me running to the brothels, shun me. I had to think about my living."

"Cry and cry. We never cared about yer sexual life." Elva said.

"No, but others in this kingdom did and still do. You know me. I am who I am. Creator forbid the queen sees me in her court."

"My father's court." Rowena corrected Paul.

"In name only, and you know it." Paul answered.

Rowena sneered. "So you betraying us benefitted you how? A place among those that mock you?"

"Something like that." Paul replied. "It was a mistake, and one I intend to correct. The Queen sent me here to lead you into a trap. Just like all those years ago. She knows of my connection to Black Hand. She wants me to betray you again. I intend to do the opposite. I regret that choice years ago, and to be honest, I'm more afraid of Black Hand than I am of the queen." Paul ran a hand through his hair. "Let me help, but be warned, this will not be easy. The army is looking for you and your army. I can get you out but that's not the end of it. No kingdom or queendom on the Falcon Coast will harbor you, but I have contacts in the south. They will help. I've been assured."

"What do you get? Can't stay here if you betray the queen." Rowena said.

Paul shook his head. "The queen said I'd be given a title and place at court, but I don't trust her. She wants you dead, and I believe she'll kill anyone that knows of this trap. I'm a liability to her. I can't stay, therefore I want to go with you. Just until the Southern Kingdoms."

Rowena knew the place well. Four nations, three kingdoms and one collection of city states under a parliamentary ruler. It was also a place much more liberal in thought and education than Lotcala.

"Are you sure you rather not stay here in this border town? Milking the Elysian nobles?" Rowena asked.

"No, I do not want to stay here any longer. I've heard that people like me can find acceptance there." Paul responded.

"You had it here." Elva commented.

"No." Paul shook his head. "I had it with you and the sisters. I never had it in Lotcala."

Rowena grimaced. "Fine, but you'll need be known as a traitor to the world." Rowena took her knife from her belt. She grabbed Paul's chin to hold him steady and slashed her blade across his forehead, making two long cuts. "There, however, if you betray us again, I swear to you I'll kill you myself."

"Understood." Paul replied.

Rowena nodded. "But first, I need to get something. We need to ride back to Lowerfield."

Elva and Hadiza looked at Rowena confused.

"Send all but twenty of our warriors on to safety. The other twenty are with me." Rowena continued.

"I'm coming with ye." Elva proclaimed.

"Me too." Hadiza said.

"No Hadiza. I need you to lead our force out of here. I need a trusted sister to take them to our rendezvous point. We have to rebuild."

Hadiza nodded. She wasn't happy about it, but she would not disobey.

"What of him? Hadiza asked, pointing to Paul.

"Paul's coming with us, too. I ain't letting him out of me sight." Elva added, grabbing the man by his shoulder.

Rowena nodded. "Then let's make haste."

* * * * *

It was two day's ride out of the way, but Rowena and what was left of her sisters made it without incident to the City of the Ancients.

"The resting place of my forefathers." Rowena stood in front of a large mound. "This is Theodorif's tomb." She said.

"Our ancestor." Elva marveled.

The mound was massive. Far larger than any other around the necropolis. Not so much a tomb as it was a mountain, reaching a height of nearly one hundred and fifty feet.

"Within this tomb is my birthright." Rowena said.

She nodded to two of her minotaur sisters. Both pushed the large boulder that covered the entrance. It made a grinding sound as it lumbered across the ground, revealing a small opening.

"I'll be back as soon as I can." Rowena said.

"Do ye want us to go with ye?" Elva asked. Agota stepped up next to her.

Rowena smiled and shook her head. "There is nothing in there that concerns me. Maybe a few snakes, spiders, or rats. Theodorif's spirit will welcome me."

Elva nodded.

Rowena crouched low and made her way into the tomb. Along the way was a narrow stone walkway. It wasn't a labyrinth by any means, instead, it was a very straight path toward the center. Rowena came to the large burial chamber and saw her prize.

"Ancestor. Forgive me, but this is my right by birth and strength. Strike me down now if you believe me unworthy of the throne." Rowena prayed.

Nothing happened. She touched the stone sarcophagus.

"Then I take what is my right." Rowena finished.

Next to Theodorif's tomb was the sword she coveted. She gripped the hilt and pulled the still sharp blade from the sheath. Rowena marveled at the craftsmanship. It was wootz steel, a pattern from the forging and folding processes. It looked like the pattern flowed around the blade as she moved the sword in and out of the light. With such a sword, she felt the throne was hers and hers alone.

Exiting the tomb, Rowena found her sisters waiting for her. Elva's eyes widen as she looked at the sword.

"Theodorif's sword." Elva said in wonderment.

Rowena nodded. "Forged by the siren Aklima with the fire from an eternal dragon."

"A sword that can kill an old god." Paul said in disbelief.

Rowena attached the sword to her belt. "Let's make haste. We've wasted enough time."

The group made their way back toward the Moonstone River. From there, it would several days floating along the current, however, that was their only path toward Elysia. Rowena was hoping for sanctuary in the rival kingdom, though Paul had warned her against hoping for such things. Black Hand, with Paul's help, had arranged for seven ships to take her and the sisters out of the city and off of the northern continent. In their current state, seven ships might be too many.

Rowena had left a wake of destruction from her war. She had razed towns, fortresses, and defeated armies of conscripted levies. However, she could not defeat her stepmother's force, not when it combined with the barons. Her one consolation was the lack of pursuers. She had been defeated, but for Lotcala, it was a pyrrhic victory. The kingdom lost so many warriors that it seemed to be content with letting her leave without a fight. That was a blessing Rowena was willing to take.

Rowena sat on the barge, taking her down river, lamenting her defeat. She had a plan to escape. It was hard to get the distaste of retreat out of her mouth. Never had she retreated from a battle. Yet, she was now out of options except to run to Zaragoza, where Black Hand was setting up a new base for her to rest and rebuild. However, Rowena knew it would take time to rebuild enough of her force to take the Lotcalan throne.

Rowena cursed her luck and the nobles that held on to their xenophobic beliefs. She cursed her brother, Alfred. Her father for his cowardice. But most of all, she cursed her stepmother. On that barge, she vowed revenge against the kingdom. Speaking to the old gods and the Creator, to any that would hear her prayer, she vowed to return and claim her throne.

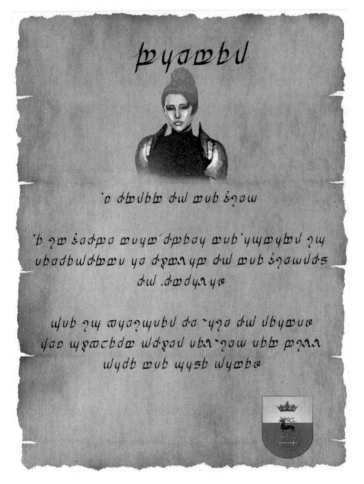

Wanted
By order of the King
Be it known that Rowena the Bastard is henceforth an outlaw
of the Kingdom of Lotcala.
She is banished on pain of death.
Any subject found helping her will face the same fate.

Three Years Later: Outlawed

ing Alfred stood in front of his throne. The houses that had maintained their loyalty to him stood in front of him, on the lower lever just beyond the raised dais. The king dressed in silken finery, and he looked happily over the crowd.

Many banners hung on the walls, though some were missing. It had been the tradition that every noble house had a banner hanging in the king's throne room, the great hall of the palace. This was a reminder that the king's duty was to the people. Yet, during the bloody and terrible civil war that had raged, during the Stag War, several noble families were stricken from the rolls. Their leaders were imprisoned and estates seized by the crown.

The war, won for the Golden Stag of Alfred, almost tore the kingdom in two, yet it survived. Barons, strong in their own rule over their lands, and their vassals loyal to them, held the peace that finally saw the war end. Yet, the most damaging toll was taken when King Charles I died in heartbreaking agony, just three years after his daughter's defeat and exile. Alfred was now the king, a role he had played for nearly the past few years while his father was grief stricken. His first duty was to set forth in finding out the loyalty of those in his kingdom. Calling all of his vassals and their vassals, he intended to usher in a new age for the kingdom.

"Lords, I bid you welcome to your fallen brethren." King Alfred said, motioning to his guards escorting the rebel houses into the throne room.

Many of the attendance murmured over the display of kingly power. King Alfred sat back down on his throne.

"Bring up the first accused." Alfred grinned. "The former baron of Hardstone."

The guards pushed the grey-haired Leif in front of the king. One guard kicked the man's knee, knocking Leif to the ground.

"My lords," Alfred began. "Lotcala cannot have rebellious barons, manor lords, or gentry fighting against its king. Simply ask anyone that remembers the Seabanes and the Goldwaters." Leif grinned. "Once loyal vassals, now rotting corpses under Carolyngian soil."

The crowd was silent. The Stag War had done more than just expose the realm to its vulnerabilities, but it left a disgusting taste in the mouths of the lords. They were not as one any longer. The common folk had joined Rowena in greater numbers. Even lesser noble houses fought by her side, leaving the liege lords without valuable commanders and men during battles. Battles that they had won when Rowena wasn't there to fight against. Still, those victories did little to mend any fear of future rebellions. That fear was seen as an act of treason and this could not stand. Yet, the usual punishment for treason would only enflame the defeated. It would prove Rowena was the better ruler, though many wouldn't admit it.

Lord Chancellor Curr had reasoned with the new king, even before Alfred was the king, and helped to show the young man a better way. An option that could heal the realm. Lotcala might have been Gota in ancestry, but now the nobles were fattened and spoiled. Needing the power that nobles had, forgetting how to live without it. This meant, Curr correctly reasoned, forgiveness was the only way to reunite the realm.

Alfred hated it, but the Dowager Queen Sirie, stricken with the grief over the loss of her son Liam, supported Curr's recommendation. It was that influence that pushed Alfred to call for the court that day, and for the imprisoned lords, or their surviving heirs, to be brought out. Humiliation would play a role in their forgiveness, perhaps more.

The king called upon each, the Lord Chancellor reading their crimes as each name was called. He then offered each noble the same terms. Swear fealty to Alfred or be executed. Each man swore such an oath. In one afternoon, fallen houses were granted a rebirth to nobility and welcomed with open arms by the other highborns. Titles and estates returned.

Alfred looked at Grainne next. The king locked her away in the years since the war's end. Captured at the Battle of Kirkhaven, Grainne received a noble's honor of being held hostage. She pursued the ancient right to sue for claims, not wanting to leave her family lands to the king without pleading her case. Though Alfred wanted to execute her earlier, Grainne had been with child. A ploy to stay her sentence under Lotcalan law. That son, born in prison, was being raised by the Grainne within the walls of Grimwolf Castle.

"Grainne, my sister's trusted lieutenant. You may find my heart softened. Do you wish to plead?" Alfred said.

Grainne, still shackled, her son watching and standing by her uncle, a knight in the Lostwood Barony, looked up to the king.

"Your Grace, I plead for the return of my family's lands and reinstatement has the Lady of Beringridge, our ancestral home." Grainne responded. "All rights and privileges returned as a gentry estate."

Alfred gave a sneer but relaxed his face. "Renounce your friendship to my sister and kiss my ring. All will then be forgiven, and you and your son can then journey to Beringridge as is your right as the lady and lord of the land."

Grainne knew the price of her plan would be her pride, but she knew the consequences of holding on to it. She leaned forward to the king's outstretched arm and kissed the gem encrusted gold ring.

"Then it's settled. Lady Cullenhun of Beringridge." Alfred grinned. "All hear me. Just a couple of years ago, and I would have had her head. Let it be known that time may heal our wounds." Alfred stepped back from the kneeling nobles.

"You lords can now count yourself among the noble few. All your ancestral privileges and lands are hereby granted under your renewed oath of fealty." Alfred proclaimed.

That was, until the king looked back upon Leif Hardstone. The aged baron, his hair matted and his body bruised from the beatings, was a shell of his former glory. All those glories gone from the agony of war and years of imprisonment.

"Leif, a once trusted friend to my father. You didn't bat an eye at the question of who you would side with during the war. Rowena, the dwarven bastard, was your choice. Your crimes are far worse than those beneath your station. You're their leader. They follow your word because of your title. A heavy responsibility." Alfred sneered. "Yet I am merciful today. Hardstone should not be a house that falls from grace."

Alfred might have spoken of forgiveness, but the wounds were fresh. Many of the lords he pardoned were Hardstones vassals, and Highwind was still at the northern border, watching over the mountains that guarded the realm from Panyakuta. Highwind lords knew no lords other than Hardstone, but they had refused to join the war. They were the only house that stayed out of the fight. The king wasn't ready to trust them to be barons, therefore, Hardstone had to be forgiven. The family, at least. Not the current lord.

"Your son Torin," Alfred motioned to the young man shackled next to Leif. "He will be the new Baron of Hardstone. Should he say the oath, of course."

Torin spat on the floor.

Alfred frowned at the sight. "That's not all. Torvi will also be my bride. We will seal our houses in a union of forgiveness, with Hollerton being the dowry."

"Never!" Torin answered.

"Shut up boy!" Leif responded. "Speak the oath, and protect yer sister."

"What happens to me, da'? Will he see mercy, your grace?" Torin asked, gritting his teeth, looking up at Alfred.

"By order of the crown, we will execute him. He supported and fought for Rowena. He influenced others to join her revolt. Since Rowena can't answer for the charge. Noble blood will have to be spilt." Curr answered. "An example must be made."

The king held a hand up to his chancellor. "However, his name will be recorded in the rolls as a hero to the realm." Alfred added. "He was my father's favorite, and an excellent warrior." The king smiled his cruel, manipulative smile. "See? I'm not an evil king." Alfred grinned wickedly. "No, only one need pay for the crimes of my sister, since she is too cowardly to accept the punishment herself. Of course, Hollerton is to make up for my brother's death at the hands of Lady Catherine."

"And what of her?" Leif asked. "Will her name be cleared?"

"She died defending a criminal." Alfred sighed heavily. The lords were watching him, curious about his next move. Lady Catherine had been popular among several of the leading houses, though not all. It was more about the precedent for executions. One accused had openly revolted. The other died defending the daughter of the former king. The entire ordeal of Liam and Catherine's duel was a grey area many saw from different perspectives.

Alfred raised a hand as if taking his own oath. "Let no one say I'm not merciful. Lady Catherine is posthumously pardoned, and restored to the rolls of nobility. Her heir may take his place as a gentry lord. Though his lands are now crown lands, so he would be no better than a hedge knight. I'm sure he'd find a home in Hardstone."

Leif and Torin lowered their heads. Torin was ready to fight back. He was as defiant as any other Hardstone. Torin shook his head, but before he could speak, he heard his father's voice.

"We swear it." Leif replied with a raspy voice. "Me son, he'll swear yer oath. We're loyal to this kingdom, and its king."

"The true king?" Alfred asked, leaning forward in his throne.

Leif sneered. He knew what the king was trying to do. He'd humiliate them, all of them. Every lord that stood with Rowena would be humiliated, and brought to kneel in front of all the lords. Alfred would cement his power as the supreme ruler of the land, while reuniting it.

He had no choice. Leif nodded.

"Aye, the true king. King Alfred." Leif responded, defeated.

Alfred again grinned. He had finally won.

* * * * *

True to his word, after the execution, Alfred had Hardstone's body taken back to the barony for cremation. The ancient way of the Hardstone family. A great scion was gone, and though Torin was to be civil on the matter and most lords saw that the matter of the war was swept under the rug, wounds were deep. Torin could have tried to plan revenge, but his sister would feel the scorn. Her children, heirs to the kingdom when they were born, could feel the scorn. Torin was trapped without being physically held hostage.

Torvi Hardstone married Alfred, an affront to the ending of the war. It was necessary, and the one consolation was that Torvi, a true Hardstone, wasn't a weak willed wife. She butted heads with her new mother-in-law and husband. Torvi was not the push over that Alfred had expected.

The "great" king that had won the war on the backs of better commanders, such as his mother, had a very unfamiliar sense of the world. The coming years showed as much.

Alfred went to work, pushing a stronger centralized base for his throne. Nobles were losing the grip on their own lands. Reversals of his father's reforms, and new taxes to pay for foreign wars, finally brought the kingdom to a halt. That is a tale that will play out for years to come, however.

Unable to secure sanctuary in Panyakuta for fear of a war, the dwarven princess and her band of sisters went south. Unwelcomed in Amazon, and even Elysia, Rowena took what was left of her sisters to

Zaragoza, and then off searching for a new land. Fame followed them. The mercenary band recruited more followers, gained more wealth, and ended up on the southern end of the Central Continent.

Rowena, the hardened warrior strengthened in the forge of battle, would one day birth a nation, a queendom, worthy of her bloodline. A nation to rival that of her homeland and father. That too, and the wars that followed, are a tale for another day. For the two monarchies will be forever linked in hatred and pain.

Aftermath: Epilogue

welve years after the Stag War ended, a new nation arose in the south. Mightily, the land of Nashoba conquered large swathes of land in quick succession until finally the ruler of the nation called for peace. The peace was hard won, years of war, countless lives lost, but to this one warrior, the conqueror queen, it was worth it.

Sitting upon her gilded throne, the queen, surrounded by her husband and retainers, welcomed a delegation from Gotistan.

Lady Elva the Exile, next to her queen, looked out over the court.

"Ye stand in the presence of Rowena, Queen of Nashoba. Rowena the Dauntless, Rowena the Conqueror. Scourge of the North, victor of the War of the Free States. Fearless among foes, vanquisher of the dragon worshipers, and rightful heir of the Carolyngian throne." Lady Elva paused. "Speak, cousins."

One of the delegation approached and bowed. The royal guards flanking them stepped closer, but Rowena motioned them back.

"What news do you have for me?" The queen asked. Her red hair, now with slivers of grey, was draped over her shoulders under her golden crown.

"We bring tidings from your uncle, Lord Robert of Lor Galdon." The man said. "He wishes to form an alliance to claim the Carolyngian Throne from your brother Alfred."

"Interesting. My uncle, the man that refused me when I called upon his aid and refuge twelve years ago, seeks my help." Rowena smiled. "Fate is a crafty bitch of a mother. What does my uncle suggest for the Carolyngian throne? Who will sit upon it?"

"Lord Robert has the intent on returning the throne to a stature of power that your father, King Charles, oversaw. As a reward, Lord Robert promises you the Barony of Antei, as is your right." The man continued.

Rowena stood. Her frame, still strong and broad, cast a long shadow in the sunlight from the stained glass windows behind her throne.

"My right, you say? Did you not hear Lady Elva tell you what my rightful throne is?" Rowena clinched her fists. "Robert wishes to usurp a pretender then take his place as a pretender. No, that throne is mine, and mine alone. I will or my descendants will claim our rightful place. Until such a time, let it be known that we are no friends to usurpers!"

"Robert is being more than fair." The delegation representative said. "The people of Lotcala suffer under Alfred, but they still will not follow a dwarven ruler."

"That is their mistake." A woman said from the shadows.

The delegation turned to see Agota cradling Rowena's infant daughter.

"A gorgon?!" The man exclaimed.

"A sister." Rowena corrected. "Tell me more about how my people shun me still."

"My lady, you must understand-"

"Your grace!" Rowena interrupted, correcting the envoy. "You are addressing a queen!" Rowena returned to her throne. "My uncle will have an answer." She motioned to her guards. "Bring out a barrel of pickling brine. Kill all but this one." She said, pointing to the man that had been speaking to her. The guards rushed in and began restraining the members of the delegation. "Send their heads to my uncle in the pickling barrel. This one..." She paused, looking at him. "He'll return, but castrate him first. Send that piece to my brother with a note that I haven't forgotten whose throne he stole."

Rowena waved the guards away to do her bidding.

The man, being restrained by the other guards, pleaded. "The rules of hospitality demand you let us leave unharmed!"

Rowena sneered. "We have no such laws here."

The screams of the men as they were taken away echoed throughout the throne room and the corridors.

* * * * *

Within a year's time, the war, later known as First Gota Succession War, was brought to a close, though the implications were great. Alfred won the war against his uncle, but his nepotism and mismanagement of the war brought a renewed call for rebellion from the barons. Soon, it was Alfred that found himself locked in Grimwolf Castle while his four-year-old son, Edemir, was named king. To prevent any attack from the south, Baron Canton acted as regent and protected the boy. Alfred was found dead soon after, yet no one could agree as to how he died. Few saw the body. Many still thinking of a southern attack strengthened the borders and their alliances for just such an occasion.

Yet, no attack came. Rowena, though never forgetting her vow, had settled into life as a queen. Her husband, the underboss of The Company, Gerald Blackhand, comforted her in the darkest nights.

"They hate me." Rowena said, sitting up in her bed against the headboard.

"Who hates you? None in this realm." Gerald smiled. He gingerly rubbed his wife's shoulder.

"You know who. They call me the cruel, the dwarven whore, Rowena the bitch. Worse, the false queen of Lotcala." Rowena sniffed. "I could take that throne from little Edemir with such ease that my hordes would storm over the lands, leaving nothing but wastes for their hatred. They do not see the mercy I am extending to my nephew. To allow him to grow up and be a different king than his father, than his grandfather, with hope. No, they still call me the merciless, the pretender, and kinslayer." Rowena scowled at the last word. "I struck no one that was my blood. Lady Catherine killed Liam, my poor little brother, in a fair duel. Had he just listened to me, he would be alive. My sweet little Liam." Rowena fought back her tears. "If only he had lived."

"He would probably be the king."

Rowena sighed. "Maybe, but he wouldn't stand to listen to such horrible lies and names thrown at his beloved sister."

Gerald sat up and wrapped an arm around his wife. "Those are just words meant to sow seeds of distrust to those that know better. You are known to Nashoba as the liberator, the fearless, the dauntless, and more importantly, mother." He pulled her close, her head resting on his chest. "You broke centuries of tyrannical rule. Yes, you have been strict in your rule, but also fair. You are firm. That was needed. The lords here proclaimed you queen, and still pay homage to you." Gerald rubbed his wife's pregnant belly. "Our children will take your example and continue to shape this country into a great power that none will stand against."

Rowena turned and kissed him. "Let us sleep. Tomorrow, we can think of names for our newest little one."

* * * * *

A very pregnant Queen Rowena walked down to the docks, her royal guard flanking her. A slow walk, but one with energy for the pleasant day. Lady Elva behind her. The queen had received a letter. A letter with wonderful news, but one sent in secret.

"She seems to have been able to prosper in the years since our separation. Five more children since the first one she was carrying when we left. Three boys and two girls." Lady Elva said, as she walked along with Rowena to the docks.

Rowena smiled. "Grainne has rebuilt her house."

"Aye, with a Hardstone cousin." Elva replied. "And now she risks it all."

Rowena waved her friend's concern away. "Proactive. She doesn't fully trust the lords of Lotcala, and why should she? She is sending Finn here to learn how to be a warrior, and to protect her house. However, she has made some friends in the north. We might have allies in case we ever need them."

The pair, along with the royal guards, reached the docks. A young boy, no older than eleven, wearing the arms of a black hound on a blue shield, was disembarking from a longship. Several men at arms, all bearing the same sigil as the young boy, were at his side. The young lad, guided by his attendant, walked up to the queen.

"Your grace." He said, bowing to Rowena.

Rowena bowed her head. "Young master Finn Cullenhun. Second son of the great scion, Lady Grainne." She cupped his chin and gently turned his head. "You look just like your mother." Rowena released her grip. "I'm your aunt Rowena, and this is your aunt Elva." Rowena motioned to her friend. "We've known your mother since we were about your age. She is our oldest and truest friend."

"A pleasure to meet you, your grace. Lady Elva." The boy smiled as he bowed again. "Is Lady Agota here?" He asked, looking around the docks.

"Aye, she's in the palace with the princess. Ye'll be meeting her soon enough." Elva said with a grin.

"Your mother has been telling you about her travels?" Rowena asked, smiling.

Finn beamed. "Every night before putting us to bed. They're our favorite stories."

Rowena beamed. "Then come, let's go meet your other aunts."

About the Author

Joseph S. Samaniego is a historian from North Carolina specializing in medieval European History. He has a Master of Arts in History and has future plans to receive a PhD.

In his daily life, he is not only a Fantasy author 6 titles to his credit, he also writes non-fiction and is a gifted fantasy cartographer.

When he is not spending time with his family, Joseph spends time reading, writing and playing video games.

Made in the USA
Columbia, SC
24 September 2024

42964382R10170